CHOSEN

FOR SUCH A TIME

Maryann Remsburg

TERRORISM IN THE WHITE HOUSE

Text copyright 2018 by Maryann Remsburg

Jacket art copyright 2017 by Bobbi Menger

Author picture by elliegrover.com

ISBN-10: 0692057692

ISBN-13: 978-0692057698

This book is a work of fiction. All modern day characters and events are the product of the author's imagination to show the biblical story and characters of Esther in today's world. Any resemblance to any modern day person, living or dead, is coincidental.

DEDICATION

My Lord and Savior - you gave me the idea, the inspiration, and the perseverance to finish this book. All I have and all I am is yours.

To my children - Corban, Anya, Ella and Caleb. Studying Esther has encouraged me not to let fear, or anything else, hold me back from what God has for me. I hope this book might encourage you to do the same. God has created each of you so unique and amazing and He has an awesome adventure just for you. I love you forever and thankful to be your mom.

Chapter 1

ESTHER ON THE HOT SEAT
ESTHER THOMPSON – POLITICAL SCIENCE STUDENT

In the silence of the moment, the panic rises within me. Their eyes on me—I assume mocking. One set of eyes darts to another and the slight raise of their eyebrows make their feelings clear.

"Well, that's an interesting theory, Esther. A little far-fetched that Iran actually has hurtful intent."

Professor Fraser and everyone else here must think I'm an idiot. Why did I even bring up the Iranian Government and Russia when they are all focused on talking about North Korea's nuclear program? Again the awkwardness of silence.

If I could only break the awkwardness of the moment. Maybe if I could speak with indignant passion like Uncle Cai. Or even crack a joke like Leeann. Anything to get their eyes off of me.

"Of course, there is a lot more to understand," I squeak out.

My weakness betrays me as I feel the emotion welling up in my eyes. I blink rapidly and look at my lap—willing the tears away.

1

"Now would anyone like to respond to Esther's claims?" His emphasis on the word claims takes me off guard.

Dr. Fraser usually has a neutral stance during debates. Not this time.

I clench my hands together. Now I'm angry as well as embarrassed. The voices of my classmates start to chime in all at once—everyone seems eager to pounce.

"Iran has agreed to dismiss their nuclear program. They obviously want peace."

"We need to have patience and follow the inspections as agreed on. Rushing in will only push Iran into action."

"What is the benefit in Russia helping Iran take over the Jordanian Valley?"

I slide further down in my chair. *Maybe awkward silence is actually better than this onslaught of accusing peers.*

"Zip it y'all," a booming voice rings out from behind me. Even without looking, I know the voice belongs to Cord. "Ms. Thompson here knows what she is talking about, even though all y'all can't see it."

Now I'm being defended by the guy who no one takes very seriously - partly because of his demeanor and partly because he acts like a know-it-all. Our views are not that different, but his mannerism puts me off. I sink in my chair even lower as Cord continues. Everyone has quieted down to hear him—probably to give more ammunition for the next round of attacks. *As long as they aren't directed at me!*

"Time is exactly what these countries with aggressive nuclear programs need. Meaningless sanctions and agreements are a gift. In the case of Iran, it lets them keep the west happy while they do exactly what they want."

The opposing condescender in the room, Clayton, speaks up. "The problem with you two is that you have a doomsday mentality. You look for the worst and do not understand that these things take time. Frankly, you are ignorant about modern day politics."

With a clearing of his throat and a pointed look, Dr. Fraser lets Clayton know he has gone too far.

This international policies class is one of my favorites – as long as I don't speak up too much. Exactly because of that word— ignorant— and here I am, being called it anyway.

Another student now – a woman speaks up. "Esther, why do you think agreements won't work for countries like Iran and Russia when top government officials obviously do?"

Oh great, on the spot again. I think her name is Kara or Karen or Kate— something with a K—maybe Kathryn? Focus and don't let fear take over! I take a deep breath and sit up a little taller in my chair.

"I am looking at the warning signs. What they have done in the past and what they say they will do in the future. For example, Russia convinced the Ukraine to give up their nuclear program and then pushed in instead of the protection they promised.

"But that was really Russia's land—it was decided upon in a signed agreement back in '94." The voice is to my right.

I respond, "It shows their power hungry nature. They are now supplying Egypt with weapons for the first time in over forty years. Teaming up with Iran. Makes me wonder why?"

Clayton smirks as he responds. "Your evidence against Russia looks like interactions as a good neighbor. Iran is no problem either."

Voices of agreement break out around the room.

I am not good at explaining myself, especially in politics that are difficult to truly understand.

"Let the woman talk." says my unplanned partner in this debate. "Go ahead Esther."

Why does Cord keep dragging me farther in this debate? Although I do admire his confidence—wish I had it.

Clayton shoots an icy glare past me to Cord. He does not like being shushed.

"Iran is my biggest worry without a doubt." I begin tentatively. "In recent years, the west thinks they have used diplomacy to shut down their program, but they have actually opened the door for it to continue with the okay of the global nation. Iran has no intention of letting anyone oversee their nuclear program."

I hear a snicker. *Just keep going. Uncle Cai encourages me to do one thing every day that makes me just slightly nervous. This is my thing for today—and for tomorrow too!*

"The U.S. and the U.N. say Iran is not moving forward in their nuclear plans, while Iran says the exact opposite. They have been very clear that they want to wipe out entire countries, including Israel."

Groans go up from students throughout the class. Israel is not a favorite in this class. Some of my fellow students accuse Israel of not really wanting peace while wanting the support and sympathy of the United States. *Of course, I care about the future of Israel, being Jewish myself. I am done talking.*

Cord again, "Go on Esther and tell them more."

Oh Lord, can this class just end already?

Hesitantly I go on, "The Jordan Valley is key to the area. Jordan has allegiance to Russia for past help. I think if Russia can gain control of the area, they will let Iran come in and wipe out Israel for them." I stop talking, taking in that I am talking about the destruction of Israel.

Uncaring eyes greet me as I turn to look back towards Cord for support. He gives me a small nod acknowledging his agreement.

"Why always so pro-Israel, Esther?" Clayton asks. "Their prime minister is always looking for support with their 'poor us' complex. You can tell that even President Susa is tired of talking to him." Many chuckle with him as he laughs.

"Poor us complex?!" Cord's roar from behind causes me to jump. "A country with near nuclear capability constantly threatening to destroy his country and people and you think Prime Minister Holon has a poor us complex?"

I do love Cord's passion for Israel. And he couldn't care less what anyone else thinks of him. Why can't I be more like that? Why do I feel badly for what I think?

From the woman with the K name again, "What about the Jew's over-reaction in Europe? A few incidents of people not shopping at their store and they cry boycott."

"Actually," Cord booms, "Reports of anti-Semitic boycotting has become such a problem in Europe that thousands of Jews are fixin' to return to their homeland to escape the persecution."

Cord is getting angry now. I wonder why he is so passionate about Israel?

"Kayla, you do realize you are talking about European Jews don't you?" Cord retorts.

Kayla! I knew it started with a K.

"You so easily slid from impatience with Israel to impatience towards Jews in other countries. So, are you saying that just Israel over-reacts or Jews all around the world?"

What a great point. How easily the tide could turn against both Israel and Jews around the world—my people.

Kayla just shakes her head and dismisses Cord with a wave of her hand. I look ahead to see that Clayton is tapping the top of his table, visibly agitated as he speaks.

"Israel—the Jews—both. They better know who their allies are and be careful not to lose them. The U.S. is going to be around for a long time and they would be wise not to push us away."

Clayton glares towards Cord, then towards me. Nothing from Cord. I turn around to see he is scribbling something into a notebook, seemingly unaware that he has been challenged.

Oh fine, I'll respond again. I have to.

"Do you think our country is so invincible that even though we are in an economic and moral downward spiral, we are somehow going to escape the two hundred year cycle?"

"The two hundred year cycle of what?" Clayton demands.

"The cycle of democratic nations."

"I have never heard of this—another one of your doomsday beliefs?" The laughter from Clayton sounds hollow, even to me.

Cord is back with us, "Go on now. I want to hear."

"The typical cycle is that a country starts in bondage, but they have spiritual faith which brings great courage. With this courage, they gain liberty and abundance follows. After abundance comes selfishness which leads to apathy. This apathy calls for dependence, usually on the government. Eventually, this country finds themselves back in bondage again."

The room is quiet. *Either trying to follow the cycle in their minds or again thinking I am an idiot.*

I venture, "Where do you think the United States is in that two hundred year cycle?"

Nothing—quiet—complete silence.

Breaking the hush, Kayla quietly asks, "If you think so little of our country's future, why exactly are you getting a masters in political science?"

That is a good question. Why exactly did I decide to go back to school instead of continuing as an advocate?

"Whether the U.S. is on top or in decline, it is my country. I want to do whatever I can."

The condescender smirking at me says, "I'll work for a super power country. You are welcome to work for a country that is past its prime."

Loud clapping draws all of our attention to the front of the room where Dr. Fraser is giving us a standing ovation.

"And that discussion is exactly why I spend my days teaching political science students instead of running the country myself."

And that debate makes me want to run home and never show my face in this class again.

~~

Chapter 2

A PLAN FOR THE PRESIDENT
ALEXANDER SUSA – UNITED STATES PRESIDENT

"Are you even listening to us, Xander? Considering this is your marriage and career we are discussing, I would think you might be a little more interested."

Thanks Preston, always ready to make some condescending remark in the name of advising.

I respond in what I hope is an interested tone, even though Preston is completely right.

I should not have been awakened out of a perfectly good sleep for this.

"Yes, yes, of course I'm listening. I'm with you, but quite honestly, those European guys sure can drink. I tried to stay up with them, if you know what I mean. My head might not be quite as clear as I would like for this conversation. Let's start again at the top please."

I look around at the table of my advisors, the men and token woman who have helped to shape my presidency. There are a few more White House staff seated along the edges of the room. They all look so serious this morning, which does not seem necessary considering our successful week with the

Peace Summit. This must have something to do with Vanessa. There is a vague memory from last night of me being upset with her, but now I can't put my finger on why.

The anxiety around the table is probably Preston's doing. He is an organized chief of staff, but is always getting everyone all riled up about this or that. I look at Preston. He seems frustrated with me. *Not the first time. I actually find a secret joy in ruffling his feathers a little.*

"Of course, Mr. President, let's go over the particulars. We need to inform you of the details, give you options, and then you need to quickly execute."

Seriously Preston, why the word execute? I think you like to ruffle my feathers just as much as I like to ruffle yours. Preston looks at Thomas, my trusted advisor, and gives him a nod to lead the conversation.

"Mr. President, we all realize this is a sensitive issue as it combines your personal life with your presidency, but we must talk openly and candidly." I nod.

"At the culmination party last night, you made a request of your wife to come down to visit the assembled heads of state. What was your reason for making this request?"

I reach deep into my clouded memory. Part of the reason I was upset at Vanessa comes to me. *That's right, I asked Vanessa to come downstairs so I could show her off to the men. I thought she might take it as a compliment because when I think of sexy women, she is the first to come to mind.*

"It was really no big deal. It started with Andres, the Panamanian head, saying women in Panama were the most beautiful in the world. You know how that kind of conversation goes, even if the men are heads of state. One boast led to another and in my drink induced mind, I decided to show off Vanessa to the men. I guess she got a little upset about the whole thing."

Thomas opened a folder and began looking over something inside. *Why are they making such a big deal about all this? It's just something between Vanessa and me. I'll smooth it over with her, like I have a thousand times before.*

"Sir, I know you are aware Mrs. Susa never made it to the party. But we need to inform you of all the events that followed your request. Mrs. Susa was coming to you, however, she was headed off by Monique."

I didn't understand. "Why didn't you let her come in?" I quickly demanded.

"Well," Thomas says, "Mrs. Susa told Monique in livid tones, and I quote from the file notes: If Xander wants an American woman, then I am coming to show him and all the men assembled what a real American woman looks like. I am going to take my last scrap of dignity and slap my husband across the face with it."

I begin laughing. "There is no way Vanessa said that. Monique, you must have heard her wrong because that does not sound like my wife at all."

12

Thomas pauses, nodding his head toward the White House assistant sitting against the wall. Monique gently returns the nod and begins speaking, tentatively.

"Yes, Mr. President, those are the exact words she used. There were two Secret Service present who also heard the same account. I'm so sorry Mr. President, but I have never seen your wife so angry or upset during the two years I have worked here."

Quickly jumping in, Thomas adds, "Monique had the quick thinking to involve the guards and divert Mrs. Susa outside to the garden to cool off rather than enter your gathering in that state. Preston quickly arrived to make sure you and the heads of state were not interrupted by Mrs. Susa, which could have damaged the positive relationships you have been working to build."

"Well, thank you all for your help with this little marital conflict. I do remember it was awkward to save face after Vanessa did not show. I don't think there was any harm done with the progress made in the peace process this week because of it though." I give a little wink to let them know how confident I feel. "As far as Vanessa and me, we have been through a lot worse than this. My wife is always fine after a little scuffle; nothing a new purse can't solve."

I get up from my chair. *I need another cup of coffee. That night was too short and my advisors are way too tense for me this morning.* I can quickly tell the meeting is not over as everyone appears agitated. Preston takes the lead again.

"Mr. President, there is much more about this situation we need to discuss if you would not mind sitting down."

13

Although he stated it as a request, I can see I do not have a choice. I settle back in with a confident smile. "Monique, I'm going to need something to drink if I'm going to make it here much longer. Coffee please, unless you really want to make my day. Then go ahead and make it a scotch."

"One coffee coming up, Mr. President." Monique smiles.

Oh well, at least I tried. Maybe if I had chosen another line of work I could have a scotch for breakfast.

"Okay, what else do you need to discuss about this little marital saga of mine?"

Thomas starts speaking again, referring to his file folder notes. "When Mrs. Susa was diverted from entering the gathering, she did agree to go outside and asked to be left alone as she walked through the garden. Mr. President, what none of us knew until this morning when we saw the news reports, was that your wife spoke to a reporter when she was outside last night."

"What do you mean, she spoke to a reporter?" I ask. "It was late, were there reporters here?"

"At the time Mrs. Susa went outside to the garden, there were a handful of reporters still here waiting for one last comment from the International Peace Summit. With you and the leaders of so many countries together, there have been reporters here almost around the clock all week long, hungry for any statements or footage."

I take a moment to smile and savor what Preston said. *This business with Vanessa is small beans. I don't even know why we are taking precious time meeting about it. The International Peace Summit is what we should be focusing on—now that has been something. No one but me has ever brought as many leaders together in one place before. No leader has ever built such connections as I have built during this last week.*

"Hasn't it been amazing boys...and, of course, lady. Watching these leaders let their hair down the way they have. No team has ever made such progress in international relations as we have. I congratulate you all. Having a place for the leaders to just enjoy themselves and make memories together. Real diplomacy that will go farther than anything else we could have done."

Taking me down from my moment of reveling again. "Preston, you look like you are about to jump out of your skin say something."

"Mr. President, no one doubts the International Peace Summit was a huge success, but the news we have to share with you this morning could possibly jeopardize all that success."

I can't imagine what they're talking about. *I'm sure it can't really be all that bad, but you gotta love Preston's enthusiasm.* I try to put my serious face on.

"Yes, by all means, carry on then."

"Mr. President, as I was saying, your wife spoke to a reporter while she was out in the garden. We are speculating the reporter was also stretching her legs and they met by chance, since no one could have known Mrs. Susa would be out there at that time in order to plan the meeting with her."

Okay, so what? Vanessa has talked to thousands of reporters.

"Mrs. Susa gave permission for the reporter to audibly record their interview. It is the cover story of every newspaper and newscast worldwide this morning. The first bit of information was leaked to us just over an hour ago. By that time, it was much too late to stop the onslaught of reports."

Preston took the controller in his hand and gestured towards the screen. "Mr. President, we thought you should hear what your wife had to say for yourself."

Well, it can't be that bad. Vanessa has always stood by my side and been completely loyal, even when I probably didn't deserve it. She's a smart woman and she realizes all she gets out of our marriage.

After a brief introduction by a national broadcaster I know well, a picture of my beautiful wife of sixteen years comes on the screen. Her voice accompanies the picture.

I listen as Vanessa's words tumble out. "My smile always stayed the same. When my mother died, my smile stayed the same. When Xander became a senator and I walked in on him with his hand up an intern's skirt at the celebration party, one of many women I knew about, my smile stayed the same. When we lost our little one so late in the pregnancy, my smile stayed the same. And even now when Xander is the President of the United States and everything looks so perfect to the outside world, inside I'm dying. It might seem to you that my smile has faded in just one day, but in reality, it has been crumbling away little by little for years."

Could this be a hoax by an imposter? There is no way Vanessa would say these things. She doesn't even think these things.

My wife goes on telling my short-comings as a husband, my weakness in leading our family and her loss of hope for any change in the future. When Vanessa's voice and picture fade, the room is silent except for the hum of the projector running through its cooling cycle.

I guess everyone is waiting for me to say something. But, what am I supposed to say? There is truth in what Vanessa is saying. She knows me better than anyone and knows I was never really cut out to be a husband. That it has been hard for me to be loyal to just one woman. I probably have been the reason that her happiness has been slowly evaporating. I do love her, always have. But come on...should she be all that upset about her life with me? Vanessa certainly has never been upset with the clothes or the jewels or all the admiration she gets from this marriage and title of president's wife.

I put these thoughts in the back of my head and instead grab the charm and charisma that has gotten me out of more sticky situations than I would like to count.

"I see it's going to take a little more than a purse this time, but nothing that can't be solved by diamonds. Just watch and learn. Vanessa and I will be back to normal by dinner time."

"Xander," Preston leans in closer to me as he speaks. "This time purses or diamonds are not going to solve the problem. This is bigger than you realize and affects not only your marriage, but this country, as well as all those international relationships you have been working so hard to build. More than anything, this problem with your wife affects your possibility of re-election. "

What does he mean this could affect my re-election? How can my spat with Vanessa affect my next term as President of the United States of America?

Thomas's fatherly voice breaks into my thoughts. "Xander, your reputation and Presidency will not survive this kind of character attack by your own wife. The public has been supportive of your shortcomings because of your charisma, but your ratings are already low and these statements are too blatant and harmful for the majority to swallow. Even during the last hour, we have talked to many of the heads as they prepare to leave Washington D.C. They are starting to turn on you as they hear these statements. With you being portrayed as an unfaithful and selfish husband who is not a strong leader in your own home. I'm sorry to say but many have already said they are not going home in support of your presidency. If the world does not see you in control of your family, they will certainly not see you as a strong leader for the country come re-election time." Thomas looks at me quietly for a moment to let his words sink in.

"Xander, either you will be destroyed by these comments or Vanessa must be."

Destroy Vanessa—could I do that? She started as my friend that first year at grad school. Even though we went our own ways to follow our careers as lawyers, she was always the one I thought about. Vanessa, the girl who blossomed into a gorgeous, elegant woman by the time we re-connected years later. As I bid on a Senate seat, Vanessa agreed to become my bride and with that decision gave me the most perfect political wife I could have asked for. How can I destroy this woman?

As I look around the room at my trusted advisors, I can see that the tide is quickly shifting against her.

I do love Vanessa, but there is no way I am going to give up my presidency to protect her and save our marriage. All is quiet at the table for a moment while I gather my thoughts and shake off my feelings of regret about Vanessa, as I have done a hundred times before.

"Well, I guess you all know which one of us I want to see standing at the end of this."

That one comment opens up the floodgates of conversation and suddenly the table is full of chatter, even from the other four members who have been sitting quietly up to this point.

"She has to be seen as the unfaithful one who talks badly about her husband."

"All the things we've covered up over the years: her affair, excessive shopping on the taxpayer's dollar, it all needs to come out and more."

"You have to look like the victim in this marriage, Xander. Your re-election depends on getting the sympathy of the voters."

Quickly, brainstormed ideas are scrawled out—making me look like a Boy Scout and Vanessa, the self-centered woman I have endured all these years.

19

Not reality, but believable with the right spin. It is necessary though. Even she will understand when she looks at the facts of what she has said and done. I'll make it up to her though. She will be set for life financially and maybe she'll be happier on her own anyway.

A moment of regret settles over me again.

~~

I keep reminding myself of why this is necessary. The next weeks and months are a constant blur of cover-up and interviews, putting a false front over my feelings, and constantly keeping the facts spinning. *I'm the best at this and even I am exhausted.*

A few months without my wife and a hole of loneliness is growing inside me. *Was this the right thing to do? I did keep one promise though and Vanessa is well taken care of financially. Of course, it came with the legal obligation to never speak about our marriage publically again. But that is a small price for her to pay for the level of style she can afford to live in for the rest of her life.*

As I walk down the White House hall for yet another interview, I feel my mood slipping to negative. *I can't keep up this facade of confidence. It was all decided too quickly and now I am not so sure what we did was right. I miss Vanessa.*

In the room, I meet Siana Tyler. She quickly stands and walks towards me. "Mr. President, I'm sorry for all you have been through." She reaches up for a quick hug. *Sympathy from the women, congratulations from the men. I can see the topic of today's interview is my personal life, like most of them lately.*

Following a few short questions about health care, Siana eases into the questions I know she is dying to ask.

"Mr. President, let's go back to that morning when you found out about the hurtful comments your then wife, Vanessa Susa, said about you. What was the first thing that went through your mind?"

"Pain...hurt. I was devastated by the comments my wife made. I knew then that I had to be honest to the world about our marriage. No, I was not a perfect husband, but I tried hard for such a long time to make our marriage work. When Vanessa decided to make accusations against me, I realized our personal life was now the business of our country. I would need to be open as well."

"In your openness, Mr. President, you shared very critical information about your ex-wife. Why had your wife's issues of alcohol abuse, excessive spending, and even a male prostitute in the White House never come out before?"

"Siana, when you love someone, you want to protect them. You want to help them turn from unhealthy behaviors to a more positive pattern. I thought I could help Vanessa turn from those behaviors. In the end I had to put the American people above my love for my wife when she refused to be an example for our country."

Siana and I are both quiet for a moment. I can tell a sentimental question is coming as she looks into my eyes with softness. "Do you miss her?"

"Of course, I miss her every day, but I have decided to be the best president I can be. I will hold onto my country, to my people, as my bride."

I watch as tears brim in Siana's eyes.

I'm done playing this role of the poor president, jilted of a happy marriage, but holding on strong for his country.

I walk back to my office after the interview accompanied by Preston and Thomas.

"That was another excellent interview, Mr. President," Preston said, "You are playing it just right. We believe your ratings should begin to turn upward very soon."

I stop in the hallway and turn to face them. These two men have been so influential in the course of my presidency and now my personal life as well.

"You two are the ones who have created this, created me through this. Your salaries are clearly not enough for bringing me through this potentially career destroying mess. Siana Tyler cried, what more could I want?"

By the look on their faces, I know they can see there is more to my thoughts than wanting to congratulate them. They both looked worried. *Good, maybe I want you both to look a little worried.*

"But boys, I'm getting tired of this. I'm tired of all this rehashing the pain of my marriage, which really was not that painful at all. It makes me wonder if this was really the right thing to do."

Their faces show they are starting to panic. *Good, maybe I want you both to feel a little panic too.*

"And there's another thing. I miss Vanessa. She was the one who knew me and loved me. I need to call Vanessa and talk to her. Maybe I'll just fly down there tonight so I can see her in person. We need to hash some of this out." Without waiting for their response, I turn and continue walking down the hall.

I wish I could see their faces with the bombshell I just dropped.

Thomas and Preston quickly follow me. Both begin talking at the same time, rapid fire. I can feel their panic rising. "Xander, no! That cannot happen. That would ruin everything. You cannot talk to Vanessa, you cannot meet with her. You will be seen as weak if you try to get involved again with a woman who has treated you so poorly. That would be the end of your career. You will not win re-election if you and Vanessa reconcile."

I continue walking down the hall towards the Oval Office. I like the feel of being in control for the first time in a long time. I respond to their onslaught, "Maybe I need Vanessa back to get my…my," I cannot come up with the right word, "My normal back."

Preston puts his hand on my shoulder and stops me. He looks straight into my eyes. "Xander, if you get back together with Vanessa, you may have your normal, but you will certainly not have your presidency," he says in a calm, but commanding voice.

Well, there goes my moment of feeling like I was in control.

In my office, I pour myself a scotch and sit down to think. I want to make my own decision, but I know what they are saying is true. *I will not risk losing my presidency for a woman, even if that woman is Vanessa.* Thomas and Preston wait for me to speak and finally I do, resigned to their arguments.

"Preston, you have ladies accompany me to all my events. You would think this would be perfect for me— companionship and no commitment. But honestly, I'm tired of meeting new women. I am ready to have the same woman to come home to every night." I give them a small smirk, "At least on most nights."

They smile back, I am guessing from relief that I sound like myself again.

I did try to be good when I was married. There were just so many beautiful women. But I do want the rock of having one woman at home. Maybe I am changing my ways. Sitting on my couch and drinking my scotch, everything goes quiet. I am consumed in my thoughts.

Thomas, who always has the right words to guide me, comes and sits beside me. His words immediately calm me. "Xander, you sound like a man who is realizing you need love in your life. Vanessa is not an option for love anymore, but there are thousands of other women that are. What you need is to fall in love again. You will find a love just as deep, if not deeper than your love with Vanessa. You will find a woman who will help you find your normal."

Preston sits down on the chair opposite Thomas and me. "And we will help you do just that. We have an option that

24

we think is perfect. You want love in your life. You also need to boost your ratings before heading into re-election."

I turn to Thomas and he continues, "Xander, we will find you a beautiful woman, who is intelligent and kind. She will know the kind of pressure you are under as president and will support you."

Thomas has always been there for me and I trust him. Even Preston, who is twice divorced himself and does not care about my love life, certainly cares about my re-election.

"Okay, boys, what you are telling me sounds perfect. I would love to fall in love again. I need to be re-elected. If you have a plan to make both of those things happen, then your salaries really do need to be doubled."

Preston's face breaks into a huge smile at my words. "The details are in rough form right now."

I cut him off. "I don't care, I want to hear it now! How are you going to find me this perfect woman?"

Preston and Thomas exchange glances and nods.

Preston begins, his voice low with intrigue. "Mr. President, you have called the United States your bride and now we will make that statement a reality. There will be a nationwide search for the most eligible women this country has to offer. They will be everything the wife of the President of the United States needs to be. You will have the opportunity to meet the top candidates from this search and narrow them down to women you want to get to know, and possibly fall in love with, before you choose your wife. This

25

process will undoubtedly boost your ratings sky high as most of America will be captivated by your journey to fall in love. You will be happily married long before re-election day and much of America will think of you being that way all along. This is a win-win situation for everyone."

"I love it! I truly love the whole idea. The excitement of it, the romance, and the ratings it will undoubtedly bring." *I'm impressed that Preston thought outside the box on this one.*

I nod to Preston with approval. I look from him to Thomas and break into a smile. My energy and hope for the future are renewed. I suddenly cannot contain my enthusiasm.

"Well, you certainly have a lot of work to do to get this ball rolling between now and our next meeting. Good work, boys. This is excellent, just excellent! Go make my dream wife, and the sky high ratings that go along with her, a reality."

~~

Chapter 3

REVEALED IN DREAMS
Mordecai Allenby – Oregon Attorney General

My eyes meet Esther's as the bell over the door signals her entrance at our favorite little Thai restaurant. I love the big smile she throws my way. Quickly, I'm standing to greet my dear girl and help her take off her rain-soaked jacket before we hug our hellos and sit down.

"So, what is it about today, Uncle Cai?" She asks, nodding towards my book resting on the corner of our table. She takes a long sip of the Thai iced tea I have waiting for her. "I haven't gotten too far into this one yet. It's about the prophecies of Ezekiel chapters thirty-eight and thirty-nine."

It may look to her as though I was reading while I was waiting, but in reality I couldn't concentrate on a word. Not with everything on my mind that I want to say.

In her teasing tone she says, "Do you want me to get you some cardstock so you can make a sign to carry around that says, 'The end is near'? Maybe a megaphone would help too!"

Her lighthearted humor only makes me feel worse about what I need to say.

"You know that might not look so good though," she continues, "for the Oregon Attorney General to be pacing the streets during his lunch hour, wearing a message of doom."

"Well, maybe not then," *My lightheartedness is forced.*

Approaching our table again now that Esther has arrived, Marion gives a small bow of her head. Palms pressed against one another as though in a prayer position.

In her thick Thai accent, "*Sa wat dii kha*, Esther, you look as lovely as always."

"Thank you, Marion, you too. Something new with your hair?"

"Oh, stronger black to hide the grey, that's all!"

Esther smiles, "Grey—I can't believe it—you are much too young for that!"

Marion beams. "Mango and sticky rice on the house for you today. What else for you my dear?"

"You can take Uncle Cai's order first while I think."

Marion shakes her head. "Cai's no fun, I have his order memorized for the last ten years. Lettuce wraps and Pad Thai. Never changes." She looks with mock disapproving at me, but breaks into a smile instead when I shrug my shoulders at her.

Marion and I patiently wait as Esther flips through the menu, indecision pasted all over her face.

"Everything is just so good!"

"You say that every time, Esther. You know I always love to hear it."

"Okay, I got it, Marion: a bowl of chicken Tom Yum Soup—that is if Uncle Cai doesn't mind sharing one of his lettuce wraps with me?"

Esther looks at me with a hopeful smile on her face—the same face she has given me since she was a little girl.

"Of course, Esther, you can have one of my lettuce wraps."

"And Marion, we will take that mango and sticky rice, but we must pay for it. You already give us too much food."

Marion just smiles and now it's her turn for a shoulder shrug.

"Thank you, Marion—*Khop khun.*"

Esther looks around the restaurant as she speaks. "We have been coming to this restaurant for such a long time."

How can I say the words that I know she will not understand? That she will resent?

Esther continues, oblivious to my inner turmoil.

"I remember being here one time when I was really young. I don't remember how old I was, maybe seven or eight. I think there was another part to it back then. I remember someone dropped a platter and the crash of dishes scared me so much I jumped. The most delicious smell in the world came from that pile of broken dishes. I'll never forget it. Sometimes I go back to that feeling of being a little girl when we are here—the same delicious smells."

I can't help but smile. "I love the way this restaurant takes me back too. Although, this restaurant never had another part to it. I think you just grew up."

"Are you sure, Uncle Cai? I could have sworn there was more to it back then?"

I just smile and shake my head no. "Would you like to hear about my first memory of bringing you to this restaurant?"

Nodding for me to continue—Esther already looks nostalgic. *This isn't what I planned on talking about, but maybe a good way to start.*

"You know that your mom introduced me to this place way back during high school—I think it was her senior year and I was just a lowly freshman when we found it. We would come hang out here—especially because our parents didn't like spicy food and so it was our own special place for years. This was back before Thai food was so trendy."

Obviously enthralled by my memories, Esther leans forward in rapt attention.

"I attribute your love for Thai food to the fact that your mom kept coming here throughout her pregnancy. She would come with me—with your dad—with anyone who would come."

Esther's smile is clouded by sadness. "I always think of my mom and dad when we are here. Sometimes I try to picture them sitting at one of the tables." Her smile comes back quickly and she encourages me on with her bright eyes.

"Well, the first time I brought you here on my own, it had been a really rough week for both of us. It must have been at least three months after the accident. I tried to come earlier, but had not been able to force myself to stop. Drove by often, even parking once, but I just wasn't ready yet. My grief was still too strong."

"You had not slept much that week. Crying and crying. Begging for your mommy and daddy. You would run out of my arms into Davide's room to pick up his teddy bear and tell me that he needed it—could we please take it to him?"

I glance up and notice Esther's eyes are watering. It's still hard for her to hear—and hard for me to talk about the car accident that took them all away from us too soon.

"We were both exhausted from lack of sleep—emotionally raw and alone. That particular night, I could not get you to fall asleep. We had read stories—I had walked with you—I was completely out of energy and ideas. For whatever reason in my sleep deprived mind, I decided we needed to come here. I strapped you into your booster seat and off we went. Although not so late for a bachelor to go out to dinner, it was late for a preschooler. It probably showed my lack of expertise at being a father to everyone in the restaurant."

Reaching out for my hand, Esther squeezes. She dabs her eyes with the napkin in her other hand.

I continue. "As soon as I came inside and saw all the faces I'd seen here with your mom and dad, I began to feel lighter. I ordered your mom's favorite soup—the one you just ordered."

"While we waited, I cuddled you in my lap with your blanket wrapped around you. I told you stories about your mom and dad and big brother. Your green eyes were so wide. I stroked your head and your eyes became heavier and heavier until you dozed off. By the time the soup came, you were in the deepest sleep you had been in for a long time."

A tear slips down Esther's cheek and she grabs a new napkin to wipe it away. "It's still hard to hear," she gently says, "But good—it's good to hear. We have been through so much together—and in this restaurant."

"Yes, right here." I look around for a moment, picturing my quarter of a century younger self—a new and inexperienced father to this precious girl—a grieving brother—a lawyer struggling to keep my practice alive in the midst of it all.

"It was Marion's father here that night and he would not close up the restaurant because he did not want to disturb your sleep. They all knew how much we were going through. I finally realized how late it was, thanked him, and bundled you up to go home. That was the first time you slept through the night without waking up crying."

Esther chokes up and struggles to clear her throat.

"You know Esther, that was the night I knew we were going to be okay. In the months before then, I was not so sure. But that night, I knew."

Memories consume me in the quiet of the moment. *Come on Cai, remember what God has told you. Focus—do not compromise.*

Picking up my glass of tea, I drink the rest of it and try to compose myself before I begin to speak.

"I do want to talk to you about something else today."

"Of course, Uncle Cai." Esther dabs her eyes again and sits up a little straighter in her chair.

"I know you have been looking at your options after you finish your masters and I have an idea for you."

"I figured you would want to talk about my plans for a job today. I'm kind of stumped at the moment."

"It's probably not something you have thought of. You might even think it sounds a little crazy, but I hope you will hear me out."

"Uncle Cai, I don't think in all my childhood I can remember you saying you have a crazy idea for me," she responds, leaning in with eagerness.

She won't be so eager once she hears what I have to say.

"A few weeks ago, I had a very vivid dream. You were in it. You were waving to me from the front door of the White House and you blew me a kiss just before you turned to walk inside. There's more to the dream, but I'll tell you the rest later."

Esther looks curiously intent. "Won't you tell me the rest now?"

Nodding my head no, I pause to think a moment before I keep talking. *If I tell her about getting tackled to the ground and arrested it will make her worry.*

"I had the exact same dream the next night and the next and the next—ten nights in a row."

Esther sits back now, sipping her Thai iced tea, obviously intrigued.

"What a bizarre dream—and to have it over and over."

I realize I am clenching my jaw a little—my shoulders are tight—the anxiety of what I am about to say. Trying to relax, I continue, "A few nights into the dreams I had a strong impression that it meant something important. I began to pray I would understand any meaning this dream might hold."

"Did you find the meaning?" Esther looks excited.

"Yes, Esther, that is what I want to talk to you about."

The moment she realizes the meaning of my dream—everything will change. Her countenance, her curiosity, maybe even how she feels about me will change. With resolve I almost wish I didn't have, I carry on.

"The morning after the tenth night of dreams, I woke up to hear about President Susa's search for a new First Lady."

The scowl on her face makes her feelings perfectly clear—even before her words do.

"I have been watching that on the news too. Totally disgusting. I assume you heard they decided to put on a nationwide search with screening centers where women can come 'try out'. The whole thing is pathetic on so many levels."

I look down at the table. "It does make me sad."

God—really? Are you sure I have to say this?

Esther tries to lighten my obviously heavy mood during the silence of my prayer. "But it sounds like people love the entertainment of it all. I'm guessing this is all just a publicity stunt to boost the president's approval ratings. I don't think he will really go through with it."

Looking up at my dear girl, I see she is now shaking her head and smiling, almost in amusement. She continues, "Can you imagine the poor woman if he does choose a wife? It would all be about the looks. She will have to be the silent type because you know she won't be allowed to say a word after what his first wife said to the press."

Esther falls quiet—*probably realizing the awkwardness of my quiet.*

I inhale slowly—composing myself as best I can. "Esther, the morning I saw the news about the nationwide search to find the president a new wife, my ten nights of dreaming suddenly became crystal clear. I prayed about it over and over and God confirmed it. Something that does not make sense, even to me. However, I have learned that sometimes God tells us to do things that don't make sense in our eyes."

I straighten up in my chair. Esther's hands are on the table in front of me and I take them in my own. *This is the hardest thing I have ever had to say to her. The most confusing moment during a lifetime of following Christ.*

"Esther, I think you should go to a screening center. I believe God wants you to become the First Lady of the United States of America."

"WHAT?" She practically yells as she pulls her hands out of mine. Instantly she looks around, probably realizing how loudly she responded. Esther quickly lowers her voice to a strong whisper and leans in towards me.

"There are a hundred reasons why I would never do that. I can't believe you would even suggest it!" Quickly stopping her response and looking down at the table, a smile begins to spread across her face as she slowly shakes her head back and forth.

"Oh, Uncle Cai —that was a good one. You completely got me—although that really wasn't funny at all." Her eyes meet mine and by the sudden drop of her smile, I can see she realizes I am completely serious.

It takes all the strength I can muster to respond. "Esther, I am sorry, but I am sure of it."

My sweet Esther is silent for a few moments. *Dear God, is this really what you want? How can this be the plan you have for her?*

Her face shows confusion—then anger. Finally, she takes a deep breath to speak. "Uncle Cai, when you said you had an idea that was *a little crazy,* I assumed you meant crazy as in fun or interesting. This would be humiliating."

I just sit quietly. *She has to work through this on her own.*

"You know me—this would be horrible for me! Where do I even begin with all the reasons? First of all, this is probably just an attention-seeking ratings scheme by a desperate president. So, the women involved will be humiliated in the end. Second, even if it is for real, it is still humiliating. A man shopping for his new wife as though he is shopping for a new car. Third, if he actually does want a wife, I don't want to join my life to a man whose marital drama and self-centeredness has been the headline news story for months. He brutally threw his wife and marriage aside in one night. He destroyed Vanessa Susa in every way for his own gain. He probably will do the same thing to his next wife as well. And last, but most important. I love God and would only want to marry a man who loves him as well. That is definitely not the president."

Esther has never looked at me like this before. She eyes me like I am the enemy and have betrayed her. "God, help me be strong in what you have told me. Please, let us stay close. Esther and I have been through so much already."

Esther finally holds her tongue and sits in angry silence, looking down at her hands.

"I understand and even agree with what you are saying. I still know what God made clear to me and wanted me to share with you."

Shaking her head, she looks straight at me. "Be honest, Uncle Cai, what is your angle on this? What are you hoping to get out of me marrying the president?"

Her words cut me to the core. *After all these years lovingly caring for her, giving and sacrificing, that she thinks I am using her for my own gain.* I try to separate my response from the hurt I am feeling.

"Esther, I hope you would trust me enough to know that I would never ask you to do something for my own gain."

A tear glistens in the corner of her eye. I want to tell her to forget all this, but I can't do that. *I have to hold strong.*

"I agree that this is not the kind of marriage I would have dreamed for you. However, I am confident that God has this plan for you. He has made it clear to me, even though I don't know why." My voice cracks with emotion.

Esther takes a deep breath. "I don't actually think you would use me, Uncle Cai. But I don't understand why in the world you are suggesting this?"

"Maybe God has a plan for you in this position. I love you and value you and believe in what He can do through you."

Esther lets out a muffled grunt.

I remember her doing that when she was younger and did not agree with my decisions as her parent. Just as I did then, I hold on to what I believe is right and leave the changing of her heart to the Lord.

Marion returns with our food. We both take the momentary distraction to calm down from this emotional conversation. I watch Esther lean over her bowl and inhale the spices coming off her Tom Yum Soup.

She does that every time she gets her food; ever since she was a little girl.

In the quiet moment, watching Esther, my love for her wells up so strongly.

"It's not that I think I would be chosen to be the president's wife, but it's the fact that you want me to try." Pausing for a moment, her look changes from anger to concern. "Is it possible that maybe you are going a little too far in your faith? Would God really tell you something that completely goes against everything both you and I think is right?"

"Esther, I would never want either of us to live our lives outside of God's best. You will have to pray about this and see what God tells you. All I know is what He told me."

There's anger in her eyes again. I've seen that righteous anger before when she would tell me stories from her work of the abused and oppressed women and children in human trafficking. Her anger burned as she told me about the atrocities people inflict on others. I always agreed with her anger and supported her efforts to make change. This time, her anger is pointed at me. Maybe she is feeling that same sense of injustice and oppression.

"Really, Uncle Cai, I don't see you giving up your career to follow some crazy idea God gave you." Her tone is harsher now. "I don't see you marrying someone horrible in the name of God." Another deep breath and a more controlled

39

voice as she speaks again. "You know I love the Lord. You know I want to live my life for Him and follow His plans for me. But I cannot believe for one second that this is God's plan for me. To be the pretty girl used, or better oppressed, by the president for his own gain."

Esther's beauty has actually been a challenge in her life—the guys wanted her and the girls wanted to hate her. She really is beautiful. Tall like my sister, with long chestnut hair and deep green eyes.

Keeping the boys away from her had been practically a full-time job. In junior high, the high school boys were interested. When she was in high school, it was the college boys or even older. So beautiful in her spirit and personality too—truly gorgeous in every way.

Now, rather than encouraging her away from an older man who would love to have a young, beautiful woman on his arm for the second time around, I am actually encouraging her.

"Let's assume for just one second Uncle Cai that I end up marrying him. Then what? Wait for him to divorce me?" Shaking her head and taking a spoonful of soup, she seems to have finished speaking for the moment.

"I have thought about all of this Esther and agree completely with everything you are saying." By the look on her face, I can tell this only frustrates her more. "However, despite these less than perfect circumstances . . ."

"Less than perfect circumstances!" Esther interjects with the combination of exasperation and sarcasm.

"Yes, even in these circumstances I still believe God wants you to do this for a reason." I look over my untouched Pad Thai at my Esther. Her jaw is clenched tight and her nostrils flare out slightly as she breaths.

"All I can do is encourage you to ask God what He has for you. If this is His plan, then He will be just as clear to you about it as He has been to me. Esther, just promise me you will pray about this and ask God to show you what He wants."

Her eyes quickly dart to her keys sitting on the edge of the table.

She is getting ready to go. This isn't how I want to leave things.

As she reaches for them, I gently put my hand over hers. "I am asking you, Esther, please just pray about this possibility."

Without making eye contact, she pulls her hand away with her keys clutched inside. With a large breath in and out she answers, "Fine, I'll pray—even though I already know what is right. I have to go."

Nearly colliding with Marion as she pushes back her chair, Esther starts to mutter an apology. It catches in her throat and something resembling a sob emerges instead. Her hand flies to her mouth to cover it.

I stand up to comfort her, but she extends her arm to me as a barricade as she hops up and darts around Marion and flees out the door. I watch her go. The jingling from the bell on

41

the door signals our relationship might never be the same. I slump back down into my chair.

Lord, please do not destroy my relationship with Esther. Even more, please do not let her be destroyed through this.

A hand on my shoulder causes me to look up. Marion's bewildered face looks at me with confusion. "Mr. Cai, everything okay?"

With the spices of uneaten Thai food still filling my nose, I unsuccessfully try to muster a smile at Marion. *What can I say? Nothing feels okay in this moment.*

"Marion, I have to trust it will be okay."

~~

Chapter 4

WRESTLING WITH GOD
ESTHER

My feet beat the pavement in the rhythmic pattern of my run. Maybe I can get my anger to fall into a manageable rhythm as well. This is my way of handling stress. With each splash of my feet on the wet ground, I think one word at a time of how I am feeling. They are angry words. Some are even curses I would never say out loud, but in my head they are screaming. After a few blocks, the words turn into incomplete sentences. I can tell I am thinking more clearly: *How could he? What do you expect? How could you?*

A mile or so into the run I feel the weakness of my body as I grow more tired. The drizzling rain has left me wet. A sense of vulnerability comes. This is usually the point in a run I hate and I love; where I feel close to the Lord as his weak child, who needs His help every step of the way. Some of my most passionate times of prayer are while I run. Today though, distrust and anger fill my heart—instead of that usual close feeling.

"Honestly God, I don't want to be open with you. I do not want to pray because I'm afraid of what you might say."

As I continue to tell the Lord I do not want to pray, I find myself already talking to him about it. With resignation and a sigh, I continue. *"I am frustrated and angry at Uncle Cai and at you too if I am honest. Why in the world would he want me to do this? Is he becoming some religious fanatic?"*

Since childhood, Uncle Cai taught me about his faith as a Messianic Jew. Born and raised Jewish, both he and my mother had learned about the saving grace of Jesus during high school. Their choice was not received well by their parents. Over time, my grandparents pulled farther and farther away from their children. Eventually they gave them an ultimatum, "Continue on this path and you will be choosing the Jesus of the Bible over your family." They continued on the path and eventually there was no relationship between them.

Is this really what Uncle Cai wants for his only family member? To marry me off to a man like the president? I can't imagine my mother would ever ask me to do this. She would understand how this feels from a woman's perspective."

As I pour out my frustration to the Lord, a sense of calm begins to fill me, almost like a hot cup of coffee warms me after being out in the cold. As the feeling of calm grows, my shoulders and arms, all the way down to my fingers feel tired after holding tension. My anger has worked itself out, but in its place I still find confusion and questions.

"It is not fair for Uncle Cai to put this expectation on me. You know President Susa is not the kind of man I want to marry."

As the sky darkens overhead, I start going over a list in my head of pros and cons on marrying the president.

The president is a womanizer = Con. It is his second marriage and it will be in the shadow of a scandal = Con. The president's wife lives her life under the spotlight with every detail scrutinized = Con. President Susa and I do not share values, beliefs, or common morals = Con.

Uncle Cai's words suddenly ring through my mind, "Please pray about it." *Okay, I'll pray about it if only to confirm that this is not from the Lord.*

I try to push away all the negative reasons flooding my mind. I begin to talk to the Lord again—this time out loud to keep me focused. "Father, you know there is no part of me that wants to marry the president. The whole idea is absurd. If you really spoke to my Uncle Cai … then you will have to make it completely clear to me."

As my prayer ends, so does my desire to run. I head home just as the rain picks up intensity. Something about the rain coming down all around me gently reminds me of the Lord's constant presence. *I feel loved and lighter, more open.*

As I step through my apartment door, the chill of being caught in the rain sets in. I head straight to the bathroom and run a hot bath.

When I step into the bath, it is hotter than I think I might be able to stand. Slowly, I ease myself in, gritting my teeth as I go. *I always love it once I get in if I can just make it through the initial pain.* Finally, settled under the water and adjusting to the heat as the steam rises around me, I remember what I heard about a frog in hot water. A frog will hop right out if it is put into a pot of boiling hot water. However, if a frog is put into a pot of room temperature water and the water is slowly brought to boiling, the frog won't even realize it is being boiled to death until it is too late. The irony of that story is not lost on me, as I compare myself to that frog.

If I even consider getting involved in this process of marrying the president, it could be a pot I never get out of. The embarrassment of trying out could haunt me forever. Then there is the unlikely chance that, God forbid, I do end up marrying the president. I would be stuck in a pot of shallowness, hurt, and pain. I force myself to lay back and relax. To think. To pray. To let the Lord take my mind where He wants it to go. My thoughts are still jumbled.

Come on Esther - focus, pray about this and be done.

Just a couple of minutes into quiet prayer and my mind is again playing out the consequences I would suffer for getting involved in this process. *Why hasn't the right guy just come along already and I would not even be praying about this.*

A book on the shelf next to my tub grabs my attention. I've been wanting to read it about secret believers around the world. *Maybe it will settle my thoughts to read.*

The first story tells of a man who planned to go to a secret meeting of Christians. Before he went, a friend warned him that the police had been tipped off about their meeting. In the closed country where he lived, it would mean certain imprisonment and possible death if he was caught attending. The man took time to pray with his wife about what to do. He felt a strong urging to go to the meeting. The man kissed his wife and young children goodbye, possibly for the last time and went to gather with other believers.

Part way through the service, the police burst through the doors as he had feared. Everyone was ordered to lie face down on the ground. With guns pointed at them, the police captain said, "Deny this Jesus and you may go home." A few did leave. He stayed where he was, face down on the ground, preparing to die – maybe this was the plan God had all along. Then, the captain of the police asked those who were left to sit up. He motioned for the guns to be lowered. As the man and the others sat up in confusion, the captain asked the remaining believers if they could help him and his guards find Christ as their Savior as well.

How could a man be willing to give up his family, his future, and even his life for the Lord? What kind of strength must it have taken to stay; to not have run from fear?

I am slightly shaking as I lay the book down on the side of the tub.

I would like to think I would be willing to sacrifice my life to share my love for Christ. But would I? I don't know if I'm strong enough.

I think about those in my life who I would like to see know Christ personally. The girl at the beauty school who does my hair and talks to me about her struggles to know if God is real. My sweet neighbor, who is so kind and hopes she will be saved by her goodness. The little Kenyan boy, who made such an impression on me in a village years ago."

I say I want them to know Christ, but what have I sacrificed to tell them? As I add more hot water to my bath, I think back to that little boy in Kenya. I was working as an advocate with a campaign against female circumcision. My group and I peeled ourselves out of the four-wheel-drive after the teeth-chattering, head-shaking, bumpy ride to get there. We were greeted by a large group of children. They surrounded us with big smiles; white rows of teeth showing through their pink lips on a background of dark chocolate skin.

The children encircled me. Their beautiful brown eyes were on me and their hands reached out to touch my skin and hair. Their calls of *"mazungu, mazungu"* echoed through my ears. I knew this as a friendly greeting to someone with white skin. My surreal moment came to a quick end as I felt a sharp pinch on my arm. I suddenly began to feel crowded by the large number of children pressing against me. I looked towards the source of the pain on my arm and found a little boy no more than five or six-years-old with his thumb and forefinger still locked on my skin. He was wearing nothing except a tattered pair of shorts and a grin that matched the twinkle in his eye.

I put my hand on his and gently took his fingers off of my skin. I asked him, "Why did you pinch me?"

The little boy responded in English, a language he seemed excited to try out, "It hurt you?"

"Yes, it hurt me, just like it would hurt you," I told the boy as all the other children watched this interaction with curiosity.

I was fascinated when the little boy's smile lit up even wider and he said, "That's why I pinch— to see if your skin hurt like mine."

A smile burst across my face at his response. I wanted to share with him that there is a God who loves him, but I never got to. Armed with new knowledge, the curious boy ran off yelling his discovery about white skin to the rest of the village.

My initial question of what I would sacrifice to share the love of God comes back to me. *I don't think I am as strong as the man in the story to die in that moment of crisis.*

My book sits on the side of the tub where I laid it a few minutes earlier. I pick it up again—reading one story and then another until I am completely engrossed in the lives of these secret believers. The theme of each life is the same: *Ordinary people believing in God and doing what he asks them to do, even if it means giving up their comfort, their families, or their lives.*

The cooling bath water signals the passage of time. Shivering, I dry off and dress in comfy clothes. I make a cup of coffee and settle onto the couch with my Bible.

God hasn't given me an answer yet, but I feel more open.

My phone lights up. A text has come in. It's Leeann.

I completely forgot about meeting her and friends for dinner!

I call her immediately.

"Leeann, it's me."

"Hi, are you coming? We are already at the table."

"I'm so sorry. I had quite a day and I completely forgot about dinner."

"What's going on Esther? Are you okay?"

"I'm fine, just a lot on my mind. By the time I could get there, you'd be done anyway. Go on without me."

"No problem, but do you want me to come by after? I can bring some food."

"You are sweet Leeann, but I'm good. Just thinking."

More friend's jovial voices chime in to say hello. "Hi everyone!" I respond.

"Leeann, can we talk in the morning?"

"Sounds good. We'll all miss you tonight." The jovial voices again wishing me goodbye. *I am glad I do not have to put on a happy face tonight.*

"Thanks, good night."

"Night Esther, sweet dreams." *Funny Leeann should mention my dreams. A few of the stories I read today mentioned God using dreams in people's lives. Maybe God will send his thunderbolt or voice from heaven through a dream tonight.*

In the quiet, I wait for something from the Lord. Bible stories come to mind about others who sacrificed. Stephen, whose face was like an angel as he was dying became the first Christian martyr.

Ruth, who stayed with her mother-in-law, Naomi, and gave up any known possibility for her future. Job, the ultimate man of suffering. He continued to praise God when everything was taken away from him.

The disciples who gave up their lives of normalcy and comfort for Christ.

Then I remember the story of Hosea. I open my Bible and find the story in the book with his name. I read how Hosea took a prostitute, Gomer, as his wife just to proclaim the love and goodness of God to his people. They had three children, although in her unfaithfulness the third was not even Hosea's child. Hosea stayed faithful. Gomer eventually left Hosea for another lover, only to be sold into slavery. Although it seemed more than any man could bear, Hosea obeyed God again when he went and bought Gomer out of slavery and took her home. *Honestly, this story has always really bothered me. How could God ask Hosea to go through all that just to explain his love to Israel? Was that really fair?*

Sitting still and listening, I feel God's presence. I half expect him to answer me out loud, although that has never happened in my life before. I listen to the clock counting away the seconds. There is the engine of a car revving outside. I hear thunder in the distance telling of the continued rain. *"God, I want you to help me understand."*

The loud answer I want never comes, but just a tiny thought. *Hosea knew that my plan for his life was more important than what he hoped and dreamed for himself. Do you feel the same way?*

That was it. In one question, God summed up everything! *Do I trust him with my life?*

"God," I pray out loud, "at any other time I would easily answer yes. Yes, I want my life to follow your plan. I always thought that your plan and mine would be pretty similar, but now I'm not so sure. I worry that if I say yes, you are going to ask me to do something I do not want to do."

In his still, small voice of my heart I feel him answer. "I might ask you to do something you don't understand. Something that will be difficult. Will you do it?"

In this very real situation where God's plan could be worlds apart from my own, will I submit to him?

In my mind and will, a battle is raging. In my mind, I know whatever God has planned for my life is far better than anything I could plan for myself. My will is having a hard time letting go.

I fall to my knees and bury my head into the couch. I begin crying as I pray through my inner struggle. My will does not want to submit. My mind tells me the only life I want to live is submitted to Christ. Like Jacob wrestling with the Lord, my own wrestling match goes on and on. I completely lose track of time. I go from telling the Lord I will obey whatever He says, to making up excuses why I will not.

"Maybe this is just a test. Is that it? Just testing to see if I will do whatever you ask?"

God continually tells my spirit He is not satisfied with my half-hearted submission. He encourages me to truly give over my will to Him. Our wrestling match continues.

A thought comes to me again and again. *"Go to a screening center. That is what I want you to do."*

What? Lord, don't ask me to do that.

Time goes by, only my aching knees give a clue to how long. I finally give up my will and a peace washes over me. I speak the commitment out loud to the Lord. "I will obey you Lord and go to a screening center. It is against what I would choose, but you have made it clear. I trust you. To the screening center."

I use my arms to push off the couch and support my legs in standing.

I can't believe I actually changed my mind about this and have agreed to go to a center. I've heard it said that the greatest miracle is a change of heart. After tonight, I agree. It is late and I am exhausted, but I fall into my bed knowing the only life I want to lead is the one that God has planned for me.

~~

Chapter 5

THE RED PASS
ESTHER

"Leeann, where have the last two months gone? How can it already be this embarrassing day! The long days of dread crawled by, but now that it is here—the time went too quickly."

"It's been fun watching the other screenings. The thirty-seven women going to the meet and greet at President Susa's home in Colorado look respectable, don't you think?" *Leeann's chipper response makes me think she is actually excited about today.*

I respond glumly. "But the lines of women waiting to get into the centers were so long and they were not all respectable. Cameras are everywhere for the entire world to see. That is why I have been so anxious."

We are speeding up I-5 from Portland to Seattle. The northwest screening will be a media extravaganza like all the rest. I shuffle through the paperwork I brought along, while Leeann drives. I have my criminal background check, copies of my diplomas, an eight by ten picture of myself, and my resume—all in my portfolio.

Holding the portfolio up to Leeann I say, "See, this just proves how ridiculous this whole thing is. Who has to submit a resume when looking for a husband? Obviously this is a job, not a real marriage. Not even a job I am interested in getting."

"Esther, don't worry so much. It won't be that bad. This is just a fun day out."

I nod at Leeann and give her a half-hearted smile. My thoughts are running away. *Why didn't I just get up that next morning after praying and pretend I never heard from the Lord. It had been a late night and no one would expect me to keep a commitment I had made halfway through the night.*

I know God—I know. I always come back to the same answer. You and I know. And my life will not be the same if I build a wall between us.

My thoughts are back to the car and Leeann. "I know I've told you before, but thank you again for coming with me today. I don't think I could be driving up this road if it wasn't for you."

Leeann has been my good friend since running track together in high school. She was the instigator of our silliness. Leeann would roll down the windows of her car and sing along to her music at the top of her lungs and encourage me to do the same. She got me to dress up as Marilyn Monroe one time when we went shopping. Her motto was, "An adventure waits around every corner; you just have to turn the corner."

"Thank you for helping me go through this . . . humiliation!"

55

Leeann smiles sideways at me, "No humiliation—just fun. Besides, it's not every day I get invited along to try and marry the same guy my friend is interested in." She laughs at her own joke.

"I'm not even interested in him. I'm just going to the screening center, that's all," I quickly respond, flustered. "You'll probably end up marrying him!"

"Nope, you are the one who felt like you were supposed to come. It must be for a reason. Maybe God wants you to lighten up and have some fun." Her humor is not always so funny.

I think back to when I told Uncle Cai about my decision to go to the screening. I thought he would respond differently, at least happy or satisfied I took his advice. Instead, he sadly said, "God has a plan in this Esther. It might not even be about you."

Might not even be about me, it sure feels like it is all about me right now since I'm the one who is doing this.

Uncle Cai told me I shouldn't mention to anyone at the screening that God told me to come. *I agree completely.*

I explained some of it to Leeann. She understands listening to God, but she thinks of this as a fun adventure from God. Not me.

I groan. Then taking a deep breath, I try to relax.

Uncle Cai sounded so secretive, so worried. I still have a nagging thought he encouraged me to do this for some political reason. Why else would I have to be so hush, hush about everything? About being Jewish? About being related to him?

We ride in silence except for discussing the directions. Leeann maneuvers us off the freeway and we find the convention center parking garage.

As we pull in, I say, "I'm not feeling so good about this. Look at all these cars and the TV crews. I don't think I can do this." This moment is one I anticipated needing Leeann by my side.

"You, my friend, are going to be fabulous! There is not one woman here today with the combination of brains, beauty, and kindness that you have Esther, except for me, of course," Leeann says with a smile, "and I'm only here for moral support!"

I take a big breath encouraged by her confidence and lightened by her humor.

With such different values, I don't think I am the kind of woman the president is looking for. Hopefully that will mean my day will be over soon. I'll have obeyed the Lord, but be back in Portland and my normal life by tonight.

"Now let's get some lipstick on and get out there." Leeann whips open her purse and holds out two lipstick choices to me—soft pink or bright red.

I force a smile after applying the soft pink lipstick. Leeann throws open her car door as I tentatively reach for mine, wishing I could just stay inside. We meet at the front of the car, join arms, and begin walking toward the convention center. The doors are scheduled to open at 10:00 a.m. and even though it's only 9:40, we see women streaming to get into a long line that is already formed. Television crews are swarming. Interviews are already taking place.

"The circus I was dreading is here in full force," I whisper to Leeann, as we take our place at the back of the line. I can't help but notice the woman just a couple up from us dressed only in a bikini and stilettos. *Really, is she kidding? That is exactly why I did not want to come down here, to be associated with this.*

Leeann gives me a nudge and nods her head towards a woman getting in line, wearing a large white wedding dress with a veil and full train.

Leeann and I both quickly look away and try to suppress our giggles - my first moment of relief. *Good to find some humor in this madness.*

Just as quickly as the relief came, it is gone. I'm filled with dread again as a camera crew looks towards our part of the line.

"Leeann, I am feeling sick to my stomach. This decision seems worse and worse the more I look around."

"No, it's fine. Look, at that lady up ahead. She looks professional." Her eyes scan the group again. "And up even farther, there's a whole group of well-dressed women. And over there in the power suit," she motions to a woman walking towards us. "She could be the CEO of a company."

As I look around, I see the majority really are well-dressed, calm, and collected women. "It looks like we all got the memo on the outfits. I was thinking job interview clothes." I look down at my black skirt and pink dress shirt that looks strikingly similar to many of the ladies in line. "Maybe we won't stand out as much and get the focus. That is fine with me, since I do not want a camera anywhere near us."

The minutes tick by slowly as we wait for ten o'clock. I think Leeann is sensing my tension because she keeps bringing up topics to talk about.

"Do you remember the time we waited for concert tickets all night long? I was so cold I never did fall asleep." Even though I would rather just sit quietly and wait for the inevitable, I appreciate her efforts to keep me relaxed.

"I remember—it was so cold. When we were almost to the front, they sold out. Oh, we were so upset." I smile as I think of that morning with Leeann and other friends.

"I remember we decided to use some of our unused concert money to splurge on breakfast. I have never eaten so many pancakes in all my life," she said.

Just then, the line begins surging forward and we move quickly towards the convention center doors. "Here we go."

We settle into a quiet between us until we're inside the convention center. Tables are set up all over the hall, one person behind each table, and a new line formed in front of each one. Women are presenting their paperwork, as well as themselves, to the person behind the table. Leeann spies a table with a fairly short line and pulls my arm to hurry towards it. "I guess our wait is not quite over."

"This must be the screening right here," I tell Leeann. "I thought there would be more to it than just one person behind a table." While we wait, we look around and try to figure out the system.

"Okay, so most of the ladies go back out the front doors after their turn at the table. I assume that means they are being sent home," Leeann says.

"I saw a couple of ladies wearing more outrageous outfits heading out, so that is probably right," I add.

"But some ladies walk towards that door." Leeann motions to the far end of the hall. "See, there."

We both watch a woman in a dress walk towards a side door and hand something to the man standing at the entrance, who then welcomes her inside.

"So maybe there is more to it," Leeann concludes.

This makes me more nervous. "I am just hoping I get rejected and get to go home? The only time in my life I have wanted to be rejected." We both smile as we work to keep my fear at bay.

"I'm with you Esther. If you go home, I go home."

We wait for almost an hour to get to the front of this second line. We step forward together and the man sitting behind the table greets us and asks for our portfolios. He takes the paperwork from our outstretched arms with a smile. "Let me just take a moment to look over what you have brought."

We stand patiently as the man flips through the summary of our lives. I can hardly keep myself still, but manage to hold it together by the encouragement of Leeann's small smile and a slight raise of her eyebrows. *It's as though I'm waiting for results at the doctor's office.*

"You both look like accomplished young women. We're glad to see women of your caliber interested in this process. I would like to ask you a few more questions."

He asks about our hobbies, our dream job, and our biggest regret. I look to Leeann to let her go first. When it's my turn, I try to be as honest as I can and I hope this man will see that I am not the right woman for the President.

"My hobbies include running, reading, serving at a local shelter, and I've just started learning guitar. The question of my dream job is difficult, but I know it would involve helping those who cannot help themselves—standing up for the oppressed. And my biggest regret—." I can feel myself starting to get emotional, but I don't want to do that here, so I choke back my feelings. "I wish I could have known my mother, father, and brother because they died in a car accident when I was very young."

With that, the man smiles and writes something down on his clipboard. "The rest of the president's staff and I would like to get to know each of you a little better, to see if you might be a possible match for the president. Would you please join us in the Red Room at the end of the hall?"

We nod. *No Lord, no farther, please.*

With that, he hands our portfolios back—along with a small red pass. He points us down the hall where we'd watched the other lady head just a few minutes earlier. As we start walking that direction, Leeann says in an almost giddy voice, "It almost feels like being back in middle school and we have been given the teacher's hall pass."

"I guess this means we can't go home yet? Or can we?" I hesitate for a moment with that hope that I have gone far enough, knowing I haven't yet.

"You are enjoying this too much Leeann."

"It's just an interesting day is all, so let's keep going." I shrug and Leeann leads the way as we weave through the sea of women towards the door to the Red Room. We walk by a woman standing off by herself, a scowl on her face. She looks down and sees the passes in our hands.

"Oh, I see you two are some of the beautiful ones. It seems like everywhere in this country we have to worry about being politically correct, except when the president picks a wife. If you don't have a degree, no Red Room for you. Any criminal background, you are out. If you are over thirty-five, don't even think about it. But most importantly, if you aren't one of the beautiful ones, then definitely no. So, congratulations beautiful ladies, enjoy your politically incorrect path to the Red Room! If you become the First Lady, please remember us still out in the real world."

We stop in our tracks at the woman's speech that has also gathered the attention of others waiting in line.

Before either of us can say anything, the woman walks off. Leeann and I stare at her, eyes wide open as she walks away. Looking back at each other, small giggles escape us. "Well, I guess we are lucky to be off to the Red Room, oh beautiful one," Leeann whispers.

"It really depends on how you look at it—if we are lucky or not," I reply. The woman's speech broke my nerves and I feel a little more relaxed as I follow Leeann through the crowd with the red pass in my hand.

"Lord, I agreed to come to the screening and I have done that. Please don't make me go any farther."

~~

Chapter 6

IN SEARCH OF A FIRST LADY
XANDER

"After a long days' work, do you know what my new favorite way to unwind is?" I ask Thomas.

My advisor looks over at me with a watchful eye, maybe thinking I'm going to tell him something he will have to veto.

"Don't worry! It's nothing that would get me impeached!" I laugh. "I watch footage of women attending the screening centers. The staff is compiling video for me about the one hundred ladies who have been chosen to come to my place in Colorado for the meet and greet."

Thomas smiles. "I'm glad it helps you unwind Xander. Although I think that footage is for more than just your entertainment as you need to use it to prepare for next week when you meet these women in person."

"I know, I know, don't worry, I am. There are a few women that have caught my attention. I'm watching closely and looking forward to meeting them in person. You have to admit, there are some crazy women out there too. I am also entertained by what I call the 'blooper reel' full of outrageous stunts and outfits to gain my attention at the centers. Have you seen any of them yet?"

"Not much, Xander. I think you should be more interested in watching some of the women you will be meeting next week though." Thomas just shakes his head.

"Okay, but you are no fun. How about we watch the next screening together? Since I need to be more serious about this." I use an exaggerated serious voice to joke with Thomas. I pull up the next file on my computer and put it onto the large screen to watch. Thomas and I settle onto my office couches as a voice-over gives information about the screening in Seattle. It shows a video clip of a woman standing in the receiving line. The woman is beautiful as all of the remaining one hundred are. When she smiles at the woman next to her in line, I lean closer, intrigued.

"Mm, Thomas. Look at her! Gorgeous!" I shush him when he tries to respond. The video shows the woman being ushered into the red room as the voice continues over... "Esther Thompson, age twenty-eight, performed well in the initial screening interview as well as in the Red Room. She scored five out of five on poise and appearance, five out of five on general knowledge, four out of five on compatibility, and five out of five on likeability." I push pause on the control to talk with Thomas. "How do they get those scores from the women just sitting around eating and talking?"

"At the initial screening interview, the staff look at women's education, job history, and background check. If they are suitable, they are sent to the Red Room for the rest of the day," Thomas responds.

"And of course they had a look at the women themselves." I jump in.

"Of course," Thomas responds. "The Red Room is set up to be a combination of a party, speed dating, a job interview, the Miss America pageant, and a book club all rolled into one. The women don't know it, but they are being analyzed in their actions and words. The staff rates them to give you an idea of how well each woman did."

"They all must have scored pretty well to have made it to the next round, right?" I ask.

"Yes, they would have all scored fairly high, which helped them be invited to the meet and greet. What do you think about the rating system? Does it help you narrow down who you are interested in?"

"Mm, I don't know. Okay, let's take Esther for example." I say waving my arm towards the woman frozen on the screen. "Her ratings are great, except for one point down in compatibility. So maybe there is something the staff sees that might not work there. She still has a very high rating. You never know, everything can look good on paper or everything can look all wrong, but it is really all about the chemistry."

Thomas's fatherly face takes on a stern look. I know I've said something he doesn't agree with.

"Xander, I hope you understand this choice cannot be about chemistry. If you happen to have chemistry with a woman who is right for your presidency, then great. But if you don't have chemistry with the right woman, then you are still

66

going to have to make it work. This marriage will secure your re-election. You need the right woman by your side to make that happen."

"Okay, Thomas, I know." *And I really do know what a big deal this is and it scares me. I have to choose one of these one hundred women. It will kill my ratings if I choose wrong.*

"Don't worry, I will find the right woman for my presidency, who I am also very attracted to," I say with more confidence than I actually have. I give him a smile and a wink, but Thomas does not look convinced.

"Listen to me carefully, Xander. You have to pick a wife who has high likeability by the public—that is the most important. Along with that, she has to be completely poised and loyal too. She has to have an air of almost royalty to give this union the fairy-tale feel we are looking for. Your feelings are last on the list of importance."

I nod as I think about what he said. *This marriage will secure my re-election.*

"I'm sure this will all work out. Out of these ladies, I will be able to find just the right woman for me and for my re-election. How can I not?" I wave towards the screen and remember the woman we were just watching.

"Let's hear some more about this one," I say with a smile.

As I push play, the voice continues—Esther mingles with others holding juice in her hand.

She looks calm and confident. Good choice on the juice too, not like a couple women I have watched on the bloopers reel—escorted out of the Red Room after obviously drinking too much of the champagne provided for that exact purpose.

There is something mesmerizing about this woman. I can't take my eyes off of her. "Thomas, I'm going to have to remember this one." I reach towards a notepad and pen on the coffee table and jot down her name: Esther Thompson.

"I think this next portion is my favorite part of the screening centers," Thomas says lightly. "It is almost like speed dating but without the potential groom."

"You sound like you have some experience in the speed dating world," I tease.

"There are many things you don't know about me, Xander. Speed dating is not one of them," he teases back.

The screen shows twelve tables around the room. A staff member sitting behind each with a chair in front of the table for the women. The women are rotating between the twelve tables—and answering questions. I can hear Esther speaking for the first time.

"I would not say I am one for religion, but I am definitely someone who has a relationship with God." *Oh that voice is so silky. I love when a woman's voice sounds as good as she looks.*

Hattie, one of my loyal staffers is sitting at the table and quickly responds to Esther, "This relationship to God is obviously very important to you and it sure sounds a lot like religion to me. Do you have an affiliation with any religious groups or attend any religious gatherings?"

Esther seems almost hesitant to answer. "My relationship with God is between me and Him."

Hattie and Esther continue speaking, but I cannot hear as the voice-over comes on again. "This answer about her religion is the only red flag that came up during the day. It is not of great concern as many women did not feel comfortable going into great depth about their views on religion. However, the fact that religion is important to her did lower her compatibility score."

I laugh out loud. "That is why they lowered her score, because she believes in God? What does the staff think I am, some heathen?"

Thomas stands up to get something from my office bar and I push pause on the control again as he starts talking. "Don't worry about that Xander. The fact that she is religious could actually be a good thing. It would be the good girl who falls in love with the president, the whole thing could actually help your image." He smiles at me now.

"It's interesting to know what you all really think of me." I shoot back at him jokingly. "I honestly don't care what religion a woman is. As long as she doesn't want me to get right with God or anything, she can pray all she wants. In fact, she's welcome to pray for me while she's at it. Grab me a scotch while you are up, will you?"

I turn my attention back to the screen. An image around the lunch table comes on. The voice tells about Esther's other responses during the question round—all very positive. I am not focusing on the words being spoken as much as the look on Esther's face as she looks around the table. She has a small smile on her face, as though she is trying to hold in a laugh. The food includes spaghetti, spare ribs, long stalks of asparagus, and milk tarts for dessert that are too big to eat in one bite, but messy to cut.

"Hattie let me in on a little secret—they make the food challenging on purpose. I think she's figured it out though." *Her smile and the twinkle in her eyes dazzle me.*

When Thomas holds my glass in front of my face, I jolt from my trance. His chuckle is not appreciated. "Well Romeo, it looks like the staff is doing okay finding women you like."

I grab the glass from his hand and shrug my shoulders. "Who doesn't appreciate a beautiful woman?" I go on the offensive, "Are you telling me you aren't a little taken with the ladies who want to marry me? That you don't want to be in my shoes? Women fawning all over you, picking your future wife out of a hundred of the most beautiful women in the country."

"I'm happy for you, but honestly: no! I hope I never have to go through the dating game again," Thomas smiles.

"But Thomas, what a fun game it is when all the odds are in my favor."

I give my full attention as the woman is speaking again. *What is her name again?* I look down at my notepad. *That's right, Esther, what a unique name.*

"I believe that the First Lady's most important role would be as a wife to support her husband. In addition, she has an opportunity to serve her country and make a difference to those in need."

I pause the screen again and turn to Thomas. "Esther looked nervous when she started speaking, almost like a deer in the headlights. She did okay though, once she got going."

Thomas chuckles, "You seem a little protective of her, Xander. Yes, she did just fine. It is obvious does not have much experience in front of the cameras. That is fine though because your wife won't get to speak much on camera after you are married anyway."

There's a rap on the door and we turn to see Preston enter the room. "I knew this is where I'd find you. What do you think of the Seattle screening?" He chuckles.

I lean in towards Preston as he sits down next to me. "Do you remember this woman?"

Preston wrinkles his brows at me. "Do I remember her? Of course I do. That clip of her was the one shown on all the news clips after. Everyone loves her."

"Really?!" The volume of my own voice catches me off guard. "I just watched the clip of her now."

"The public opinion from one comment isn't really that important in the long run, but it does show this process is generating the positive interest we are hoping for."

"She seems like someone special."

"Who is someone special?" He replies back to me as though he has no idea who we were just talking about.

"Forget it!" I stand up in frustration and go to get myself another drink.

There is that chuckle again. *His condescending laugh grates on my nerves. He can chuckle all he wants but after my re-election, he and his chuckle are going to have to go.*

"Esther does seem like a wonderful woman, Xander. Just don't forget all the other women you were mesmerized by before," Thomas smiles.

"Yes," Preston jumps in. "Many of them have caught your attention and they will all be in one place to meet soon."

As I lean back against the couch, I smile. "I am going to enjoy the rest of this process. One hundred women together who all want to marry me and are all beautiful. How bad can it be, gentlemen?" I look at the television screen. Esther's face is frozen like a portrait. I stare at her. "Still, put a little red lipstick on her and this woman could be my future wife." I toast my glass towards the screen.

~~

Chapter 7

MEET AND GREET

XANDER

"It's been different than I thought it would be," I say to Hattie in a low, conspiring voice. "The first night was all fun and games, meeting them with hugs all around. Now it is hitting me I have to quickly figure out who these women are and who I really like. I would hate to send someone home who is the right woman for me, just because I'm not paying attention or putting my focus on the wrong woman."

"Don't worry, Xander," Hattie replies. "We are all here to help you and find out the information we need. You just make the connections with the women."

"I just wish I had taken more time with the screening center videos. Don't tell anyone, but I just watched them here and there mostly for fun, when I should have been studying them like a school boy with a big exam coming."

Her smile at me is not condescending, just kind. Hattie has always been a staffer I trust. *Maybe I should just marry Hattie and call this whole thing off. Did she end up finalizing her divorce or not? I can't even remember.*

It's been a busy day and the purpose of Hattie and I sitting down is to do more than just shoot the breeze. She needs my initial impressions for strategic planning of the week. Hattie frantically types while I give her my opinions of women I have spent time with. Then it's her turn to talk.

"You will be having dinner with five ladies, all top candidates."

I interrupt her, "Do you remember Esther from the Seattle screening?"

"Of course I do," Hattie answers quickly.

"Will I be having dinner with her tonight?" I ask.

The huge smile that spreads across Hattie's face surprises me.

"You liked Esther, did you? I thought you would, so I have a special dinner planned for just the two of you on Saturday night. That way you will have a chance to really get to know her."

I shake my head in frustration before Hattie even finishes her sentence. "That is still two more days away. I haven't even really talked to Esther yet and she was one of the ladies I was most looking forward to meeting. She seems to be holding back."

"Be patient. This is a tough process. Some women fight for your time and push others out to talk to you. Esther does not strike me as the pushy kind of woman."

"It's true. Certain women seem to park themselves outside my wing just waiting for me to come out so they can snatch me up. There is something I like about that too—aggressive women! Esther on the other hand seems like she is not working very hard at all to get time to talk with me. I even tried to make eye contact with her across the room a few times. It seemed like she was even avoiding that."

"Maybe she's just waiting for the right time to talk to you. Or maybe she would rather not have to initiate the first conversation with you."

"That almost sounds like a challenge, Hattie."

"I think Esther is worth making time for," she encourages. "When I met her in Seattle, she impressed me more than anyone else had."

"Why, what was it about her?" I questioned.

"After I asked Esther the questions about her religious views, which you should have seen if you watched the clip of her."

"Yes I did see the clip. I did try to watch most of them," I tell her, defensively.

"Good. We were almost done when a text came in from my son. You remember, Mark?"

"Of course," I respond, *I thought she had a girl.*

Whatever, kids are not important to the story, focus on Esther here. I wait impatiently as Hattie tells me a story of Esther being insightful with the text from her son. I glance out my office window—my ranch and the beautiful Colorado countryside stretches before me. A small group of women are just heading down a path towards the river.

"There she is." I start from my chair as I point towards Esther through the window; part of the hiking group. "No time like the present," I say to Hattie as I grab my sweatshirt and head out the office door.

I can hear her voice trailing after me as I jog towards the back door of the house. "There is more we need to discuss."

"Later!" I burst through the door. I see in my peripheral line of sight, my body guards as well as two camera men startled into action by my sudden outburst, trailing behind me. The ladies are chatting as they walk down the path towards the river, but turn as the commotion of our crew reaches them. My eyes are on Esther as I call out to them. "Hello, ladies, mind if I join you for your walk?"

She looked down while the other's all smiled and answer yes. Maybe Hattie is right that she is just nervous; maybe because she wants this to work out so badly. No problem, I know how to put a woman at ease.

We all walk together for a few minutes as I lead the group from one trail onto another that will take a more winding path towards the river with a better view. *Plus, it is a little longer walk so I'll have some more time with her.*

I notice Esther right in front of me. I speed up to catch her and then match my stride with hers. My body guards position themselves with the same strides behind us. "Hello, Esther. Finally, I get a moment to really meet you." *Finally, I'll get to hear that smooth voice in person.*

76

"Hello, Mr. President. Thank you so much for inviting me to your ranch."

All other conversations die down to almost nothing behind us, probably so the other women can catch whatever Esther and I talk about. *Hopefully it won't make Esther too nervous to talk and let me get to know her a little bit.*

"I have to admit I have been waiting for a chance to talk with you," I continue. "You have made quite an impression on my staff."

Her face begins to color. A small smile creeps onto her face. *There we go. This one just needs a little encouragement to warm up.* "It has been a pleasure to meet your staff. They have pampered us and treated us so well. And now to meet you, President Susa, it is a pleasure."

"No more President Susa, Esther. Please call me Xander as all my friends do. I hope we will only continue to get to know each other better and become good friends." *Her eyes are even more beautiful in living color, so compelling; inviting.*

I'm so taken with those eyes that for a moment I almost forget I'm walking. I quickly remember as I catch my toe on a rock and start to fall forward before I catch myself. Esther's hand reaches out immediately to steady me. "See, I'm falling for you already!"

Esther smiles at my little joke, but also seems embarrassed by it. *Come on Xander, keep it smooth and put her at ease.*

"So how has this process been for you so far?" *I want to get her talking.*

77

"Well, it has been nothing like I expected."

"I've seen some of the media coverage on you ladies during the last few months."

"Yes, the media coverage has definitely been something to adjust to. I'm sure you are used to it after all these years in politics. It seems everyone has an opinion."

"That is something that comes with the territory—the vocal and very public opinion of others." *Gorgeous, that's the face I saw on the clip that I have not been able to forget.* "Tell me about someone who gave you their opinion."

"Okay…there is an elderly woman who lives a few doors down from me. The other night she came outside as I was coming home. Dorothy told me it was about time I settled down and got married and that you would be a good catch. Dorothy did say how dreamy you are – and that is the exact word she used. So you can know that Dorothy is available and interested."

I laugh at the twist in her story and she laughs with me. *There is a fun and easy-going side to her. She seems comfortable, like she isn't even working to impress me like all of the other women.*

On my right side, I can feel another woman has come up to walk beside me. I do not turn to acknowledge her though. *I just want a few more minutes with Esther; alone.* I put my hand on Esther's arm and stop by the side of the trail as I say to the others, "You ladies go on up ahead to the river, we will be just a minute behind you."

With pasted smiles the other ladies agree and continue walking, while my body guards take up their posts around us and media not far off. I see Esther spot the lens of a camera focused on us and her forehead crinkles with worry.

"You will get used to it. Before long, you will even forget they are there." Reaching down, I pick a few petals of the wildflowers that surround our path. Esther accepts my impromptu bouquet.

"Thank you, they are beautiful."

I feel a small flutter of butterflies in my stomach as our hands brush against each other. *I feel like a young boy with a crush around this girl.*

"Nothing compared to the woman holding them," I say to her. *Oh great Xander, now you sound like a boy with a crush.*

Esther reaches into her pocket and brings out a small item. "I actually have something for you as well." *Now I am surprised. So, she was hoping to get time alone with me.*

"I understand you love to go for hikes any chance you get. I got you this compass so you will never lose your way when you are out." Esther holds out the compass towards me.

"Thank you Esther, it is the perfect gift." I take the compass in one hand and reach for her open hand with the other. I give her hand a little squeeze before I bring it to my heart. The click of camera shutters in rapid succession fill the silence and instinctively I know this will be the cover picture of newspapers around the country tomorrow.

79

Esther's embarrassment is back as she instinctively pulls her hand away and looks over at the cameras that have just captured our intimate moment. I try to ease her worries.

"Like I said, you'll get used to it."

~~

Chapter 8

FINAL FIVE AT THE WHITE HOUSE

XANDER

"I have stretched this process out as long as I possibly can for media exposure, but I'm done now. Esther is the one and I need to tell her." I make this demand in front of my executive staff, plus the twenty or so extra staffers who have been involved in my hunt for a bride.

Preston quickly speaks up. "Mr. President, the time is not right. We have three weeks left of events with all five of the remaining women heavily scheduled. The event is already in the works for the proposal. We don't want to lose this momentum. Your ratings are sky high."

"Preston, honestly, I don't care about the events you have planned for me. You wanted me to find a woman and I found her. All of you agree Esther will be the perfect First Lady. I'm done with this process. I'm telling her this morning I love her and want to marry her."

"Please Mr. President," Hattie pleads.

"We all agree that Esther is the right one for you; no one is questioning that. However, you don't want to lose the opportunity for the public to see the culmination of this process. There has been too much work to create the perfect romantic moment to rush it now."

"Don't worry, Hattie. You want romance, I can do romance. I just want to do it now instead of in three weeks."

"Let's look at this from another angle," Thomas says. "We all know it is Xander's passionate and romantic side that has helped the American people love this process. Why not let him propose to Esther in a more Xander-like, impulsive way? The people will love it and the surprise could grab more media attention than even if it is scheduled." *I love this guy. He has my best interest at heart; always has, always will.*

"What about all the events already planned for the women to go to? What about the plans for the proposal?" *Preston drives me crazy. He puts his plans above everything else. Can't be flexible to do something my way. Who is the president anyway; me or him?*

"Don't worry about all the planned events. Esther can go to them as my fiancé. People will love it."

"Mr. President, how about a compromise?" Hattie suggests. "Wait one week to propose so we can set an alternate plan into place?"

"A week?" I practically shriek. "I want to go find her right now and ask her to marry me!"

Thomas jumps in as the peacemaker he always is. "I don't think there is any way we can ask the president to wait for a week. To ask him to go through the motions with other women when he is ready to ask this woman for her hand in marriage. Xander, will you wait until tomorrow? We can have television crews ready. Have the ring sized, the whole thing. You can still have your element of surprise, but with the preparations to make it perfect and get the footage we need."

Preston and others around the table do not look too happy with Thomas. *True–it has to be well documented. Of course, more romantic with the ring.*

"I can wait until tomorrow, but that's it." I look to Preston in defiance. *Good, one thing I am doing my way.*

"Tomorrow morning, she should be in the Kennedy Garden. You told me she is out there reading every morning. I want it to be a surprise though, so don't let it out. Get whatever footage you need while I ask her and you can count on the fact I will deliver on the romance."

Again, the killjoy in my life, "And you are sure she is ready to say yes, Mr. President?" Hattie and Preston exchange glances. *What, they don't think she is going to say yes?*

"Are you kidding me, Preston? Of course she is going to say yes. She's here isn't she? Which one of these women would not kill to become the First Lady of the United States of America?"

Twenty four hours later and Preston's question comes back to me. *Am I positive Esther will say yes? I think she will, who wouldn't? Esther would be a fool not to accept my proposal. Plus, I'm crazy about her.*

"There she is," I say to Hattie as we look through the curtains towards the Kennedy Garden. My stomach flutters as I look out on my soon to be fiancé quietly reading, pausing only to periodically look up into the clouds. *She is so beautiful…and sweet…and kind. Probably too good for me in many ways.*

I look down at my hands and realize they are all sweaty. *Is this because I really am crazy about her or because I don't want to go through another divorce? Or maybe because I don't know if she is ready to accept.*

I look at the large crowd around me—my staff and camera crews all preparing for my romantic proposal, which will be televised around the world. *They are not going to wait for any indecision on my part. I'm just nervous to ask her, that's all. Esther is beautiful and she seems perfect. The country loves her and I love her too, or will soon. Another term as president depends on this.* Just a moment more and a few deep breaths. I feel ready. I nod to a staffer who opens the door.

Esther's face turns towards the commotion. I can see her entire body stiffen at this sudden interruption of so many people into her time of solitude. Her face shows concern as she quickly looks to the camera crews setting up all around her.

As I walk towards her, my nerves completely disappear. I feel excited for the proposal I am about to make. *I can't wait to see Esther's face light up when she sees the ring; when I ask her to become my wife.*

Esther sees me and stands up quickly to face me, her face showing concern and her words confirming it, "Xander, is everything okay?"

I close the distance between us with a smile on my face. "Nothing is wrong, my love. In fact, everything is perfect."

Her stiffened body visibly relaxes. Her face breaks into a smile as well. I take the last few steps between us and wrap my arms around her waist as I lift her gently off of the ground. It doesn't take much effort to swing her around in a circle while I hug her. Out of the corner of my eye, I can see the camera crews are filming.

Perfect, this is just perfect. I set Esther's feet back down on the ground and slide back from her just a little so I can look into her eyes. My hands don't want to stop touching her though, so I move down her arms until they find her hands to hold. It is time to tell her how I feel and what I want.

"Esther, I know you are going to think I'm impulsive, but I can't stop thinking about you. I was at a veteran's luncheon last week and all I could think about was your beautiful smile—even though I had gone there with three other women. Last Friday, I went out for a dinner and the whole night I wished you were there. I ended up just cutting the evening short and heading home. "

"And when you and I had our date alone, it was magical. You were gorgeous and everything was perfect. I think I fell in love with you completely and fully somewhere between dinner and our ride in the horse and carriage. I didn't want to let you go and I stayed up half the night trying to stop thinking about you."

"Then I realized, why do I have to stop thinking about you? This whole process is to find the woman that is perfect for me and perfect for our country. And I have."

Esther's eyes are wide as she looks at me. I realize she has hardly taken a breath the whole time I have been talking.

Is that a nervous or excited look in her eyes? Maybe a little apprehension? Not the utter joy I'd expected, but it's probably just because the camera crews are here. I'm sure she'll give her big smile in just a moment once she realizes I'm really asking her.

"Esther Thompson, I am in love with you. I know I have so much more to learn about you. I want to explore every bit of who you are for the rest of my life, if you will let me. My search for the perfect wife has brought me to you."

Still the confusion in her eyes, the worry. Can she not see where I'm going with this? I assured everyone that she was ready, but what if I was wrong.

As my mind quickly weighs my questions, Esther has the same look in her eyes of a mind frantically working away. In an instant, I can see her calculating is done and her mind is made up. A smile is slowly creeping onto her face and is changing her entire countenance, as I knew it would. *There she is, just had to give her a minute to wrap her mind around what is about to happen.*

The ring box has been resting against my chest this whole time through my suit and I reach into my pocket now as I ease myself down on one knee. *This is the moment America has been waiting for. Make it good Xander.*

86

The look on my face is the best I can give of a man who is crazy and passionately in love with a woman. I do love her, I'm sure, I think. I open the ring box to Esther and take her hand in my free one.

"Esther, will you do me the honor of marrying me and giving me and this country the most beautiful and amazing First Lady imaginable?" The gorgeous woman standing before me swallows deeply. I feel her slender hand shaking inside mine. Giving it a gentle squeeze, I look directly into her eyes.

I believe that is actually a look of love in her eyes. Maybe she isn't here for fame or all the benefits of a marriage to me. Maybe this really will be a marriage lasting forever.

"Xander." Emotion fills her voice and she can hardly speak. "I promise to be committed to you and show love to you every day for the rest of my life. Yes, I will marry you."

The huge smile on both of our faces is genuine. I take the ring out of the box and slip it onto her finger. I give the ring and her hand under it a long kiss before I stand up to kiss her on the mouth.

I know our kiss will be broadcast around the world. I can imagine all the romantics will wipe away their tears with sighs of contentment knowing I have found my Cinderella. *I could not be more content either as I may have actually found a wife, not only for my re-election, but for the rest of my life.*

~~

Chapter 9

THREAT TO THE PRESIDENT
MORDECAI

After more than two years apart, this is not the kind of circumstance where I would prefer to see Esther, but at least I get to see her.

I don't show my pleasure outwardly. I can see the surprise in her eyes at seeing me here. We hardly acknowledge each other across the room. This distance has been difficult to keep, but I feel it is necessary. Ever since Esther and Xander were engaged, she respected my request for this distance—for safety—for the future. Although I don't even know the reason for our separation. *She certainly can't understand it if I can't.*

The White House head of security, Bob Gregory, asks for everyone's attention to begin this impromptu meeting, here in the secure facility underneath the White House. *Not where I thought I would be spending this night, underneath the White House, but here I am wrapped up in this drama.*

Mr. President, Mrs. President, members of the staff. I want to thank all of you for your immediate cooperation with the security procedures that were put into action tonight. This evacuation to the underground secure facility is in response to a threat that could potentially put the president's life in danger. "

I peak a glance at Esther just as the words spoken register across her face. Her husband, the president, who is sitting next to her, has fear written all over his face as well.

"I will give you an update on the events transpiring up to this point," Mr. Gregory continues. "At twenty-three hundred hours, just over ninety minutes ago, it came to my attention there were suspicious comments and activity being made from members of the security force here in the White House. Oregon's Attorney General, Mordecai Allenby was crucial in gathering this information and I will let him share what he discovered before I continue."

I scoot my chair back and clear my throat as I move to stand.

Interesting that Bob has asked me to give a report. Maybe because we have known each other for a long time and he trusts me. Or maybe he wants to take some of the pressure off himself in case things don't go well.

The look of surprise and confusion is apparent in Esther's eyes, as well as in many others in the room. I only come to the White House periodically and do not know many of the people here. Certainly it's unexpected that I'm involved under these circumstances. *I'm just as surprised as anyone to find myself in this situation. Just be confident in what you heard and saw. And try to ignore Esther.*

"Thank you, Mr. Gregory. Just a few hours ago, I attended a dinner here in the White House. The evening went longer than expected. Dinner was followed by dancing before speeches were to be given. I decided to slip out during the dancing portion of the evening to re-read a case I will be presenting in the morning—."

I stop for a moment to clarify the time on my watch before I complete my sentence in a little lighter tone. "This morning I guess it is."

A couple quiet chuckles come from somewhere in the room, but the mood is somber. I continue on, "I went into the conference room just down the hall from the state dining room. I was deep into my notes when I heard men's voices discussing something in hushed and urgent tones just outside the door. Something about the way they were trying to quiet their voices and the deep emotion attached to them made me curious. I could not make out their words. Quietly, I got up and moved closer to the door to hear the following exchange."

"KXS confirmed?"

"Just one detail loose, but we will be ready soon."

"You've been saying that for days. I want it to happen by tomorrow."

"Don't worry. He will be gone and we won't have to look at that smug face anymore."

The president, Esther, and everyone else in the room listen intently, hanging on my words.

"I wasn't sure what the exchange meant. The aggressive nature about someone being 'gone' made me believe this was not routine. As the men walked down the hall away from me, I could not make out anything else they were saying, but I looked out the door discreetly to see who they were just before they turned the corner. Although I did not know either of the men by name, I was familiar with both of their faces as men on the security force."

I pause and look at Bob, who gives me a nod to continue.

"I immediately went to the communications room and asked the officers to call Mr. Gregory to join me there. I have known Bob for a long time as Head Security and wanted this information to get directly into his hands. I informed Bob of what I had heard, the manner in which it was said, and who was speaking."

I stopped, feeling the rest should be reported by the White House security since I had merely been an observer from that point forward. Looking towards Bob I asked, "Mr. Gregory, would you like to take it from here?"

I tried not to look at Esther, but I could not help myself a couple times. If anyone could read my mind or her face, they would have been able to tell we are not strangers. My mind clicks back to the present.

"Thank you Mr. Allenby. We began to watch back footage from here inside the White House. There were numerous worrisome interactions between the two men in question. One verbal interaction caught on tape includes one of the men saying, 'give Xander what he deserves' while the other man hushed him and said, 'not now, but soon.'"

The room is buzzing as a few people lean towards another to talk over the last statement. Obviously, this makes the threat stronger.

"On another segment of footage, one of the men in question was using his hand as a gun and as he walked by, subtly pointed it at a picture of you, Mr. President."

I look at Xander and see his hands balled into tight fists on the table in front of him. Esther has put her hand onto his arm, but he does not seem to notice.

Bob continues, "The manner of the two men's body language and speech over their last three shifts was more accelerated and agitated. There was no conclusive evidence in the tapes to know if the men had a plan, but the clues all point to the fact that they are disgruntled and may possibly take action."

Bob looks directly at the president. "Mr. President, I felt the information we gathered was enough to warrant a search of the men's cars and lockers. Their communication accounts were frozen as well for review."

This part of Bob's speech was news to me. After the video clips were reviewed, Bob called other officers in and excused me back to the dinner hall, still in time to give my speech.

I can't even remember how the speech went. My mind had been racing with all I'd just seen on tape of two of the president's own security force conspiring against him.

My thoughts are broken as Bob continues, "The immediate search of the two men's cars revealed numerous handguns with silencers. In one of their personal lockers we also found a lethal dose of the drug Botchelin, which is a tasteless and odorless poison. I immediately contacted the entire security staff to order the suspects be detained for questioning."

"Who is it? Which men are being held for questioning?" The president's shrill voice rings out over his head of security.

I look back to Bob to see his head hanging down. *This must be tough on Bob as these men are on his staff. These are men he has worked with and trusted.*

"Mr. President, the two men in question are Darrell Harper and Alex Wisemen. However, I regret to inform you they have not yet been taken into custody."

"What?" the President practically yells out. "Are you telling me that these two men, Darrell and Alex of all people, have a plan to kill me? Yet they are still running around free in my house while I'm down here hiding out?"

I can see Bob is working hard to keep his composure in the midst of a difficult situation and now a very angry president.

"Mr. President, Mrs. President, I sincerely apologize for waking you from your sleep. When we were unable to immediately locate the two men in the White House and realized they were at large, you were awakened and brought to the secure shelter. The White House was cleared as quickly as possible with dinner guests and staff and the entire security force is working to secure the White House. I have no doubt the two suspects will be apprehended shortly. When the suspects are in custody and the White House is secured, you will be able to return upstairs."

Out of the corner of my eye, I can see Xander take a few deep breaths and run his hand through his already sleep tousled hair. He is trying to calm down. But really my eyes and my thoughts are all on Esther. In so many ways, this has not been an easy two years for Esther. To the outside world, her story book romance with President Susa is perfect. The country loved her throughout their courtship, however convoluted the process had been. No expense had been spared on their lavish wedding as the president and his staff appeared to have the goal of topping even the royal weddings in Britain.

But I can see the unhappiness in her eyes every time I see her on television. I'm sure it comes because her clothes and hair are constantly evaluated, because she can never speak publically, and because I have put a wall between myself and her.

Maybe the love between her and Xander isn't quite the fairytale everyone would want to believe as well. Her unhappiness is on my shoulders. I know this is not the life she wanted to live, but she felt led to do it. She has given up her initial dreams for something she thought God had for her, but I wonder if she is second guessing. I am consumed in my thoughts while the entire room waits in silence for President Susa to speak.

"Mr. Gregory, I appreciate your staff's quick response for my safety. But, is it possible Darrell and Alex have a bigger plan in mind. You can't find them and we are all holed up in one place. What if we are still in danger even now?"

President's Susa's tone is starting to sound frantic. Like he is just a man scared to die rather than the commander in chief.

He continues his rant. "I have never liked this death trap down here. Maybe you should get me out of the White House and to another secure location."

I look around and can see others are recognizing the growing alarm in the President as well. Preston, who is sitting near the president, begins to speak calmly. "Mr. Gregory, thank you for your work to secure the President and all of us in this obviously very difficult situation. This secure facility is reinforced and fortified for a situation exactly like this one. I commend your efforts to get the President here so quickly. Mr. President, I believe you are in the safest place possible as we are protected from any scenario that could be devised." His tone is sensitive from his usually business-like demeanor, which confirms my suspicion of the president's growing panic.

"If two members of our own security force are involved in this, how do we know I am safe from all the others?" President Susa looks around the room suspiciously at the other security officers.

The reaction on Bob's face is immediate – hurt.

"Mr. President, it is with regret we realize two members of our own staff are involved in a breach of security. However, these men and I will die for you if necessary. Our first and foremost job has been and will be to protect you. You can count on us to do just that."

"And I just might take you up on that promise to die for me," President Susa responds.

Self, self, self. Xander is the most self-centered man I have ever seen. He is acting like such a child in this situation and so ungrateful of everyone around him who is working to protect him. And there is my Esther, sitting next to him – sitting next to her husband. Why did I have to encourage her to marry this man? God, why?

The wall phone breaks the silence. Bob walks over to answer it and breathes an obvious sigh of relief.

After hanging up, he begins, "Mr. President, the two guards in question have been taken into custody and are being removed from the White House grounds. The house is being secured and as soon as we are given an 'all clear' from upstairs, you will be able to return to your residence. Thank you for your continued patience."

This news lifts the tensions considerably. I spend the next few minutes in conversation with those around me while making a conscious effort not to look over at Esther. Thirty-five minutes later when the call comes through from the security force upstairs with the "all clear" signal, the worry clears from the room completely. I watch as the president gives out a few high fives and even takes a moment to give Esther a big hug and kiss.

Maybe there is something real between them after all. There was love and commitment in her eyes, unless it is just wishful thinking on my part.

The president is talking to someone else and Esther turns and looks right at me. I give her a small smile before turning away quickly.

I wish I could go and give her a big hug, but I can't. I was always careful to keep her out of the media growing up and we have been so careful now not to let people know we're related. I miss her so much though. God, please let me have her back in my life before it is too late and she decides she does not want to be there again.

~~

Chapter 10

A FRIEND AND CONFIDANTE
ESTHER SUSA - THE FIRST LADY

"I'm sorry, Kristi. I feel like I am dumping my life on you. I need to talk to someone living and breathing, with flesh and bones."

Here I go crying again. Now that I've opened up and started talking, it is like the floodgates of my soul have been opened as well. It is all coming out through my tears.

"Esther, I had no idea you've been going through all this. You can talk about anything you want to with me," Kristi reassures.

The woman sitting in front of me works at the children's home I visit frequently. It's one of the few ways I can contribute, since so many avenues are not open to me with the tight control by Xander's staff. I connected with Kristi the first day I went. When she offered to pray with me once, we connected in faith as well.

This is the first time I've invited her to the White House. I felt like I would explode if I didn't talk to someone.

I continue sharing my frustrations at feeling a lack of purpose as the First Lady. "Xander's staff watch and limit my every move; probably for fear I will make a costly mistake."

There is so much to talk about. The lack of closeness with Xander. The pressure I feel to get pregnant and not being able to. My own regret that I made a mistake in marrying Xander.

Maybe I'll even tell her about Uncle Cai. I know I can trust her; at least I hope I can.

"You look like there is a lot more on your mind and my day is free. Whatever you want to talk about will only be between you and me." Kristi looks concerned.

I look at the ceiling as I take a deep breath and wipe away a tear.

"It's just so difficult with Xander. It is hard to really feel close to him; to even feel like I know him. Sometimes I even wonder if I did the right thing."

I feel like I just let out a big secret, but Kristi does not seem too shocked.

"But during the whole crazy dating process, the day he proposed, our engagement and wedding, God gave me a peace. I didn't want to move forward with each step, but I clearly felt like I was supposed to."

I think back to our engagement and wedding. "And it was anyone could have dreamed of. The gardens bursting with wildflowers. The food was like artwork. The music by famous artists. My dress was like one from a fairy tale. The teams and designers the White House brought in to use were amazing." I pause as I try to organize my thoughts.

"I felt like more of a bystander watching my own wedding being coordinated, but I still enjoyed it. I loved the time with Xander and like I said, I had peace. God kept confirming it in my heart."

Kristi smiles, "The way you two looked at each other melted everyone's hearts. Of course, when President Susa threw country-wide parties and gave out the economic stimulus packages to go along with your wedding, we were all thrilled."

We both smile and nod before another silence until Kristi breaks it. "You looked completely gorgeous on your wedding day." Kristi pauses, looking serious. "But with all the show, were you happy?"

"Yes, I was happy; nervous, but happy. It was a miracle, even to me, that I was so excited about marrying Xander. At first, I didn't even want to meet him, let alone marry him. But I grew to appreciate him during our unique courtship. I found him to be truly kind to the people around him. Xander helped me relax, smile and enjoy it all."

I pause for a moment and take a deep breath.

"I thought the love was growing too. Sometimes he would bring me a bunch of wildflowers to remind me of our first time together. God had given me the visual that he would plant me right where he wanted me. I told Xander that story. Even though he only believes in God as 'a cosmic being', whenever he brought me wildflowers he would remind me that God had said I was to be planted with him."

I can't help myself from smiling as I think of how Xander uses anything to get what he wants. But just as quickly as I smile, my face drops.

"There is a huge gap between us because he doesn't believe in God. Did I misunderstand what God was saying to join my life to someone who believes so differently than me? I thought God might use me to bring Xander to himself."

Lost in my thoughts, I sit silently for a moment almost forgetting Kristi is there. I look up at her and force a smile. She sits quietly waiting for me to continue.

"I'm sorry. It was a beautiful wedding and there are so many things I am grateful for in my life. That is why I feel so foolish complaining. But, I still want more."

"More of having a purpose like you were talking about?" Kristi asks.

"Yes, that is part of it. I want to feel like I can make a difference. Right now I can hardly do anything without being told it is too vocal, too strong, too public, too...too...too. I am trying to respect Xander and what he and his staff want me to do." Kristi waits patiently, maybe seeing there is more.

"It's more than that. I don't feel love between us right now."

"But you felt love at the beginning?" Kristi asks quietly.

"Yes, and I thought it was growing," I respond sadly. "During our engagement, the more I got to know Xander, the more I appreciated him and loved him despite the things I did not like. I knew his impulsive nature had down sides. I still worried about how he had hurt his first wife. His moral weaknesses scared me. But when the moment came and he asked me to marry him, I knew marrying Xander was God's plan for me." I pause and a sniffle escapes.

"Our honeymoon was wonderful. We had an entire Hawaiian resort to ourselves, catering to our every need. Mostly we just wanted to be alone together. I got to know my husband in every way. It was all I'd imagined my honeymoon would be." I give a shy smile as I talk.

Kristi confides, "You know, Esther, I was really impressed by the fact that you told the president you would not sleep with him until you were married. That was a huge statement to the entire world."

I cannot help but smile, "I honestly thought telling Xander that I would not sleep with him would be the end of being in the running to marry him. Amazingly, he agreed and I stayed."

My smile drops off my face as I lean in to confide in her what the whole country probably already knows. "I think he was sleeping with a couple of the other women during the dating process, so maybe it was easier for him to wait for me."

I gulp down the emotions of thinking about my husband with someone else. "The other women were all too happy to imply they knew Xander much better than I did."

102

Kristi responds quickly, seeing my sadness, "But he picked you, Esther. You are the one he wanted to marry."

"That's true, but I don't know if his vows matter all that much to him."

"Do you have reason to believe your husband is not being faithful?" Kristi asks so quietly I can hardly hear her.

Gently biting the inside of my cheek, I wonder. *I've asked myself this same question a hundred times; is Xander being faithful to me?*

"Xander tells me I am the only one for him forever, but honestly, what do I know? He's gone so much. One time I did see him lightly flirting with an aide when he didn't know I was standing there. He told me it was nothing. What do I really know about what my husband does behind closed doors?"

"Then believe he is being faithful, Esther. Unless you have concrete reasons to believe otherwise, trust in your husband's faithfulness. If not, you will drive yourself crazy wondering and worrying about it."

I nod my head in agreement, although I am not sure I can shut out my worries.

"Xander's love just seems to be hot and cold. At times, he'll do some big romantic gesture or give me a kiss that melts me and I feel so special to him. At other times, it feels like he couldn't care less if I'm around at all."

Here they come again. I just can't seem to keep these tears inside; probably because they have been building up in me for such a long time. I reach for another tissue and wipe my eyes, blow my nose, and for a moment try to paste a smile on my face again. *Uh, just forget the smile. I don't feel like wearing it and I don't think Kristi wants me to put on a happy face for her.*

"I know Xander has been really stressed out this week with the assassination attempt, so I'm trying to give him the benefit of the doubt. But all week he has been pacing around like a caged animal; verbally biting and snarling at everyone in his path, especially me. He is so angry to think his own guards would want to kill him - understandably so. I think it makes him feel vulnerable and weak too. Then I feel like he takes his anger and vulnerability out on me."

"A few days ago, I went to his office after lunch with his thermal tumbler full of coffee like I do on many days. It gives me a chance to say hello to him if he is free." The tears are already pooling in my eyes and clouding my vision. *I hardly even want to tell Kristi the next part.*

"He was stomping around his office yelling at Thomas when I came to the door. 'How could they do this to me? Those two are going to pay. Don't they know who I am?' Things like that."

"I stood at the door waiting for Xander to notice me. He saw me standing there and finally nodded, which I thought meant he wanted me to come in. When I went in, he didn't say another word, but just sat behind his desk. Thomas motioned I should go to him. So I took the coffee I had brought and set it down on the corner of the desk as I said hello. He didn't really respond, his back hunched over his desk." *I was only trying to show love to my husband, but part of me feels like I did something wrong to deserve his reaction.*

"Usually Xander likes when I rub his shoulders, so I gently reached out towards him. But the second I touched him, he sprang out of his chair to face me and yelled, 'Don't you touch me. Don't you understand the kind of pressure I'm under? You think you can make it all better with a back rub and a cup of coffee?' He glared at the coffee I had just set down, grabbed it, and threw it towards the rock fireplace in the corner of his office. I couldn't believe that he would act like that."

Kristi takes my hand and I realize mine is shaking. I cannot seem to get it to stop, even with her calming hand holding mine.

"Of course, when the tumbler collided with the fireplace, the crashing sound filled the room, two secret service agents came running in, firearms already pulled. Xander just stared at me with anger in his eyes and his jaw clenched tight. I thought he might spring at me next. I tried to say I was sorry, but it caught in my throat. I ran out of the office and down the hall to our residence."

My heart is beating frantically as the emotions I felt during the incident come back.

"I kept thinking, What happened to my husband who just hugged and kissed me so tenderly a few days before when we were down in the secure facility? Where is the man who seemed so crazy about me during our engagement? Is it because he got re-elected? Could it be possible our love was not real, but only for that?"

There, I'd finally said it out loud. The possibility Xander had only used me and there is nothing real between us.

"Kristi, it seems like I always need to excuse his behavior; to rationalize why he seems like he does not care about me at times. Then I wonder when I'll be told I can pack my bags and leave; he is done with me."

My chin falls towards my chest and teardrops fall into my lap. I don't even wipe at them. My strength is depleted. "I really don't know how God expects me to handle this. I'm trying to be a good wife to Xander, but it is so hard."

"Do you still love him? Are you still committed to him?" Kristi asks.

"I do love Xander, I really do, and I am committed to being his wife. From the day I promised to marry him—two years ago now—I've never thought about changing that promise. I just wish it could be easier, and not just with Xander. There is so much more to this whole situation I do not feel strong enough to handle."

Uh-oh, I'm opening up a door that will cross a line here. A line I promised my uncle I would not cross. A line I have not talked about with anyone for two and a half years.

"What do you mean, there's much more to it?" Kristi looks confused.

Should I just skirt around that comment or tell her how much I really have given up to be here. I have given up my only family for Xander and now I feel so alone.

"Kristi, I'm going to tell you something else that hardly makes sense to me, so I am sure it won't make any sense to you either. But you have to promise not to tell anyone."

"Esther, everything we talk about is only between you and me and God, and I mean that. If you would rather not share; that is okay too."

"No, I want you to know. I need someone to pray for me and help me carry this burden." Kristi's face shows obvious worry about what I am going to say.

"Don't worry, it isn't that bad, just...I don't know. When I was picked to go to the meet and greet with Xander, I had to give up another relationship to do it."

"Another man?" Kristi asks.

"Yes, but not a boyfriend or anything. I had to give up my uncle, who raised me and is my only family. He decided we needed to cut ties for a while. He didn't want everyone to know we're related. My uncle also did not want me to talk about my background. I am Jewish, actually a Messianic Jew." *It feels so good to actually say that out loud. The first time in so long to say who I am and what I believe.*

Kristi's face gives away her feelings before her words do. "I'm confused. I remember hearing about your parents dying. I always kind of assumed you were without family. I never heard anything about an uncle or about you being Jewish."

"Right, which was the point. At times, I would be asked about my family. Sometimes questions about religion or

107

even my name. I tried to stay vague and the media didn't press it too much; too focused on what I was wearing, I guess. So I married Xander without him knowing the truth of my religion or my family. If the White House staff ever knew anything, no one ever said a word."

"What about your uncle? Do you see him?" Kristi asked.

"After I was chosen to go meet Xander, we stopped spending time together. There was one reporter who hounded me about my past for a while. I waited for his story to break, but it never did. I don't know why not. Xander's advisor, Thomas, walked me down the aisle at the wedding and everyone assumed I was a woman without a family."

"Is your uncle still alive?" Kristi asks.

I chuckle at the irony of my own life. How much it feels like a soap opera. "He is alive and well and actually…the Attorney General of Oregon."

Kristi shakes her head. "I don't know your uncle or anything, but wouldn't an Attorney General be a high profile figure?"

"Yes, he is in DC quite a lot and he has even come into the White House on a few occasions," I respond glumly.

"So let me understand all this. You have an uncle, who is an attorney general, but he doesn't want anyone to know you are family?"

"Yes, that is about right," I respond, knowing how dramatic it all sounds.

Kristi continues slowly, "And he also asked you not to talk about your religious background?" Her voice goes up at the end to clarify.

"That's right," I answer. "It was my uncle's idea to keep my heritage quiet. I am so tired of the secrets though—I just want to tell everyone who I am and what I really believe in."

"You have talked to me about your love for God before," she says.

I quickly assure her, "I do love God and have a relationship with Him. And I've been open about that—it's just about being a Jew that I have not admitted."

Kristi is quiet for a moment. *Maybe this was a mistake to tell her. Saying it all out loud sounds so ridiculous. I can't really expect anyone to understand, since I don't.*

"Yet you are doing what your uncle has asked you to do. Why?" Kristi looks at me with curiosity more than confusion.

Why did I go along with Uncle Cai asked? Why didn't I just tell him no.

"I did it in the first place because of how much I respect my uncle. Then, it all just kept going as time moved on."

"And why did your uncle tell you this was necessary?" my friend asks.

"He didn't really know, but he sensed from God that it was necessary—which was enough for him and at the beginning was enough for me too. But I didn't know we would stop talking and spending time together for years. I thought it would just be for a couple of weeks, but then that led into a couple of months, and now this."

Kristi nods as though somewhat understanding. I guess she was the right person to share this with.

"Esther, I don't know how you have gone through all this alone and I don't understand why you need to. But I do know there must be some purpose behind this. God does not waste a life that is willing."

An urgent knock on the living room door breaks into our intimate conversation.

~~

Chapter 11

NEWS: ISRAEL IS ATTACKED
ESTHER

"Yes, who is it?" I call out.

My assistant's muffled voice comes through the door. "It's Gabriella, Mrs. Susa. I'm sorry to interrupt you, but there is a matter I thought you would find quite urgent."

I give an apologetic look to Kristi and shrug my shoulders as I see our time of talking has come to a close. I grab a tissue and dab at my eyes as I walk to open the door for Gabriella.

She is flustered, although she takes pause to notice my puffy eyes and the tissue in my hand. "Again, I'm so sorry to cut in. Are you okay?"

"Oh, don't worry about me, I'm just fine. What did you need to talk to me about? Is it something Kristi can stay for?" I don't want Kristi to go just yet. Maybe this will be finished quickly so we can have more time together.

Gabriella walks to the television remote. "I need to turn on the news for you, Mrs. Susa. I am sure you would want to know about this as well, Kristi. There have been some problems this morning in Israel. Mrs. Susa, I know of your fascination with the country and thought you would want to know right away."

Fascination is the only word Gabriella has ever used about my interest in Israel and I have never corrected her.

"What kind of problems?" I ask, as Gabriella changes channels. The three of us move to the couches to watch the headlining story.

The news anchor describes attacks across Israel that have happened in the last few hours, with the threat of more. She hands the story over to a young, male reporter on the ground in Jerusalem who speaks intermittently while images flash across the screen.

"The first attack took place at approximately 4:30 am, Jerusalem time. A grenade was thrown through the window of a party planning shop, specializing in Bar Mitzvahs. The shop was closed, but the shop owner and her family lived in an apartment upstairs. The entire family of four was found dead, covered by the rubble of their home and business."

"The second attack was at 7:05 a.m. just outside the old city at the home of a prominent Jewish Rabbi. His home was broken into and his three children were moved into the back bedroom while the Rabbi and his wife were taken to their living room and shot, execution style. Members of the Rabbi's synagogue are in shock and mourning, but are already speaking out against the cruelty of the attack."

Images of people mourning, screaming and crying fill the screen. *How could people kill a religious leader and his wife so unmercifully and in the same house as their children?*

112

The reporters voice marches on, "The third attack took place at 9:35 am, in the Golan Heights. A prominent Jewish American actress was fired at numerous times from a passing car as she entered a local restaurant with a friend. Ada Feldstein was in Israel promoting her new movie. Ada, as well as her unnamed companion, were both hit and rushed to an undisclosed hospital where they are currently listed in critical condition."

I've seen her in movies and she is wonderful as well as a promoter of her home country, Israel. Why an American actress? That is going to be horrible for tourism and international relations as well. And for all of these to happen in the same day seems like more than coincidence.

"Is there still more Gabriella?" I turn to look at my assistant who gives me a solemn look and a nod of her head.

"One more as of now," she quietly says with a nod towards the screen.

"The fourth attack is possibly the most gruesome of attacks I have covered," the reporter continues, obviously moved. He takes a moment to compose himself. I struggle to digest his words. I look at Kristi and we exchange worried glances. Having just told her about my Jewish background, she now knows how deeply personal this news is to me.

"Less than sixty minutes ago, just before noon, a Jewish school bus filled with children ages five and six was hijacked. Masked men stopped the bus, immediately shot the driver in the head, and dispelled an unidentified toxic gas into the bus. The men closed the bus doors and immediately fled the scene. The children inside worked

113

frantically to escape. Passing cars stopped, realizing the children were in trouble. A call to the authorities was immediately made. One man was able to break a window and help a few children escape before the emergency personnel arrived. This was too late for most of the children as they succumbed to the poisonous gas. It has been reported the death toll is already eighteen children, with an undisclosed number being rushed to emergency facilities."

I cover my face with both of my hands. The image I have in my head is worse than any horror movie. *Those poor children suffocating to death, probably clawing to get out of that bus for a breath of fresh air. How cruel can people be?* The feed goes back to the news anchor sitting in the studio. Her tone is somber and I raise my head to listen to her.

"We have confirmed through numerous sources that Iranian extremists have claimed responsibility for these four attacks and threaten more will follow on a grander scale against all Jews. We will keep you updated if attacks do continue. A press conference will be held in the White House this evening. In a statement just released a few minutes ago, the US Press Secretary said, "The events in Israel horrify and sadden not only those in Israel, but around the world. However, let us remember these attacks were done by a small group of extremists and not by the Iranian people or its government, who are peace seekers. The government of Iran sent the president a statement that they do not condone these atrocities or similar violence. President Susa stands with both Iran and Israel during these difficult times."

I think about the statement that was sent from inside my own house—from my own husband.

"What about Israel? What have they said in response?"

Gabriella seems hesitant, but finally answers, "I heard in another report that the prime minister of Israel said his sources tell him that Iran's government was aware of the upcoming attacks. That the government may have even been instrumental in carrying them out. Israel is bracing itself for further attacks and is ready to retaliate."

Now I know why she was reluctant to tell me. Israel and the United States have already pitted themselves on opposite camps of blame. Israel is vocalizing their blame against Iran and its government. The US is only holding the extremists responsible.

"Gabriella, you can turn it off for now."

She leaves the room as I stare above the blank television and concentrate on the rippled texture of my wall under the macadamia paint I picked out myself. *I can't get those helpless children trapped on the bus out of my mind. The innocent lives lost in a battle of hatred with tensions thousands of years long.* Kristi's hand on my arm brings me back from my images.

"Let's pray," she suggests.

"Yes, let's pray."

I bow my head. My thoughts of problems with my marriage and missing my uncle are long gone. Only Israel on my mind.

~~

Chapter 12

A New Inner Voice
Xander

"This is a big press conference. You will do well, Xander. You will show why you are the great leader of the most powerful nation in the world through your strength, coupled with mercy. You will exude confidence that will fill our citizens and the world with peace about the future." *I love this guy and his confidence in me. Governor Phillip Stone is going to become my new inner voice.*

I look over at Preston and see him warily watching Phillip and me as we talk. *And I'm sick and tired of your condescending voice in my head Preston. I have wanted you gone for a long time—and the time is about to come.*

Stone grabs my attention again. This time I don't look away. "You need to give yourself a pep talk like this before every speech, every interview, and every event with people. Your country loves you. Your ratings are high. You will keep it that way."

Phillip leans in close and whispers quietly in my ear, "And obviously those who don't like you, better watch it because you are a very powerful man."

He pulls back with a smile on his face as I wonder if he is referring to the deaths of Darrell and Alex. *I know he's just trying to make light of a tough situation.*

"Tell yourself things like this every day and believe it, because you are one who is going to change the world," Phillip gives me a strong pat on my arm, as he walks off to take a seat at the press conference.

Okay, I'll try it. Xander, the people of this country love you. They re-elected you because they believe in you. You will reassure your people of peace regardless of what is going on in the Middle East. You will show mercy over the deaths of Alex and Darrell. You will gain respect by turning the other cheek. You are calm and confident.

I look over at Phillip with a smile and a nod. I do like the feeling this self-talk mumbo jumbo is giving me. As I walk onto the stage, it crosses my mind that I need to get Phillip working for me in the White House full-time. It would be invaluable to have someone with his strength and expertise as more than just an unofficial advisor.

If I can work it right, he can have Preston's job!

"Good afternoon, ladies and gentlemen of the press, citizens of the United States of America, and global citizens around the world."

I look over the bank of microphones at the sea of cameras pointed my direction. This is usually about the time my butterflies kick in, but today I'm feeling a little more confident. *Phillip knows what he is doing—calm, confident,*

117

mercy, strength, hope. The usual press corps are assembled and I address them and the world.

"This is a sad, but important day for our world. A day where pain has been brought unjustly to so many. A day where some want to use this pain to tear apart the steps towards peace that have been made. Those of us who have hope and seek peace will not let that happen. The United States would like to give our deepest sympathy to those affected by the attacks in Israel. We will unite with those who want peace. We will stand strong for justice."

I stoically lift my chin and stare off towards the back of the room. I can hear the click of cameras all around me.

"You have brought your questions and I'm happy to answer them now."

I already know all of the questions they will ask. My team and I discussed the angle I should take on each one. That's why I asked Stone to come and go over questions with me related to the Middle East conflict.

He is proving himself as an expert in that area, which will be helpful when he comes on staff. Although, I'm not too worried about today as interviews and speeches are where I shine. It is probably why I'm the president today. Ever since I was young, I have been able to think on my feet and get people on my side. Even when I have to twist the truth just a little bit.

Off to my right is a regular, Toni Bryant. I acknowledge her.

"Mr. President, we have heard rumors that the two men who were involved in your assassination attempt have died.

118

Can you please confirm if those rumors are true and tell us more about the circumstances?"

"Yes, I will share those details with you," I say in a somber tone.

I almost said I would be happy to share those details because happy is actually how I'm feeling; extremely happy about this news. Even though it was all by chance it turned out this way—at least as far as I know.

"I can confirm the news is true—the two men in custody both died this morning in a tragic accident. The van that was transporting them to a maximum security facility was struck by an oncoming vehicle and forced off the bridge into the Potomac River. A guard, who was driving and will remain unnamed at this time, as well as the two prisoners drowned. Their bodies have been recovered. Three guards, also in the van, survived the crash and are reported in good condition."

The same woman with a quick follow up, "Mr. President, will there be an investigation into this accident as an assurance to the American people?"

"Of course," I answer with great feeling. "There is no one more than me that wants a full investigation conducted. My staff and I are devastated by these events as all three men were a part of our staff. Regardless of what they confessed to planning against me, I am very saddened by their passing. And of course, the guard who was driving will soon be publicly honored as a great man, lost in service to his country."

Out of the sea of hands, I choose David Ericson for the next question.

"Thank you, Mr. President. You mentioned the confessions made by Darrell Harper and Alex Wiseman. Could you please expand on those confessions?"

With my sad face on, I suck in my lips and begin nodding, "I can't go into detail at this time about the confessions as there must be formal hearings due to the men's deaths before that information can be released."

I put my head down in silence for a moment as though the information is too much for me to bear.

You bet I'll let you know more details.

That Darrell Harper was anti-American.

That Alex Wiseman was weak and manipulated into the assassination plan because his pride was damaged.

Yes, these traitors will be talked about again and again.

I raise my head and nod for the next question. The room comes alive after the moment of impromptu silence.

"Mr. President, the tension between the two I's, Iran and Israel, is escalating. The Iranian government claims no part on the attacks against Israel while Israel holds the opposite view. Israel is even going as far as saying that Iran is attacking them to destroy their oil fields that are almost in production mode and they will do whatever is necessary to protect their country and citizens.   What do you think of these statements?"

I'm going for the wise counselor look with a gentle nod of the head as though we are discussing two young boys who can't figure out how to get along.

"I think the world is watching this conflict between Iran and Israel carefully. We all hope for a peaceful solution that will bring our world closer together rather than tear it farther apart. The people of Iran want peace. They want to raise their children with a roof over their heads and food on their table just like all of us do."

"Do they have young people in their country who, in an effort to live out their beliefs, make poor decisions? Of course they do."

"The people of Israel are in the same position of wanting peace. They also want to raise their children with a roof over their heads and food on their table. Are they protective of the people of their country and their right to live safely? Of course they are. Some want to blame Iran for being the bully in this fight, while others want to pin that on Israel. We in the United States support justice and peace and I will do everything I can towards that end."

Pencils are frantically scribbling as I speak. The steady red lights on the front of each camera let me know my answer will be shared across the world. "One last question please," Preston signals my attention to the left side of the room. I nod and smile at a young female reporter.

Hmm, I have not seen her before, but Preston found a pretty one. Never hurts to have a beautiful reporter as a friend.

"Mr. President, on a lighter and more personal note, there are rumors of little feet padding down the White House halls. Is there any truth that the First Lady may be pregnant?"

I genuinely do smile at this question even though it was planned. "I'm sorry to say I don't have any news to report yet, but hopefully soon. I am as anxious as you are to find out when a little one will join us in the White House."

Excited chatter starts all around the room. It is a calculated move to tell the press so clearly that we are hoping to have a child. It will take some of the focus off Alex and Darrell's deaths as well as the Middle East crisis. I say a quick thank you through the chatter and leave the stage.

I actually do hope Esther gets pregnant soon. I'm excited to be a dad. To start a family with my wife.

As I walk down the hallway towards my office, Esther is coming towards me. "I was just thinking about you," I say as we quickly close the gap towards each other.

Esther looks almost surprised as I say it. "You were? I was thinking about you too."

I sweep my arms around her back and pull her in close for a kiss. When we pull apart, I keep her face close to mine.

"You are so beautiful, you know that? Oh, you probably need to know I just told the whole world we are trying to

122

have a baby." I put on my sweet, boyish face as I'm not sure how she'll react to this.

"You did? I didn't know we were making that public."

"We kind of needed that information. Plus, you are going to make the best mother ever and I want the world to know." *She is sure looking at me funny.* I pull farther back from her to look her up and down. "What is it? You aren't already pregnant are you?"

She almost jumps at the question. "Pregnant?! No, no, I'm not pregnant. It's just that you seem in such a good mood."

I wave off my staff and take her hand. We start walking down the hall towards our home, the residence in the White House. "Why wouldn't I be happy? I have the most beautiful wife in the world. We will soon have a bouncy baby as beautiful as his mother. I am the president of this great country with people who love me—no love us."

The smile Esther gives me as I talk is what drew me to her in the first place. And those eyes gazing at me through long lashes are what drove me wild all through our engagement. *Well, we are married now and there is no waiting anymore.* I open the door to our home and hold it in a gallant gesture while Esther walks through. I lean my ear towards the click as it closes.

"And why wouldn't I be happy when I am about to make love to the most gorgeous woman in the world?" As I pull Esther to me, I hear her giggle.

~~

Chapter 13

WARNINGS
MORDECAI

"No one even took the time to thank you for your part in stopping the assassination plot and saving the president's life. Doesn't that bother you even the slightest bit?" My assistant Ethan asks as we drive towards the Salem Courthouse. When I don't respond, Ethan jumps in again.

"Couldn't he be grateful, even for a minute, to the man who saved his life? I just don't get it." His confused tone turns to frustration. "How will you move forward waiting for things to come to you, Mr. Allenby? Don't let this opportunity slip away."

I give Ethan a look I used many times on Esther when she was a teenager and talked disrespectfully. Ethan puts his hands up, realizing he has crossed a line.

"I'm sorry sir. I just see you as someone who could be working in Washington. This is your time to make that move happen."

Ethan is a good man. Has been loyal to me. He has a strong drive, if I move up it means he moves up too.

"Let me tell you something, Ethan. I did not get into politics to have people like me or tell me how wonderful I am. I want to serve the people, serve my country, and last month I had the opportunity to serve my president. I don't really need a pat on the back to feel good about that service."

"Mr. Allenby, listen to reason though." He pushes it again. "That pat on the back could mean the difference of Washington or not. Getting the credit you deserve could mean a more productive and lucrative career."

"Don't get me wrong," I respond, as the driver pulls into the parking lot. "I have worked hard to get where I am today, but I am not going to claim the recognition for myself. If God wants me in Washington, then someone there will recognize me as an asset."

I can see the cynicism in his eyes when I go there. I care much more about Ethan than the fact the president forgot to thank me for saving his life.

We quickly get out of the car and walk towards the courthouse. Ethan runs me through the morning's events as we walk, reminding me of names.

"First, you will be observing one of our newest judges on trial, Judge Jason, standard protocol of observation followed by a mentoring meeting."

I am proud of this mentoring program I started for new judges in the state. It can be hard to make time for it, but I am glad to do some of the mentoring myself.

125

Ethan continues, "After that, Judge Allen would like to have a moment to meet with you privately, before your time at the round table. I don't know what she wants to talk about, but it sounds personal."

"Fine," I respond. Thinking towards the round table meeting I say, "I always look forward to the judge's bi-monthly meetings. Discussing where we are heading in the future, and even funny stories from court."

"Yes, Sir, I know you do. I just wish I could join you one time," Ethan says with a smile.

"You know I would love to have you. But for the nature of the discussions, we decided to keep it judges and previous judges only."

Ethan holds the courthouse door open for me. "Don't forget you'll need to leave here by quarter to one to be in time for the meeting requested by the Coquille tribe leaders."

Just as I give him a nod, I spot the former Governor, Phillip Stone, the newly appointed White House chief of staff, walking briskly across the lobby towards us. His entourage, as well as two of my staffers are in tow.

What in the world is he doing here? Phillip Stone was not very friendly when I met him as a Governor, so I wonder how he'll be now as chief of staff. Lord, I have a feeling I am going to need your help.

The look Ethan shoots at me tells me he is thinking the same thing, but we both put on cordial faces and when Phillip and I are close enough I extend my hand in greeting.

126

"Don't even try to play friendly with me, Mordecai, I know what you have going on out here." Phillip does not even acknowledge my hand as he glares at me.

I'm taken aback. *What could I have done to offend him?* I work to keep my face relaxed and my voice calm. *Father, your peace please. Love for this man.*

"Mr. Stone, what brings you to Oregon?"

"I had to come all the way out here to see what a mess you are creating. I have heard about your politics and I had to see it for myself," he responds.

I have no clue what he is talking about. Does he know something that I don't?

"Phillip, why don't we sit down and we can discuss whatever you have on your mind." I make an effort to direct him into a side conference room.

He doesn't budge. "No, we aren't going to scoot into some side office so no one can hear what we are talking about. Let's talk right here out in the open about the way you have been handling this state. Or are you too embarrassed to discuss it in front of your staff?"

I look at Ethan and the two others from my team who were talking with Phillip and give them a reassuring look. *They know everything about the job that I do and if there is anything inappropriate then they would already know it.* A few walking by become bystanders to the drama.

"Mr. Stone, my work here is an open book. Although it does not seem the appropriate place to discuss it in the courthouse lobby, I'm happy to do that if you would like."

Phillip steps in closer than my normal comfort level and begins to speak in a hissing voice. "That *is* what I would like to do. And you need to know, Allenby, that this is not your courthouse anymore. This is not even your state anymore. It is all under the jurisdiction of the president and that means you are under my jurisdiction. What I say goes."

"Mr. Stone, all of us who truly work for the people have always known that this courthouse and this state, are not ours. We are only vessels of service for the people. I do have a hearing to observe in just a few moments. Was there something specific you wanted to discuss with me today?"

Although seemingly impossible, Phillip's eyes squint even tighter in anger. I begin to pray fervently against the feeling of evil that has just come over me.

"Allenby, your protocols are a mess. Your mentoring program is ineffective. Your leadership style is outdated. You better watch yourself closely and follow what comes out of the office of the President of the United States to the letter. If you don't, you may find yourself in need of updating your resume."

What kind of accusations and threats are these? There isn't anything specific in his rant.

"We have strategic initiative in place and although progress takes time, we are continuing to do our best."

128

Stone storms back at me, "Well your best does not seem to be enough in the big leagues. Maybe that worked before out here in Oregon, but I'm watching you now and things are..."

Stone's voice continues on, but my attention is drawn to my new judge who has just stepped out of a door down the hall. The worry in her eyes is clear—why am I not inside the courtroom so she can begin? I give her a slight smile and gesture with my index finger that I will be just a moment. As I turn my attention back to Stone, I realize I have lost the flow of what he is saying.

"I'm so sorry, Phillip; my mind was with my new judge and I am going to have to go as I need to get into her courtroom." his face is beyond anger.

I wasn't trying to be rude, but his rant was not my priority.

Phillip Stone steps back from me. *He seems in shock that his bullying tactics are not affecting me as much as he would like.*

His face of anger, now turns to a smirk. "Very unwise, Allenby, but if that's how you want to play it."

With that he turns towards the courthouse doors, his entourage following in his wake.

Ethan says, "Mr. Allenby, what did you do? He is the second most powerful man in the entire United States and now he is furious at you."

What did I do? I don't think I did anything. "Did he really just come to Oregon to have that conversation with me?" I ask my other staffers.

129

Keith, just out of law school, responds, "No, Sir, he is on his way to a joint meeting with Oregon and Washington Governors, Senators, and House Representatives to garner support in his new position. We did not know that he was stopping by, but he seemed to know you would be here. I am so sorry. He sounded pleasant enough when he said he wanted to surprise you. We had no idea."

"That's okay, Keith. That whole conversation came out of left field. Nothing could have prepared any of us for it."

"Mr. Allenby, Sir, I just want you to know I respect your work and leadership in our State. I don't know what Mr. Stone is referring to about the problems we have here. I know I have a lot to learn, but I think your work is outstanding." Keith looks uncomfortable as he speaks. I pat his shoulder.

"Thank you for saying that. I don't have a clue what Mr. Stone is talking about either. Until he says something concrete we can work on, I'm going to let those remarks go."

As Ethan and I begin to walk down the hall, he speaks in a low voice. "We were just talking about getting the credit you deserve and making a name for yourself. Now you need that more than ever as it seems you have gotten yourself on the wrong side of Phillip Stone."

At the courtroom door, I pause to say, "You know Ethan, I think I was on the wrong side of Phillip Stone before I even met him. You might not understand this, but there is a hatred in Stone that is deeper than any political differences."

"Then how did you stay so calm when you were talking to him?" Ethan asks. "You didn't even seem phased by his rudeness."

"I have a relationship with God and I was asking him for peace."

Ethan could use this against me in the future, but I want to share this with him.

In a gesture I have never seen from him before, Ethan puts his hand on my arm. "I don't really understand anything about God giving you peace. What I do know is that you need to be careful. Phillip Stone is not someone to mess with."

I give him a reassuring nod and smile. "Thank you, Ethan, I do appreciate your concern for me. But, if God is for me, then I'm not too worried if Phillip Stone is against me."

We walk into the side of the courtroom where the hearing is about to begin. Despite my confident words about peace, worry and anxiety suddenly begin to pound my thoughts. *What was the heavy feeling when I was talking to Stone? Lord, what kind of enemy do I have?*

Two hours later, I am seated around a table of my peers.

I usually enjoy this time, but today I can't seem to relax. It doesn't help that the topic for the last twenty minutes is the aggression of Israel—another worry on my mind.

I stand to fill my cup of coffee while Judge Tolan, just Jeff to me, continues to condemn Israel for their aggressive stance against Iran's actions.

There is not much more I can listen to of this. If even the judges of this great state, people I truly respect, cannot see through the media's lies, how will the general public be able to? As Jeff finishes his opinion that Israel is the aggressor against a helpless Iranian public, I quietly pose a question, coffee still in hand.

"Here is a question, Jeff. Really, for all of you to consider. Would your views be different if you knew the Iranian government had a part in planning, funding, and carrying out the attacks against Israel?"

Many around the room smile at my question and begin to shake their heads at the impossibility.

"Just go with me here. Would you feel differently if you knew without a shadow of a doubt these actions are part of a plan to set in motion what Iran hopes will be the ultimate destruction of their enemy, Israel?"

"Of course, we would feel differently, Cai," Jeff says. "If there was any truth to it."

"So, you are telling me that if it turns out Israel is right in their claims that Iran wants to destroy them, you would back Israel?"

Jeff answers again. "Of course we would support them, but it seems that Israel just wants to fuel the feuds of the past rather than looking towards solutions for the future. We all know Holon is just being over-dramatic when he talks about Iran's plan to destroy Israel so that the twelfth Imam can come. No one thinks that is what Iran is planning—no one except Israel."

I pause, while the quiet in the room settles. A tactic I have long used in the courtroom. "Why do you think Prime Minister Holon, who we all have agreed is a reasonable and wise man, would be making these wild claims of Iran's plans for destruction?"

Another pause while I take a drink of my coffee before I continue.

"The Ayatollah of Iran himself has said for years that he not only wants to destroy Israel, but the United States as well. I wonder why Israel's government is the only one who is listening to these claims and taking them seriously."

The silence in the room turns uncomfortable and I hear the clearing of a throat from one side of the room. A judge shifts uncomfortably in her seat on the other.

"I wonder why we are ignoring Iran's threats of destruction. Is it because our minds cannot comprehend one group decimating another again, so we dismiss it as ludicrous? Israel is preparing to defend the lives of her citizens if Iran plans to go nuclear. It would be disastrous if we sit by and let another Holocaust happen again in such recent history."

Some have already dismissed me with their skepticism. I have definitely gone out on a limb against popular belief on this one.

Jeff does not look happy, but has been listening intently. "We have different views on this, but we all obviously want to see peace between these two countries."

"I agree Jeff, but as long as the purpose of one country is to destroy another, peace between them is impossible."

I walk back to my chair with my coffee still in hand. No one answers and the entire room is thoughtful and quieter than usual. As I sit down, side conversations are starting up as everyone senses the meeting is winding down.

Sylvia, a silver haired sage with no fear, leans in to me, "Cai, we all know how strongly you feel about Israel with your Jewish background. You can even get a little stubborn in your views. Do you think you might be a little too vested in this conflict to see everything clearly?"

I break into a smile, which Sylvia obviously does not expect. *This reminds me of a time when Esther was upset with me for not letting her go to a party. "Uncle Cai, you are the most stubborn man I know. You'll never change your mind once it is made up." The answer I gave to Esther that day is the same one I give to Sylvia now.*

"Sylvia, you use the word stubborn like it's a bad thing, while I think that trait is my saving grace. The Israelis and their government have that same personality trait as well." I take on a more serious tone now as I explain. "Israel has had to be stubborn to survive. To be resilient. To fight when needed."

Sylvia surprises me as she is the one to break into a smile now. She shakes her head side to side. "See what I mean

Cai? I guess that stubborn strength coupled with your kindness is what we all love about you."

"Thank you, Sylvia, I take that as a real compliment."

Sylvia looks at me with genuine concern in her eyes, "Cai, listen to me carefully. Not everyone knows you like I do and the stance you are taking on Israel is a risky one. I have also heard there is conflict between you and Phillip Stone. Please be careful."

I nod to Sylvia a word of thanks. And in an unusually intimate gesture of friendship here at the judge's meeting, she puts her hand on mine and gives it a quick squeeze.

This is the second warning today I've gotten to be careful. I'm starting to have a feeling that there are going to be difficult times ahead—for Israel, for the Jewish people, and for me.

~~

Chapter 14

TRUE COLORS REVEALED
PHILLIP STONE - WHITE HOUSE CHIEF OF STAFF

"We counted on the democratic thinking of the west to help us be viewed as the innocent ones in the attacks. It has worked beautifully," I assure Ahmed on the other end of the secure phone line. "Americans don't want to believe that a country's government would generate attacks on innocent lives, including children. It is easier for the average American, watching the news over dinner, to swallow that these attacks were planned by a group of angry young men rather than by the leadership of the country." I pause, waiting for Ahmed to respond. *I'm doing way too much of the talking. My comrade seems unsettled and I want to reassure him.*

Finally, Ahmed breaks the silence over the phone line. "My worry is not with the general public. My worry is with your leader and if you have him on board as you say you do."

This is my source of pride—the way I have orchestrated events and shaped Xander's thinking.

"Yes, my brother, you can be assured I have the president's ear. He is listening completely to my guidance in how to handle this crisis. Do not concern yourself for a moment with him. He is a sheep, following my lead."

"Good. That is exactly what I hoped to hear. What do you need from our side?" Ahmed asks with obvious relief in his voice.

Ahmed truly is my brother in every sense. I know him more deeply than I could possibly know a brother of flesh and blood. Even from this far, I can sense how he is feeling, his deep desire to see his life's work come to fruition.

"Keep the statements coming with a strongly sympathetic voice towards Israel's death toll. Have our father, the Ayatollah, proclaiming condolences to Israel, while speaking about working hard to help the misguided youth. Have him portrayed as Father Iran, struggling to mold his wayward children toward peace."

I can hear Ahmed's agreement and picture him in his office, leaning back in his chair and looking relaxed as he responds. *His relaxed posture never gives away the intensity that he is feeling; especially now, as he prepares for the monumental event that will change all of our futures forever.*

"Israel will continue to be portrayed as the bully, ready to strike out against an innocent Iran, who is doing their best to promote peace. This caring stance by our father, while at the same time patting the attackers on the heads like little boys he is proud of, will infuriate the Little Satan. We will keep leaking intelligence to Israel that we are ready with a nuclear strike. Israel won't be able to keep from attacking. Israel will tell the world an attack is in self-defense, but they will be alone as they open up the door for our retaliation."

Following his words, the laughter coming from the other end of the phone is intoxicating. I find myself breaking out in laughter as well.

Ahmed finally quiets his laughter and begins to speak again. "I know I don't have to describe to you, Phillip, the thrill I feel at this moment. I could never have imagined when I met you, an unbridled American youth staying at a hostel in Tehran, that our lives would bring us to this moment. We are about to change the course of history by crippling our enemy and promoting the coming of the Twelfth Imam." Suddenly, I feel a catch in my throat and emotion overwhelms me. Ahmed knows me as well and gives me a moment to gather my composure before I speak.

"Ahmed, what if you had not found me when you did—flailing in uncertainty, looking for my purpose in life, where would I be today?"

My brother quickly responds, "It was not me who found you brother, it was Allah's plan. It was never coincidence that an American boy just out of high school traveled through Turkey, followed a girl into Syria, and then was drawn to Iran where he found his home and true family."

"You are right, my brother. Do you remember the first day we met? I was almost out of money, cleaning rooms and working the breakfast at the hostel to be able to stay. You had come in for something." I pause as Ahmed jumps in to help with details I had forgotten.

"I could not get my car out. Someone blocked it in while I was in the mosque to pray. I was looking for the owner in the neighborhood."

"You came through the door, made a beeline for me and immediately began asking me questions. We ended up talking right there in the lobby for over an hour. You listened to my frustrations about the hypocrisy of my country. Your passion and beliefs were contagious. You immediately gave me a desire to fight for something."

Ahmed picks up the trip down memory lane. "At first, I was drawn to you out of curiosity. I planned to immediately hate this American infidel. Instead, I found someone frustrated with the United States and open to new ideas. We had the same spirit."

"That was a tough time for me. I was so disgruntled with everything American - Vietnam and Nixon – I did not know how to express it until you helped me understand. Not only Islam, but the mission of my life and the difference I could make."

Ahmed chuckles again, "Remember how I repeatedly had to tell you to stop calling me Mr. Al-Sadoon?"

"Well, you were a few years older." We both laugh. "It took a few times together before I could call you Brother Ahmed, but it stuck, didn't it?"

"Yes, it did. We talked for hours over hummus, flatbread, and olives, about the things that mattered most? How America and Israel were bedfellows of greed and corruption. Always against us. Once you gained a vision for our future and embraced it completely, you were the one whose passion was contagious. You made me believe we could do something more than just dream. You made your

139

dream a reality, even more than we could have imagined. Look at you, the White House chief of staff."

"It never would have happened without your guidance. You came up with the plan and worked in Iran to position yourself and our comrades both militarily and politically to act. The General of the Army with the entire government on board." I pause for a moment. "You know, I might have never left Iran if you had not told me I needed to. I wanted to stay forever."

Over the phone, I can hear a rustle of movement and know Ahmed is leaning forward on his desk now, more intent. "I know brother. You have sacrificed your life for the cause. You have become a part of the system you despise and been patient for the time to come. Your time of sacrifice will soon be over and you will be home and embraced with open arms. You will be called by your true name once again. When we succeed, *Inshallah,* we will be a part of one of the biggest events in history since the Prophet Mohammed, peace be upon him, lived on the earth and gave us the holy Koran."

Ahmed continues, "We must succeed, Brother, we must succeed. Stay focused now. Nothing can go wrong." Memories are over and the intensity in what is about to take place is back.

"Everything is going according to plan on this side. Are you and the comrades prepared for the timeline as previously discussed?" I respond.

"Yes, brother, everything is in place. I am like a child the night before Ramadan begins, I am anticipating this so greatly!"

"Allah is obviously on our side," I conclude.

~~

Two hours later and I urge my driver to hurry as I am running late to meet the president. *That conversation with Ahmed left me more emotional than I have been for a long time. Maybe it's because the time is drawing near. Maybe I'm ready for forty years of preparation to finally pay off. Maybe I'm anticipating returning to my true homeland and being able to stop living a facade. Ahmed is right, I need to stay focused.*

~~

"Xander, how are we this morning?" I exclaim, walking into his office a few minutes later, and shooing other staff out of the room with a wave of my hand.

I love how they skitter away like little rats when I tell them to. I had to gain the president's complete trust. I just had to stroke his fragile ego and give him a vision of himself as the ultimate leader with me there to support him. Then, there was the staff to deal with. Thomas obviously had to go immediately. Then I drew a line in the sand to find out who was with me and replaced those who were not. And here I am as the sole advisor to the President of the United States.

I sit down next to Xander as he begins. "Good morning. I am glad you are here, I need your insight."

"Of course, Mr. President, you know I am only here to assist you," I respond, humbly.

And lead you my sheep.

"Thank you, Stone. I have always appreciated your vision and focus coupled with service to our country."

If Alexander Susa was not obviously such an idiot, I might actually like the guy.

"I assume you have been briefed on the message we received this morning from Prime Minister Holon?" he asks.

"Yes, sir, I would have been here earlier, but I was on the phone with contacts in the Middle East this morning, already preparing a possible response for you to consider. I know what the message says, although do you have the exact wording?"

"Of course," Xander says, as he lifts the paper on the desk to me. "I should have known you were already on this. That is why I consider you a gift to our country. You know I tell everyone that, don't you?"

I force a humbled smile. "Thank you, Mr. President, I am honored you think so. I am proud to be working with a man full of greatness as well as such wisdom."

Great and wise are about the farthest thing from this man, but I need to keep him close during this critical time.

After reading the two pages, a summarized version of the much longer message it came from, I put down the paper and look at Xander. He has been anxiously watching me while I read.

"Mr. President, there can be only one response to this request." I take a deep breath for effect. "The simple word, no."

Xander locks his hands behind his head and props his feet onto the desk. He begins shaking his head back and forth with obvious worry. "The rest of the staff don't think so. We have been allies with Israel for years, Phillip. Prime Minister Holon is asking for our support and I feel obligated to stand with them in their decision to strike."

He sounds so presidential with this bold statement, feet up on the same desk so many presidents before him have used. I must handle him carefully to not lose him. I stand up and begin pacing slowly in front of his desk, as though deep in thought about what he has just said. I can see his eyes tracking me as I walk while he waits for me to speak. "Mr. President, you know I have been doing this for a long time. I have seen many conflicts in the Middle East. Many have come and some have gone."

I take my time with my words and slow down my steps before I stop in front of the desk to turn and look directly into Xander's eyes. "I know we have stood with Israel in the past, but there is a line Israel is considering crossing that we cannot be a part of. They have blamed a whole country for the actions of a few and are now about to mercilessly punish the innocent. Holon is planning a large scale attack on Tehran where thousands of innocent lives could be lost. If we stand by Israel now, we are standing with those wanting to crush the prospect of peace."

143

As though concluding a speech to a large crowd, I look up over the president's head, "No Mr. President, we have to look at the direction our so-called allies are heading and see they are not moving towards a world of peace. We cannot be a part of their violent path. It goes against everything the United States stands for."

The discussion continues as Xander asks questions and makes comments. I gently sway the moldable president to see my point. Finally, Xander is quiet. He slowly pulls his feet off of his desk and sets them on the floor in front of him. His head follows the motion as he falls forward onto his elbows, his forefingers pensively rubbing the temples of his head.

With his head down, I can still hear his muffled question. "How do you think staying out of this conflict will affect my ratings? Will I be seen as weak and fickle for not supporting our allies?"

I have to tone down the joy in my response as well as the smirk on my face, knowing the president is coming around to my way of thinking.

"On the contrary, Mr. President, I know the American people will not support an attack by Israel. This decision to not back an aggressive and violent nation will only strengthen your position in the eyes of the country. They will see you as wise and prudent. Your stand on the side of peace will do nothing but garner you more support.

Just be quiet, Phillip, wait patiently. He is almost there. The moments ticking by feel like an eternity until Xander blows out a big breath and raises his head out from his hands.

"Okay then, the decision is made." Xander quickly stands up and begins to shake my hand as though agreeing on a business deal.

"We will sit tight and let Israel sort this one out without us."

When I leave the Oval Office a few minutes later, I can't help the grin slowly spreading across my face. *The whole plan has almost been too easy. The attacks in Israel were arranged easily enough by the Iranian government. The threats of more, including a nuclear attack was all it took. Knowing Prime Minister Holon's style of leadership, his response of retaliation was almost a given. Now, I just convinced the President of the United States to withhold help that our long-term allies are asking for. Without the United States supporting them, Israel will look like a rogue bully. As soon as they strike Iran and their citizens, no one will defend them as the entire world will turn against Israel.*

Once inside my office, I shut the door and immediately go to my computer. I log in through a virtual private network so it looks like this e-mail is coming out of Los Angeles, pull up my secure e-mail and begin to type. Emotions about all the years leading up to this point begin to well up inside me. *It has taken most of my adult life to get to this moment. Finally, my comrades and I are almost in position to carry out our mission.*

"Dearest Brother, no support will be given from this side. Give me an immediate update on testing from your side."

I quickly encrypt my message into a picture for added security. *I could probably skip this step, but I must be extra careful now.*

I push the send button and sit anxiously waiting for a reply. Knowing Ahmed, he will still be up and I will get an immediate response.

As I wait, I run through the details. I do wish there was another way besides sacrificing the lives of Iranians to the hands of the Israelis. However, the decimation of life we will ultimately inflict on our enemies will be worth every sacrifice.

The ping of a new message jolts me from my thoughts. "Alhamdo lellah, praise be to Allah. We will be ready, Inshallah. Testing is almost complete. As long as your pieces are in place, it is almost time my brother."

I feel like jumping out of my chair and screaming for joy, but I sit calm and composed as I have for so many years. Ahmed's word choice of "pieces" is appropriate. It's been like playing a massive game of chess. Every move has gone as planned, almost like playing against children.

"Pieces in movement. We will be ready. Time for our comrades to create a fear of the Jews in America—begin the operation to make sure the public and press stay on our side. You prepare Israel and I will prepare the American Jews for D-Day."

Leaning back in my chair, it is my turn to put my feet up on the desk. *I am in control.* I want to gloat, but only my office walls and computer know the mastermind I am. In a few moves I will have "checkmate" and the game will be complete. Then the world will know I am a mastermind and I will be a hero of Iran forever.

~~

146

Chapter 15

SECRET MEETING
ESTHER

The treadmill is not the same as running outside. It feels like an artificial run with the ground moving beneath me to help. I can't relax the same while I am thinking about the potential of falling and scraping my face across that moving ground.

I am trying to respect Mr. Stone's instructions for me to stay inside for safety reasons these last few weeks. With Israel's air strike against Iran as well as the violence here in the United States, my freedom has been restricted even more. *It's driving me batty. Here in this room, under the artificial lights, with everything that is happening racing through my mind, I just can't relax. I miss the fresh air and the sunshine.*

Round and round the moving ground goes. *Too much time to think. And then there is Uncle Cai. I don't know if it's smart to meet up with him today. But he was so insistent, which is ironic since he is the one who wanted to stay apart for so long. At least I will be able to talk to someone about everything that is happening. Probably all the talking to myself is driving me mad as well.*

A quick rap on the door jolts me from my inner dialogue. "Come in!" I yell through the door of my exercise room. My assistant, Gabriella, comes in with a glass that looks like another protein concoction she has made.

"Thank you, Gabriella, you are keeping me healthy and hydrated."

"I added carrots this time, so you are going to love it. Lots of good vitamins."

I push the large stop button on the machine, the one designed for emergencies where you have fallen, although I'm not sure how I would reach the button at that point. When the moving ground stops, I reach for the drink.

Gabriella's phone is in her other hand, she consults it— probably looking at my schedule—although these days there is very little on it. *I hope she doesn't make a big deal about this meeting. I'm just going to try and downplay it and see how it goes. Gabriella has been loyal as far as I know and I hope I can trust her with this.*

Her eyes glance up at me in question, "Mrs. President…"

"Gabriella," I say interrupting, "please remember, when we are in the privacy of my home, I want you to call me Esther."

I know she doesn't want to do this because of Mr. Stone's direct instructions to staff about titles and respect. Leaning in closer I say, "If anyone is around, you can call me Mrs. President, but when it is just you and me, I want it to be Esther. Okay?"

"Okay, Esther," Gabriella says smiling. Although I can see she feels awkward saying it. She continues, "You wanted the early afternoon left free. Is there anything you need me to do for you?"

"Thank you, Gabriella, but I am just going to have a low-key afternoon here. I have a few things to do, probably just pop downstairs for a bit."

Gabriella looks at me in confusion. *Oh, that was such a bad excuse. Now she really thinks something is up, more than if I had just told her I had a meeting. But then she would have wondered what kind of meeting. What should I say?*

"I am meeting someone today to talk about all this mess going on in the world and get some perspective on it. It has been a tough last couple weeks."

"Don't worry Mrs. President, I mean Esther, I understand this has been a difficult time in our world and our country. It's okay if you are going to talk to someone. In fact, I think that's a great idea. I had to do that once during a really stressful time a few years ago and it helped. "

"Right, thanks." That is all I can manage.

Now I feel like I've lied as she thinks I'm going to see a counselor and I went along with that. What will she think if she finds out I'm meeting with the Oregon State Attorney General instead?

An hour later, Gabriella is wishing me well as I leave to "pop" downstairs for a bit. I appreciate her gentle squeeze on my arm and little smile, even though it's probably meant as support for my therapy session. *Maybe I should see a counselor. They have patient confidentiality rules. Maybe I could get some help with what I should do about the mess of my marriage, my lack of family, and the stress I am feeling about Israel and the Jews. But today is time with Uncle Cai.*

I tentatively walk towards the small conference room. This room is as far away from Xander's office as possible and without a camera. Uncle Cai said in his e-mail it will be the best place to meet, even though there is still a risk. I hardly care anymore if everyone finds out we are family, so I guess the biggest risk is for him.

The scent of lemongrass and ginger fills my nose as soon as I enter the room and I'm taken back to all those years at our little Thai restaurant.

My eyes begin to well up with memories when I see Uncle Cai sitting at a table waiting for me with the food he has brought. He turns to me with a big smile, just like he has so many times before. I am taken back to the feel of my youth for a split second, before it seems so far away again. In that moment, my Uncle and I were so close again with no thought of ever being torn apart. As he gets up, I close the door behind me and he gestures for me to lock it, so I do before coming towards him.

My steps quicken and I walk into Uncle Cai's open arms. As we hug, my shoulders, and the tension I did not even realize they were holding, begin to relax. My eyes are suddenly wet with tears. We hold on to one another.

"I have missed you so much Uncle Cai. I feel so alone," I finally said. *This is not how I planned to greet my uncle. I meant to say hello like a grown woman, with confidence. Maybe with a little reserved distance to let him know I am upset with him. Here I am acting like a child.*

I pull out of the hug and try to laugh off my emotion. "I guess just hugging you again reminds me of how much I have missed you these last couple years."

"Esther, I miss you too. And I still love you as much as I ever did, even more."

My cry catches in my throat at his remark and I quickly silence myself, remembering we need to keep quiet to not attract attention. In a hushed whisper I say, "I guess sometimes I have not been so sure of that, so it is good to hear you say it."

I sniff and wipe my tears with the back of my fingers. The only earthly father I have ever really known gives me a peck on the head. "Now, let's eat and talk. We should not be here too long."

Once we are seated, we clasp hands to pray, just like we used to. Uncle Cai quietly thanks God for being with each of us, even as we have been apart from each other. "Amen" in unison. A small squeeze of our hands. *Just like we used to.* For a moment, I can pretend that things are how they used to be.

Opening my eyes to reality, I remove the lid from my soup bowl. I lean over as the spicy steam rises to hover around my face for a brief instant. I inhale the scent before the steam quickly disperses. I look up to see my uncle smiling at me. "How a scent can take me back," I respond to him with a smile of my own.

Uncle Cai says, "This soup makes me think of you as a little girl. Even now, every time I eat it." Once we have eaten a bite of soup, I can hardly contain my words. "I am so glad

151

you wanted to meet. I have been dying to ask you what you think about Israel."

Uncle Cai just nods as he continues eating his soup, as though thinking, so I continue. "And why are Jewish Americans choosing to voice their frustrations through violence? Don't they realize they are only antagonizing Americans against our people and Israel."

Uncle Cai sets his spoon down and I can see he is ready to talk. I force myself to shut my mouth, except for the occasional bite of soup slipping through. In teaching mode Uncle Cai begins, "Esther, this is exactly why I wanted to talk to you today. The danger for the future is even greater than you can imagine. I need you to understand in your critical position as the president's wife. The rest of the world is blinded, but you cannot be."

My silence and intent look must be enough to convince him I am listening well because he continues talking.

"Let me start with Israel's attack on Iran. It was a massive strike; over one hundred confirmed dead. The world has condemned Israel for so brutally killing innocents in retaliation for the deaths of just a few. The part of the report that is missing is that the targets hit were nuclear weapons production and testing sites. Iran had placed them near and even under schools and mosques."

I gasp at the picture of what my uncle has just said. *Iran wouldn't really put nuclear facilities under schools, would they?* My look must give away my disbelief.

"Israel knows how close Iran is to being ready to launch nuclear weapons at them. Their attack was an attempt to save their country from destruction."

I sit in silence digesting what he has just said. It sounds too much like a movie to be real life.

Uncle Cai breaks into my thoughts, "Did you hear about the earthquake in Iran last week?"

"No," I respond, confused.

"Exactly," Uncle Cai counters. "It was hardly reported there was a quake, even though southern Iran is not on a fault line. An earthquake confirms the existence of a suspected underground nuclear testing facility. It proves they are putting towns on top of these centers as at least four hundred people who lived over the epicenter of the quake were killed."

"Uncle Cai, if this is true, why didn't the media report this information?" I question.

"The media saw the earthquake as insignificant because they did not make the connection that it came from nuclear weapons testing. But this deadly quake is only one of many signs that Iran is in its final testing phase and ready to attack." I nod with Uncle Cai as he finishes talking and understanding dawns on me.

"I knew there had to be another reason Israel went after Iran so hard. If Iran fires a nuclear missile against Israel, the whole country could be virtually destroyed." My throat catches on the word destroyed as I think about that reality.

Uncle Cai slowly responds, sadness in his eyes. "Yes Esther, my sources tell me that is what Israel is fearing. That is why they felt they had to make an effort to attack the nuclear sites before it was too late."

"But Uncle Cai, why didn't Israel just wait a little longer? The UN is working towards a peaceful solution. Why did Israel have to retaliate so strongly and turn the whole world against them by acting against the advice of her allies? Don't they realize they now look like the aggressor and Iran as the defenseless victim only wanting peace?"

"Esther, there cannot be a peaceful resolution to this conflict while the objective of Iran is to destroy them."

I sit quietly thinking. *He makes it sound so hopeless. The UN is working towards a peaceful resolution. Wouldn't both countries truly want this?*

"What worries me is Iran is garnering under the false pretense of peace. The world has almost completely turned against Israel and now that same hatred is spilling over to the Jews in America as well."

My mind races between the fear of Jews being hated in America and the worry that my uncle is being over-dramatic again. *Look what he has done to our relationship, almost completely severed it, and for what?*

"Uncle Cai, think of all the times in history when there have been conflicts in the Middle East. They always have some type of resolution and the tension dies out."

His look is almost pity towards me as he shakes his head and begins to speak. "Esther, if you really think the tension towards Israel has ever died out, you do not understand the depth of hatred against them. No sanctions put in place by the United Nations will remove that."

We sit in silence for a moment. I am frustrated by his gloomy outlook on the future and he appears frustrated at me too. "Esther, I believe the current political situation is creating a scenario where Jews around the world could be persecuted again."

I quickly cut in. "Some Jews aren't exactly helping that situation. With the Jewish Americans the last couple days lashing out in violence; of course the rest of the world is scared and upset. I don't understand why our people are doing these things."

Uncle Cai nods, "It looks bad that Jews in America are so angry they are turning violent, but don't be so sure that these events are not being manipulated to cause this reaction."

What is he talking about? How do you manipulate violent events?

He continues over my thoughts, "It is not only society who has blind eyes, but they are in the White House as well, Esther."

Although Xander and I have our challenges, I am loyal to my husband and don't want to hear him slammed by the very man who encouraged me to join this marriage. I look into my lap and try to listen without being upset.

"Esther, your husband is not open to see the true intention of Iran towards Israel. He is being swayed by Phillip Stone to support Iran despite warning signs."

When Phillip Stone is mentioned, I nod my head in agreement. "That I do see. Mr. Stone seems against Israel in every way. And he has such a hold on Xander. I remember the first time Xander introduced me to Mr. Stone and his wife, Tricia, at a state dinner. It was right before he became Xander's chief of staff. The excitement Xander had in introducing him peaked my interest. He was enamored with him. It should have been a warning of things to come. Since Mr. Stone has been around, things have changed."

Emotions course through me. I feel grief for all those who might be killed in this conflict; both Israelis and Iranians. Fear for the future of Jews around the world and here in my own country. Worry that my husband is being used as Mr. Stone's pawn for some ulterior reason.

Uncle Cai covers my hand with his, "We need to keep in prayer. Pray that we will be wise and have courage." I quickly nod and my uncle prays over the worries on both of our minds. Finishing his prayer, his hand gives mine a gentle squeeze as he scoots back his chair. As we stand facing each other, my uncle puts his hands on my shoulders and says, "Esther, be alert and ready."

He is scaring me. Our parting hug is not quite as emotional as the first, but I hold onto him for an extra moment.

"I love you Uncle Cai, let's do this again soon," I ask, almost pleading.

"You know I would love to spend time with you, but we just can't right now unless it is absolutely necessary."

"But why?" I question.

"I'm not exactly sure why, but we need to be careful."

Uncle Cai quickly walks out of the room and I nervously clean up our lunch remnants, half expecting someone to come in and ask me what I have been doing here with him. *I want to see Xander. Maybe because I worry for my husband and where he is leading our country. Maybe because I am scared and he is the man I love.*

Outside the Oval Office, I see a new aide sitting at the desk, "Good afternoon, I don't believe we have met before."

The aide responds cordially, but distantly, "Good afternoon, Mrs. President, my name is Cyrus. How can I help you?"

"Hello Cyrus, it is nice to meet you." *His look is cold, as though he does not like me already. Most people treat me warmly around the White House. Must have been hired and trained by Mr. Stone.* I almost chuckle out loud at my inner sarcasm. I aim to warm up this new aide with kindness. "Have you always lived in D.C. or did you just move here?"

The cold stare I get in return to my question surprises me. "Mrs. President, do you have some business here today as I know I do."

"I understand and I'm sure you are very busy." I am trying to keep composed, but I can't believe how rude this man is acting. "Cyrus, I just stopped by to see my husband for a minute. Is he in a meeting or is he free?" I ask politely.

Cyrus immediately responds, "The president is not available to any personal interruptions. From now on you will need to schedule any meetings through the chief of staff."

I try to gently laugh off his response as he must not understand me. "Oh, I don't need long with my husband, Cyrus, certainly not a meeting. I understand what an extremely busy man he is. Just a minute to say hello, that's all."

His steely face only hardens. "Mrs. President, I will make the instructions I have been given as clear as I can and then you are welcome to discuss them with Mr. Stone. There are to be no unscheduled interruptions to the president at any time during the day or night when he is working. Every event on his schedule goes through Mr. Stone—including you, Mrs. President."

Confusion fills my mind and I'm sure my face as I struggle to understand what Cyrus is telling me. *I'm not welcome to go in and see my own husband? Who does Mr. Stone think he is? This is too far. What will Cyrus do if I decide to go into the office anyway?*

Cyrus must see me glance towards the doorknob because he nods to the Secret Service agent who steps from beside the doorway to right in front of it.

Seriously? Has Mr. Stone told them to block me from getting in the door to my husband?

I work to smile since I'm not sure exactly what I want to do about this blockade. "No problem, Cyrus, I'll just see my husband when he comes home tonight."

His cold voice responds, "Mrs. President, I'll be sure to let you know if the president requests your presence for any reason."

I tell my face to keep smiling, but Cyrus's last comment makes it almost impossible as I nod goodbye and turn to walk back towards my residence. *I feel like I have been told I'm just another one of the people who work around here, not Xander's wife. 'We'll let you know if we need you'. Almost like they would say to a plumber, 'We'll call you again if one of the toilets overflows; otherwise we have no need for you."*

My tears are on the edge of overflowing as I open the door to the home I share with Xander. *Does he not want to see me or is this just Mr. Stone controlling him again?* Safely inside, my tears begin to slide down my cheeks as I process out loud.

"I can't live like this if Xander does not even want to see me. I walk to the kitchen—open the refrigerator door—close it—turn around to the cupboard—open it and reach for a glass, having to steady it with both hands because of how badly my hand is shaking.

"Tonight, I'm going to ask Xander about this. I will find out if this distance is what he wants or if Mr. Stone is coming between us."

When he comes home tonight I'll ask him; if he comes home tonight. He hasn't come home for quite a few nights. I don't even

159

know where he sleeps or if he is gone. Could it be he is with another woman? Is that what this is about?

The tears are dropping from my chin.

God, I don't think I can handle it if Xander has someone else. With the stress of everything else going on; it's just too much for me.

I slump to my knees in front of the couch and I begin to pray. There is nothing else to do.

~~

Chapter 16

BLINDSIDED BY THE PLAN

XANDER

"Mr. President, these are fearful times. Jews are acting out in violence against their fellow Americans. The Jewish violence in the Middle East is now here in the United States."

I look up as my trusted chief of staff pauses and runs his hands through his tousled hair. I can see the dark circles under his eyes and know he has not slept much this week.

"Phillip, I have never seen you so worried. Can this Jewish violence really be all that different than the other crime which daily plagues our streets? Are Jewish Americans really pitting themselves against the rest of the country?"

I'm tired and would like to go to bed. Maybe we can talk more about this tomorrow.

Phillip sits down next to me; the fingertips of his hands pressed against each other. He takes a deep breath and looks like he is about to explain the wonders of the world.

Nope, I don't think I am getting upstairs to bed again tonight. This will be almost a week since I have made it home to sleep. I have just been working and sleeping right next door in a makeshift bedroom.

"Xander, the rising up of American Jews against their own country is completely different than other violence because of their intent. These individual acts are just the beginning of a movement that could create civil unrest if we are not careful."

"Phillip, you know I completely respect your opinion, especially when it comes to the type of peacekeeping we need right now, but I don't understand how this could possibly lead to civil unrest? There have just been a few unrelated incidents of Jewish violence this week—that is no indication of civil unrest."

He nods his head in agreement although his jaw clenches tighter as though he is upset. "You are right, Mr. President, to the untrained eye, these incidents look unrelated and harmless enough. Let me assure you this is the precise moment when you knew you would need me because together our eyes will understand clearly the danger of what is happening so we can stop it."

Now I am the one nodding my head in agreement and with a smile I say, "Okay Stone, earn your keep and open my eyes to what is really happening."

I stand up to punctuate my own sentence. "Although I think I want a drink before my eyes are opened, you?" I walk towards the bar to pour myself a scotch.

"Yes, thank you. You might want to make them both a double as this is going to be a lot to take in." He smiles as though he is trying to keep a positive attitude in the midst of a hopeless situation.

162

Now I am starting to feel worried. I bring two scotches back and sit down to get ready for Phillip's explanation.

"It all started small a few days ago as you know. A Jewish American man in Chicago was picked up by the police for vandalizing his neighbor's house with anti-American and pro-Israel slogans and killing his dog by slitting its' throat. What is most worrisome about this violence is the man who did these acts and whom he chose to do them to. The perpetrator was in his mid-forties, a family man, successful with his own business. The neighbor he terrorized was a soldier who had served in Iraq and lost a leg during his tour of duty."

As Phillip pauses, I add, "Horrible, just horrible, but the man denied any involvement in the case."

"Let's not be naive here, Xander," Phillip quickly responds. "There were two eyewitness accounts by other neighbors placing him at the crime scene. No alibi there."

Phillip continues, "This Jew's actions show a movement against the United States military for their lack of action in supporting Israel. It also shows hatred is coming from the everyday Jewish American, like this family man, not just from radicals. You see that in all the other incidents so far as well, which all scream of civil unrest or even a civil war."

Phillip lifts his glass to his lips at the same time I do, giving a natural pause for our thoughts. *How is the country I am in charge of suddenly on the brink of civil unrest?*

He continues, "There was the Jewish accountant who threw a hand grenade out of his car window towards the doors of

163

a post office in New Jersey, killing one and injuring twelve more. His car was full of revolutionary material about the Jews rising up and fighting America from within."

"Wasn't that man in a fairly groggy state when they took him into custody? Some on the scene said he could not have been responsible for the blasts."

In a steely tone he answers me. "Mr. President, please do not take your information from unreliable sources, which includes the news. Yes, the man was recovering from the blast as he was taken into custody, as was everyone else he injured in the nearby vicinity."

"Of course," I quickly answer realizing my blunder.

Phillip nods and continues talking, obviously upset, I assume by the violence.

"There was the Jewish teen who used himself and his car as a weapon when he drove it straight into the front of his local bank in Los Angeles. Two adults and a child who were exiting the bank were struck by his car and killed instantly. The attacker was taken into custody wearing a shirt with a handwritten message: Israel will survive—Death to America!

What this young man shows is youth are playing their part in this Jewish movement against America. The young Jewish Americans are willing to die for it."

I take another drink. *The idea of civil war is not so distant anymore.* "And I briefly heard about the old man last night, but what were the details?"

"He shows the older generation of Jews, some with money and prestige, are angry and willing to fight against the United States for their home country of Israel as well," Phillip echoes back.

"The man made calls to local businesses, schools, and restaurants with the claim there was a bomb inside their building. The police were able to trace the number the calls were being made from and surrounded the home of a retired Jewish banker. The police found him sitting at his kitchen table with a list of fifty names and numbers in front of him. He had notes written all around his list saying, "America will pay". Bomb squads were quickly called in, but were not in time to find the home-made bomb that went off in a local restaurant. Ten were injured and three people were killed." Phillip pauses in his explanation of the latest attack.

"What old man builds home bombs, plants them, and then calls the cops in?" I say trying to think through the details.

Phillip continues, "Did you know that one of the men who was taken to the hospital with injuries was a 9/11 survivor? There is no way that was a coincidence. This attack was purposefully planned to retaliate against all things and all people that stand for America and her freedom."

"Cruel and unusual to go after someone who has already suffered so much. What about the other forty-nine bombs? Have any of the others gone off?"

"No, not yet." He assures me. "The bomb squads have secured almost all the locations, although it is likely the man had accomplices and more have been planted."

165

Phillip stands up to pour another drink for me as mine is already gone. "Xander, these incidents point to the fact that the Jews as a whole are revolting against the United States because we did not side with Israel in her latest conflict."

He hands my glass to me and I take it, even though I was not planning to have another. I respond, still unsure of what to think. "I understand some Jews are frustrated. They may even feel abandoned by us as their long-time allies. But Phillip, I still don't understand how these incidents will lead to civil unrest?"

Phillip now paces in front of me as he does when we are discussing something he is passionate about. "Mr. President, in only a few days, revolt has broken out among Jewish Americans. There is obviously a pattern to these attacks and shows a wide spectrum of participants. There are undercurrents of unifying this revolt and then it could grow until it is a full-blown war within America. This is how they begin."

I work to take in what he is saying. I am starting to feel the effect of my tiredness and these drinks as my processing time is slowing down. *This is how I end up falling asleep down here every night lately.*

Phillip continues pacing. "Honestly, Xander, I am extremely fearful for our Jewish community if they do not get a hold on their rage. They could draw the rest of the country into a war within. We must remind them they cannot act in violence. While at the same time, we must help to protect them against their own anger until everyone calms down a little."

It all makes sense what Stone is saying. If the Jewish Americans keep up this violence, their neighbors around them will retaliate. Eventually the police and the government will have to get involved. He is right—it could become a full-fledged civil war.

Full of worry now, I ask, "What can we do? How can we stop what is already spreading so quickly?"

Phillip finally looks calm for the first time in this whole conversation. "Mr. President, you do not ever have to doubt that I have a plan to help keep our country peaceful. I have already set tentative plans in motion to give the Jewish Americans a safe place to go, to calm down from this rage where they will also be protected. Together, you and I will keep peace in our great country and not let anyone challenge that."

Phillip holds up his glass towards mine and I feel a sense of reassurance at the clinking sound. I give him a genuine smile of appreciation as I finish my drink and set down my glass.

"You are so good to take care of my presidency and our country." A wave of emotion comes over me. Maybe it's the alcohol, maybe I just want to sleep, but I feel so strongly. *Where would I be without Phillip's guidance over my presidency?* "Truly Phillip, listen to me, you are the best. Whatever you have planned to keep the peace; do it. You have my full support." My eyes feel heavy and I want to let my blink linger closed for just a moment, until Phillip's voice opens them again.

"Thank you Mr. President, I won't let you down. I know you need to rest, but let me first read you a statement I would like to send out immediately to remind everyone across this country that the White House stands for peace."

I try to shake off my tiredness and stay alert, "Go ahead; I'm fine."

He begins, "The White House is concerned about the safety of our citizens, from all nationalities and backgrounds. Anti-American hate crimes will not be tolerated and will be seen as a lack of allegiance to the ideals of the United States. The president asks the citizens of this country to be vigilant in keeping their streets and towns safe from those who would harm democracy and what Americans stand for. The American spirit will not be crushed, either by those outside our borders or those within. Rather, the American spirit will live on while those who would like to see it tarnished will be the ones to fall."

Contentment comes over me at the confidence of his words. "Beautiful Phillip; just beautiful. The strength is there, the optimism, and the leadership. Yes, it sounds perfect." With that, I slide down on the couch from sitting to lying down. *Oh, that feels so much better.*

Even though my eyes are now closed, I say, "Thank you Phillip. I know I can count on you."

~~

Chapter 17

THE PRESS FUELS THE FIRE
MORDECAI

"Open your eyes and look at what is happening in our country, in the United States of America, the land of the free." I lean in to the gaggle of microphones at another impromptu press conference outside my Portland home. The press has been here most every morning since I spoke out against the White House's peace plan.

I take a question from a reporter. "Attorney General Allenby, what made you decide to put your job and reputation on the line to speak out against the White House?"

"Thank you for that question," I reply in appreciation of it not being a backhanded slam disguised as a question like I usually get.

"For the past two months, the president and his chief of staff, Phillip Stone, have acted as though Jewish Americans are the enemy of the country, who need to be separated. It began with accusations against Jewish Americans of crimes that were clearly set ups. The White House's response to those accusations of violence was to encourage the people of the United States to protect themselves from the Jews."

I pause for a moment as I take in the cameras, the hand-held devices, and even some archaic pencils and paper recording my every word. My worries turn into prayers.

"After the White House's encouragement to the American people to protect themselves, a wave of violence against the Jewish people began that was unimaginable in this modern world. For the last fifty-four days, the nightly news has shown the effect of the White House virtually granting permission for violence against the Jews of our country."

I look directly at the reporter who asked me the question. "However, the government's plan to separate and relocate Jewish Americans, supposedly for their own protection, is appalling. I am Jewish and the last time my people were separated from society and put into facilities was during World War II by Hitler's forces. We all know the deaths that happened there."

There are a few responses in the crowd of reporters and onlookers gathered. I am guessing it is because of their disbelief that something like the Holocaust could ever happen again, especially here in America.

I continue. "Freedoms are being infringed upon. People are being locked up for nothing more than being a Jewish American."

"Mr. Allenby," a reporter curtly breaks in with a yell, "You say that the American Jews are being locked up, but isn't it in fact true that Jewish Americans are volunteering to go into the secure facilities for their own protection."

I can feel the frustration rising inside me. In all my years of politics, in all the time I have heard people ignore and twist the truth, in all the years of blind eyes not seeing the truth; I cannot believe the lies and the distortions that people are swallowing now.

"Our government is supporting attacks against the Jewish people so strongly that violence is spiraling out of control. At the same time the White House is trying to hold to the facade that they are "protecting the Jews." There are a small number of Jewish Americans, the ones you are referring to, who have voluntarily checked into the Secure Facilities. Some of those individuals were paid to enter, some were threatened with their lives or businesses, and some were truly scared for their safety outside. However, you are ignoring how many have been forcibly placed into these Secure Facilities against their wills."

The same man yells again. I realize he isn't a reporter after all, but just an onlooker. "And yet you are still here, Mr. Allenby. If people are really being taken against their will, why would you still be here? I think it's because we all know this is America and people are not hauled off against their will."

I look at him and ask, "I don't know why I am still here, but I am guessing one of these days you'll come to see me and I'll be gone. Will you remember what I said? Will that make you believe?"

The man just laughs at my statements and so I continue. "And what makes you *not* believe America would haul a group of citizens off against their will? Look at our recent history."

"The history of slavery in this country is enough to show the injustices that are possible. In more recent years, there is the detainment of the Japanese population during World War II. Right here in the United States, the Japanese were taken from their homes and held against their will to protect the United States from the possible enemy within. Of course the United States of America is capable of holding a group of people against their will."

The man waves his arm as though dismissing me, "We are wiser now and that won't happen again." I can tell the mood of the crowd is a little more subdued after the remembrance of the atrocity of the Japanese detainment.

Since speaking out against the White House, I am the biggest entertainment these last few weeks. I have microphones in my face all day long. But I still have a job to do and need to get to it. I can hardly believe I haven't been fired yet, but I will keep working and keep talking. I'm sure my media frenzy is actually keeping me safe.

"I can take one more question before I have to go." I can see my car and driver waiting for me along with my newly appointed body guards, who are now by my side. Ironically, they were sent by the president himself. They came along with a statement for the press saying how important the Jewish people are to our country and how the president is working to protect all of us, whether with body guards or in secure facilities. *Even I have to admit that was pretty smooth of Phillip Stone; he knows how to work public opinion.*

I nod to a reporter off to my left to take her question. "Mr. Allenby, the president has come up with a practical plan to help 'your people', as you say, either by entering the secure facilities or by generously funding their 'Relocation Option'. What do you think of that option?"

"The Relocation Option is just as concerning as the secure facilities," I begin. "There are so many red flags about this program, even though on the outside it looks like an extremely generous opportunity by the government for Jews to relocate to Israel. I cannot go into detail yet about what I am discovering."

A yell from the man in the crowd. "That's because you aren't discovering anything!"

I continue, "There are huge problems with a program whose plan is to ship thousands of Jewish Americans out of the country at the same time to be dropped off at Israel's borders. I worry for the future of those families."

Looking at the man in the back, I finish, "And I will keep you informed of more details as soon as I can."

I back away from the microphones and begin to move towards the car as more questions come from the crowd. "I'm sorry. I must get to work now." I duck my head into my car and am followed in by one of the bodyguards, who feels more like my prison guard.

That's truly why Phillip Stone wanted them here—to watch me and listen to me. Maybe more. I'm sure every single thing I say and do goes straight back to him.

Once I'm in my office, with my bodyguards securely stowed outside, I can try to connect with Esther again.

That girl has the audacity to refuse my attempts at contacting her.
I have tried to call on her private cell and she won't pick up. My
secure e-mails have gone unreturned. I even scheduled meetings in
DC last week, hoping for a meeting in the White House with no
results. Doesn't she see what is happening to our people? This is
her time to stand up and help. Esther is hiding herself away in her
White House tower.

Although my work is piling up, I must get through to her, so
I compose another email.

> My Dear Esther,
>
> I am frustrated I have not heard from you. I hope
> you are seriously weighing what I have written you
> and are considering what you might do to support
> your people.
>
> You have always had a kind heart and stood up for
> those in need. You have been an advocate for others
> and now it is time for you to advocate for those you
> love—the Jewish people. Do you see how the
> government is trying to villainize the American
> Jews? Do you understand the severity of the plans
> for separation and relocation?
>
> I will be praying for you to have strength to know
> how to stand up for justice at this time. This is the
> time to share your background and use it to the
> advantage of your people.

In the middle of writing this secure e-mail where I am about
to tell Esther that we must meet to talk—a knock on my
office door jolts me out of my thoughts.

My assistant, Ethan, calls through the door. "Mr. Allenby?"

"Come on in, Ethan," I say as I quickly close my e-mail. In the middle of the most stressful period of my life, Ethan has surprised me by being a loyal support. It could be his political downfall.

"Good morning, Ethan, how are you?" His face breaks into a smile as I ask.

"I'm doing fine, Cai, but I am a little more worried about you. Just saw you on the news again. I'm not sure how long you'll be able to stay in office while speaking out so clearly against what the White House is trying to do."

"I agree completely," I respond, "In fact, I expect these bodyguards to haul me out the door and off to a secure facility any moment now." I am making light of it, but it really is a worry for me.

I have everything in order and ready for that day. Everything except getting Esther to stand up for her people.

Ethan looks concerned, "Are you worried Cai, because you look so calm?"

I smile at Ethan's kind worries. "I'll be honest with you Ethan, I am very worried. Not so much for myself, but for the Jewish people as a whole. I'm not the kind of man who usually gets frazzled easily. I've had to keep cool during election debates, in life-threatening situations like the one with President Susa, and so much more. But lately I am feeling a panic rise in me for my people and that is not something I am used to feeling."

Ethan's voice is serious, "Cai, can I ask you another question?"

"Of course, Ethan, you can always ask me anything."

"Why didn't you go directly to President Susa and talk to him about your concerns? He might have listened to you. It seems like by going to the press and speaking so openly, you have most certainly shattered your career and everything else you have worked so long for," Ethan concludes solemnly.

Ethan is a good man and I see he actually cares about me in the midst of all the politicking in politics.

"I actually did go to President Susa and talked to him before I ever spoke to the press."

I can see his surprise. I never mentioned my meeting with the president to anyone. I continue, "I went to him to plead the case of the Jewish people. I explained to him how hurtful detainment is because of our past and how it could damage all of our futures."

Ethan still looks surprised. "I should have known you would try to talk to him first. So, what else did you say to him?"

"I explained to the president how separation and relocation will actually increase the violence in our country to new levels. It will create long-term hostilities among citizens, as it did when the Japanese Americans were taken from their homes and separated. The guilt of the government and the pain instilled on the Japanese of that decision still lingers today, as it will for Jewish Americans in the future as well."

Ethan is on the edge of his seat, "And what did he say?"

Sadly, I look up towards the ceiling for a moment and swallow before being ready to speak. "President Susa hardly seemed interested in what I had to say. He was not open to thinking through the ramifications or potential problems I spoke to him about. He just sat with a little smile on his face as I spoke. I don't think he has a clue about the decisions he is making. I think it is all due to the influence of Phillip Stone."

"Did you confront Mr. Stone about separation and relocating Jewish Americans?" Ethan asked.

I nod. "Phillip Stone came into the president's office just as my arguments were being dismissed for the last time. He looked pleased with himself when he saw the direction the president was taking with me. With a grin he told me, 'You know, Cai, the secure facilities are for everyone. In fact, someone in your position should probably find yourself a place quickly, before something horrible happens that you would least expect."

"No, are you serious?" Ethan exclaimed, "I can't believe he would threaten you so blatantly."

"So now you understand a little better why I went public," I tell him. "With the president dismissing me and Phillip Stone threatening me, I decided I had to begin speaking publically about this threat to the Jewish people."

"But Cai, don't you worry about your safety? Or worry about your career?"

"When I first spoke out, I knew I was placing myself as the obvious target to all the hatred and violence brewing in the country toward the Jewish Americans. I have been able to keep my voice as the media has branded me the spokesperson. They have kept a microphone in my face almost everywhere I go. I actually think my speaking out has kept me safe and in my job up until now. But my career and even my life are not all that important compared to whatever I can do to support the Jewish people during this time," I explain.

"Do you feel like what you are saying is making a difference?"

"I sure hope so, Ethan, although sometimes I am not so sure. With the media portraying me as irrational, I hope I'm not making things worse for the cause." I sigh, "I am finding out details that make me believe there may be a very sinister plan in place for the Jewish people. Everything just doesn't add up with the secure facilities and the Relocation Option. I don't believe he is actually doing anything to protect them from harm, but rather the opposite."

Ethan stares wide-eyed at all I have just told him.

"So, it could get a lot worse and I have to figure out a way to help. I have lost my voice to the president and any information I give to the press will be twisted and tainted. So, I am doing a lot of praying for another way." I finish. *Esther is the voice to stop this, especially with the new details I am discovering through the sources that will still talk to me.*

Ethan stares at me, but says nothing. *Maybe it was a little too much information for him all at once.* In a lighter tone I say, "So, what do you say we grab my prison guards and go get some coffee before our ten o'clock meeting?"

Ethan manages to stammer out, "Cai, how can you just keep going on with all this on your mind?"

"Until God tells me to stop," I tell Ethan, "This is the path He has put me on and I will keep walking it. So come on, let's go."

With that we leave my office together, guards in tow.

~~

Chapter 18

THE PLAN OF IRAN
PHILLIP

"Of course these attacks were the mastermind of a revolutionary movement of the Jews from within," I respond to the young reporter at the evening press conference. My tone lets him know I think his question is idiotic at best.

"Excuse me for pressing this point Mr. Stone, but how can a group of confused, sometimes unconscious men be leading a so-called *revolution?* Is it possible that these men are being framed?"

Now this guy is really starting to tick me off. He won't have his job by tomorrow morning.

"Son, I don't know what kind of sources you have that are willing to disregard the safety of the American people. The violence has escalated to extreme heights on both sides. The White House is working to ensure safety for all of our citizens. Our president will not sit back while the beginnings of civil unrest are afoot. I would think you, and all Americans, would appreciate that." I glare at the reporter.

"No more questions for tonight." *That's all I want to go into. I need to get home and talk to Ahmed as soon as possible. We can't hold off the relocation date much longer.*

Two hours later and I am secluded in my home office. The door is locked, my extra thick walls protecting the sounds of my wife and boys from coming in and from letting my words go out. I open the industrial strength file cabinet with the double locking key system. Inside is the untraceable satellite phone I only use to call Ahmed.

"Salaam," Ahmed begins in Persian. He knows mine is limited since I have not been able to practice in all these years. *When I get back to Iran I can learn it again.*

He switches immediately to English as we cannot risk any miscommunication at this point. "What is this I see tonight on your news? You sound defensive to the press. Is everything going as planned?"

"There is no problem brother, Allah is watching over us. Everything is going according to plan, but we need to move soon." Emotion grips me as I speak. "Our life's work is coming into place right before our eyes."

"Our testing is almost complete and we will confirm the exact day and time. Tell me—how did our agents perform?"

"Their work was superb. Well trained and acted with discretion. There are no serious suspicions as far as I can tell. High commendations should be made when they get back to Iran. Although for the time being, they need to stay in their covers as I will use many of them."

"Of course. They will be at your disposal until our mission is complete when you can all return home together."

181

"Thank you Ahmed. For years, I have been dreaming of the day I can come home." I take on a lighter tone, although there is seriousness in my heart in what I am about to say. "I hope you are preparing a place for me."

I expect to be treated like a king when I get to Iran. I've given up so much to live this lie. To not have been with my brothers for all these years. I hope Ahmed will help me make up for my lost time.

"Brother, you can be sure you will be rewarded for what you have done." Ahmed sets my mind at ease.

"What else?" Ahmed asks. I sense the strain in his voice. *It must be because relocation day is getting so close. His stress is extremely high; as is mine.*

"The anger and suspicion that quickly rose against the Jewish Americans after the attacks could not have been stronger. With support in the press, we have swayed the view of the public. The people wholeheartedly swallowed the fear that Jewish Americans, who have lived here their whole lives, now have a stronger affinity for Israel than America. The people believe the Jews would give their lives to bring revenge on the head of America." I pause for a moment to make sure Ahmed is still with me.

"Soon after the fear in the country rose, utter chaos followed as we hoped. Jews were attacked and then began attacking back. Our agents are responsible for starting the vicious circle of violence that is thankfully spinning completely out of control."

Ahmed's positive murmur is encouraging.

"The country is scared for the future. President Susa and I have the plan to save them."

"Are you sure then the President is completely on board with the secure facilities and the relocations?" he asks, almost accusingly.

"Of course, Ahmed. He follows exactly where I lead him. He and the rest of the world see the operation we have called 'Relocation Option' as a gesture of goodwill to Jewish Americans wanting to get back to Israel."

I pause for a moment, reveling in thinking about what is to come. "I can almost convince myself that the secure facilities and relocations are necessary for the Jewish Americans to be safe." With a smile, "If I didn't know they are all headed for death."

"We are on the right track Phillip. Do not let us get off it." I can sense Ahmed's smile on the other end of the phone. Finally he takes a deep breath as though releasing his tension.

"No, Brother, I will not. Inshallah, we will complete our life's work together soon."

He murmurs agreement. "Inshallah, if God wills."

"How many do you have now in the detainment camps?" Ahmed asks me.

"We call them secure facilities," I lightly remind him. "We have over fifty facilities set up, with a higher concentration on the coasts and big cities. They are averaging one to two thousand in each area. Almost sixty thousand people total," I know he will not be pleased.

"Not near enough. Set up more. Get more people in."

He wants big numbers, but has no idea of the logistics.

"We are using camps, dormitories, gymnasiums, even hotels and prisons. Anything we can get our hands on to house people."

"Do better, Phillip. These people are not to be housed, just held. We need more people."

"Yes Ahmed, but it must continue to be seen as protection. As safe havens viewed in a positive light."

"Get more people inside. They must be concentrated and ready to move on relocation day." He sounds demanding now.

"Their movement to the designated ports is an incredible undertaking as well. Getting them there by rail, by bus, by plane has been a challenge without causing alarm. The agents are working on this."

"Phillip, you just told me things are moving along smoothly. Are they or are they not? Will you be able to move the people? You know the kind of numbers we want to see."

"Of course, Ahmed. It is a challenge, but one that will be done." I can tell Ahmed is frustrated. *He dreams of destroying over one hundred thousand lives and I am doing my best.*

"What about the numbers for the Relocation Option?"

"Just over thirty-thousand and growing." I brace myself for the outburst that I know will come.

"Phillip, this is not enough. These numbers are even more important as they will transport themselves to the ships. I have secured the commercial vessels. Do you have the naval ships secured?"

"Yes, Ahmed, of course. Those ships are already being re-routed to the correct ports. The Relocation Option is the easier one to organize, but we cannot control the numbers except to promote it as a gift to Jewish Americans. Many Jews want to repatriate to Israel, to make Aliyah."

"Then get more people to accept this *gift* and quickly." His accentuation on the word gift breathes sarcasm. "It must be done, Phillip. The people must all be contained in one place. All the Navy ships being occupied is also a necessary part to the operation."

"Ahmed, I know all these things," My frustration is building with him as well. "You act as though I have not been with you every step of the way in planning. You talk as though I am not the one who has slowly made these ideas palatable to the American public."

"It is the worry speaking, my brother. Of course you know. Of course you have been there all along." *The apprehension is causing us to lash out at each other.*

"Here in the US, I will keep the fervor of fear about those on both sides of the cultural divide at a boiling point. The balance of fear and the need for protection is vital. The deaths will continue on both sides. If they wane, we will boost them back up. This balancing act will only stay upright for so long though. I need the exact date and I need It soon."

"We will finalize our weapons testing this week. Then I will give you the date. We will be prepared to attack."

Quick farewells and we end the call. As I sit in the quiet, I think through the details of what must happen. In an instant, fear of failure pours over me. I begin to sweat and my hands start to shake uncontrollably.

"There will be no failure," I say out loud to my condemning thoughts. "We will succeed in cutting the legs out from under our enemies."

I imagine walking onto one of the ships, pushing a Jewish scum ahead of me. The scum, Mordecai Allenby, stumbles ahead of me as I throw him down the stairs to the ship's tank below, full of hundreds of other Jews.

This image thrills me. I find the silence of my office broken by a shrill and evil laughter. The laughter is my own.

~~

Chapter 19

AN OLD FRIEND
ESTHER

"Leeann, I can't tell you how good it is to get to talk to you."
I look out my bedroom window as I am on the phone.

"You too, Esther, I miss you."

"Miss you too. How is Virginia doing?" I work to keep my
voice upbeat as I ask Leeann about her little girl.

"She's doing fine. Her walking just turned into running. I
can hardly keep up with her. She is my own little personal
trainer right now," Leeann stops her sentence there.

*I can tell she doesn't want to say too much. I am truly happy for
her that she has her little girl.*

"And Joel? How is his firm doing?"

"Joel is great. He's busy though at work, but he enjoys it. His
dad took a fall off the ladder a while back. We have been
spending more time helping out his parents."

"I'm sorry to hear about Joel's dad."

"No, he's really doing fine, just a little recovery time. It's actually been nice because Virginia loves playing with Grandma and Grandpa every time we go."

There is silence between us for a moment. I think about the Grandpa and Grandma that were never there for me. Leeann is quiet. *Probably doesn't know what to say that won't be hard for me to take right now.*

"I'm really happy for you, Leeann. Just wish I got to see you more. Portland just seems so far away from Washington."

"Maybe I can come out to DC in the fall for a visit. I would love to see the leaves changing. I have heard it is beautiful."

"That would be great." I respond, wondering what my life might look like by the fall.

"How is life at the White House? I still can't believe I get to ask you that question?" Her voice is upbeat.

"I'm doing pretty well," I try to sound convincing.

"Really?" she presses.

"A little lonely sometimes. I miss all of you and there are not a lot of people I really connect with."

"The political wives still chilly?"

"That's putting it mildly. I think being the second wife and so much younger puts me at odds with many of them." *I don't want her to feel bad for me.*

188

"But there are some I call friends. My aide, Gabriella is great. A lady from the children's home I used to visit has been a support."

"I'm glad. How about you and Xander? Are you two doing okay?" *My friend knows that even though my life looks like a fairy tale on the outside, it's not.*

"You know, Xander has been so busy traveling and with meetings. With everything going on right now, I really don't get to see him. That makes me feel a little lonelier too."

I am not sure I want to go into details about this, even with my best friend. The fact that I can't see my husband unless scheduled by Phillip Stone. The fact that those meetings hardly ever happen as Stone tells me Xander has too many pressing details on his plate. The fact that lately I don't even know where Xander is sleeping. The worry that there could be another woman or even women. The fact that I feel like a prisoner in my own home "for my safety" Stone tells me.

"Oh, I'm sorry. That is no good when work gets in the way of spending time with your husband. We've had times like that before too when Joel is so busy at work." Leeann laughs out of embarrassment. "Although I'm sure Joel's schedule is nothing compared to Xander's."

Xander is still just a man. He usually takes time to eat, if he doesn't forget. He used to sleep at home every night unless he was traveling. He exercises, he takes coffee breaks, and every once in a while will watch a movie. Xander suddenly being too busy for me altogether is something new.

"Yes, I am sure it's just for a little while with everything that is going on," I assure Leeann.

"The things I am seeing on the news and on the streets here in Portland are shocking." Leeann's tone is concerned. "I can hardly believe the anger and violence. Who would think this could happen in America? Esther, you must be so upset by everything."

"Yes, of course I am upset. *We probably shouldn't talk about this on the phone. I wouldn't be surprised if my line is tapped.*

Leeann continues on with her concerns.

"What about these places for Jews to move into? And the option to relocate to Israel? It worries me."

If Stone is listening to this conversation, I'm going to reassure him that I am not against him. Maybe that is part of why he is keeping me away from Xander.

"Actually, Leeann, many Jewish families are seeing the secure facilities as a wise option for a little while. Just to weather this storm until it is a little more peaceful. You know so many cannot afford to move out of their communities, even if they feel unsafe. Now they have the option to go somewhere. And some Jewish Americans have dreamed of moving back to Israel their entire lives. This is their chance for making Aliyah on the American government's dollar."

"Really, Esther? I thought you would be upset about everything." I can tell by Leeann's reaction she does not agree.

"I am very upset about all the violence, but I see positive steps for peace with the secure facilities and the relocation option. There are some potential problems, but for the most part they could be good things."

Later I can tell Leeann more, but now I am focusing on the positive for Stone. I don't really know what to think about everything anyway. Xander is supportive of the peace plan. Uncle Cai has been on the nightly news saying it is dangerous. Probably the truth is somewhere in the middle.

"Wow, Esther, hearing you say this is so surprising. There are some who seem to know what they are talking about and they say this is disastrous for the Jewish Americans. I'm sure you know who *they* are."

I've asked Leeann never to say anything about Uncle Cai out loud. She is barely respecting that request.

"They say it is too similar to the Jews being rounded up and slaughtered during World War II."

"That wasn't in America though. It's different here."

I'm not just speaking out of fear for what Phillip Stone might hear anymore. I want to believe what I am saying. I want to believe my husband would never let an atrocity happen during his presidency.

"It was here in America though that the Japanese were detained. They lost their homes, their businesses and their communities. Doesn't that seem very similar to what is happening to the Jews today?"

"Leeann, you know I care for any people that are being oppressed. I'm just not sure anyone who is agitating the system is doing any good right now. I think if everyone will just go along, it will calm down soon."

I guess Leeann and Uncle Cai still talk and I need Uncle Cai to get the message that he needs to stop talking to the press. He has no idea how angry Mr. Stone is. He has made it clear to the entire staff that Mordecai Allenby is an enemy to the state. Uncle Cai is no longer allowed at the White House. No one is to have any contact with him. I can't believe he still has his position.

I realize I am missing what Leeann is saying as I'm lost in my thoughts. "...just sorry," is all I catch.

"What is it you are sorry for?" I ask.

"All you are going through. Your stress of being there. The fact that you feel alone."

I start to get choked up as I feel her care for me. *It has been so hard not having many people in my life who I know genuinely care about me.*

"Just know you aren't alone. There are so many of us supporting you and loving you. Even when we aren't there, the Lord always is."

It takes me a moment to control the lump rising in my throat.

"Thanks. It's been hard lately to feel close to Him. I'm trying though. I know he loves me."

"Don't give up hope, Esther. God is not wasting your life."

I would say something, but I can't get anything out.

I hope she is right. It sure feels like He might be throwing my life away for nothing.

~~

Chapter 20

NIGHTTIME VISITOR
MORDECAI

I am gathering the children, protecting them from gunfire—from the bombs. I cannot protect them all. The startling noise of the bombs in my dream becomes the reality of someone repeatedly rapping on my door. I open my eyes once reality registers. It is dark outside. My clock reads 3:45 am.

The time has come as I knew it would. They have finally come for me. There is no rush, although the rapping on my door becomes more fervent. *I could call the press. I told them that one day I would be gone and tomorrow morning I will be. I have said what I can say. Now my silence will speak.*

If only I could have gotten through to Esther.

With my hand on the handle, I take a deep breath. *"God, please give me strength. Once this door is open, my life will probably never be the same."*

My shock stuns me to silence for a moment once I open the door and realize it is not Phillip Stone there. It is not armed men ready to escort me to a secure facility. Rather the woman that stands before me is alone. She looks nervous.

I don't know her. At least I don't think I do. Although something seems familiar about her.

"Do I know you?"

"Mr. Allenby. I'm so sorry to wake you, but we need to talk."

The woman's eyes look through her large glasses to my open home behind me—searching. She quickly turns her body and checks behind her, as though looking for someone. Her actions make me nervous.

"Are your bodyguards here?"

The question puts me completely on edge. My fight or flight instincts are coming alive.

I'm not going to fight her and I can't run away. She looks harmless enough. If she is to take me to the secure facility, or worse, she is playing the role of a scared female quite well. Still, there is the feeling that I have seen this woman before.

"My bodyguards get here at 6:00. I am alone." I try to stand tall. *If this is the end for me, I am ready.*

The woman looks relieved. "I'm here for my friend. I would feel more comfortable talking inside. Can I come in?"

I hope this is from you Lord. I feel like I should trust her. I move aside to let the stranger enter my home.

If only I could place her. Then I would know if she is a friend or not.

Once we are seated in the living room, I look to her expectantly as she takes a deep breath. "Thank you Mr. Allenby. My name is Kristi Wright and I am here for your niece."

I quickly suck in air at the surprise of her words. She sits quietly, gauging my reaction. "Wow. Sorry. I just can hardly believe it." I rush over my shocked statement with another. "I am pleasantly surprised; very pleasantly surprised." In just one moment, my sense of hope is renewed. *Finally Esther is making contact. Hopefully she is ready to stand up for her people after all.*

"So, Esther told you we are family. She must trust you very much, Kristi. How do you two know each other?"

"Esther and I met at the children's home where I work. We hit it off right away."

That's where I have seen her. I watched footage of her and Esther at a ribbon cutting for the new wing at the children's home.

"Yes, now I remember you."

Kristi's face falls to the floor in dread.

"What is it?" I ask quickly, suddenly worried.

"It's just that you recognize me. What if others see me and they put two and two together? Esther told me again and again how I had to be so careful. I couldn't tell anyone anything. I had to come early so no press would see me. If you recognize me so easily, what if others do too?"

"You thought the guards might be here. What about them seeing you?"

The look on Kristi's face is one of embarrassment. Her face and neck turn a deeper shade of pink. She takes off the large glasses and sets them on the table in front of her. Then she pulls back on her black hair until it gently slides off, revealing a redhead underneath.

"I tried," she says with a shrug of her shoulders.

"What if they asked who you were?"

The color on her face and neck turns an even brighter shade of red.

"I was going to act like we are..." she pauses for a moment, before she chokes out, "special friends. I'm so sorry Mr. Allenby. I didn't know what else I could say to get in and talk to you alone."

My small smile grows thinking of the courage of this woman. Her face relaxes as she watches my expression until she breaks into a smile herself.

To come here and talk to me. To disguise herself. To create an alibi. All for Esther, for me, for the Jewish people.

"Very impressive, Kristi. Don't worry. When we are done talking we'll figure something out to get you out of here without being seen. And please, call me Cai. I think we've been through enough already to be on a first name basis."

Kristi nods her head.

197

"You had me scared for a minute when you first came."

"Oh, I'm so sorry, Mr. Allenby. I don't really do this kind of clandestine work at the children's home." She is still nervous despite some attempts at humor.

"Would you like anything to drink?" I ask, just remembering my lack of hospitality.

"No, no, I'm just fine. Thank you."

"How is Esther?" I ask eagerly.

"Esther is good. Well, kind of good. She is worried about you—about everything going on. That is why she asked me to come."

"I can't tell you how happy I am. My attempts to contact her have gone unanswered."

"She did ask me to apologize that she has not contacted you sooner. Mr. Stone is not allowing her to leave the White House right now, for her own safety. He is closely monitoring all contact in and out of the White House."

"Why? Does he suspect something?" My fear is suddenly on alert for Esther. I picture Phillip Stone, having found out she is a Jew, keeping her prisoner in her own home under the pretense of safety.

"Esther doesn't think he suspects anything. She isn't sure exactly why Mr. Stone is keeping her on such a tight rein except to keep her away from the president so he can be the only one influencing him.

Kristi goes quiet. *There is no time to wait. Esther must do something before it is too late.*

"Kristi, I am so glad you came. I will tell you what Esther needs to do."

Kristi's face is a mixture of confusion and worry.

"Mr. Allenby, I mean Cai, that is not why I came. I need to deliver a message to you from Esther."

"Well, go right ahead." I want to hear it, despite the fact Kristi's face is telling me I'm not going to like it.

"Esther wants you to stop talking to the press. She says you cannot talk about the secure facilities, the Relocation Option, or anything else related to Israel or the Jews." Her face shows the serious nature of her message.

"What?" I say louder than I mean to. "I'm sorry Kristi. I know you are just the messenger."

"She didn't want me to write anything down for security leaving the White House, so I hope I don't forget everything." Kristi fusses as though at her own memory.

"Phillip Stone is extremely angry with you for your statements to the press. He has made it clear to the whole staff that you are an enemy of the state. Esther worries he is planning something to harm you. She wants you to stop aggravating the situation. She says if you will be patient, and quiet, this will hopefully end soon. Esther begs of you to keep safe." Kristi takes a deep breath. Her eyes are determined, but she looks like a child who has just spoken back to a parent. The child who knows they have crossed a line.

"Thank you for delivering the message Kristi. I'm sure that was hard to say." I am quiet for a moment as I think about her words. It is the exact opposite of what I thought and hoped it would be.

There is no pacifying Stone. We cannot sit by idly and hope that the situation will go away. The horrors are about to get worse.

"Kristi, my niece trusts you enough to send you to me. So I am going to trust you as well.

"I will tell her whatever you have to say."

"My Esther is a caring girl. I know she loves the Jewish people and I hope will help them if she knows the truth. I'm not sure where to start."

I take a deep breath and try to organize my thoughts.

"First of all, tell Esther that Phillip Stone will never be pacified. He wants the Jews dead. Make that clear to her. Our people will not come back from the secure facilities. They will never be relocated to Israel. They are going to be massacred."

Kristi sits stunned for a moment. "How do you know?"

"Information pieced together from many different sources." *The few who will still talk to me at this point.*

"There are bits of intercepted phone calls implying there is more than the innocent plan the world sees. Trains and buses are being re-routed from areas around the secure facilities to the relocation ports. Naval ships are being brought into those ports. The amount of ships ordered is much higher than the amount of Jewish Americans involved in the relocation plan."

Kristi is listening intently with the will to understand clear on her face.

"All these point to something that doesn't add up. The most convincing evidence is from Iran itself, who I believe is behind the coming onslaught. We have evidence that they are in the final testing stages of their long-range nuclear weapons. They are preparing to move them into place for launch. Top Iranian military have hinted that they will soon wound The Great Satan and The Little Satan. That is America and Israel respectively."

"Why haven't you told all of this to the press? They would have to believe the facts, wouldn't they?"

She might be right. I have questioned myself about not telling the press about Iran once I had all the information pieced together.

"Something held me back every time with sharing this new information. The media has not received my views well up to this point. They have made me into a mockery. I don't want to throw away this knowledge and I'm afraid the truth will be discarded because it is coming from me."

This is hard to say out loud. Giving up my pride, even to the point of being treated without dignity, has been more difficult than I want to admit.

A silence comes between us. Understanding fills Kristi's eyes as she speaks, "They may trample on the truth, not knowing what they have in front of them."

I can see she is getting what I am saying and will hopefully explain it to Esther as well.

"What do you think it will look like—the attack?"

 "I believe the day being called "Relocation Day" will be the day of the attack. Those choosing to relocate will go that day to naval ships." Kristi looks at me with rapt attention.

"I think Iran plans to attack the loaded ships at the relocation ports around the country. They will use long-range nuclear weapons based on ships off port. My sources say an attack will happen simultaneously against Israel."

"There is more - huge amounts of commercial and cargo liners are being scheduled to go to relocation ports. Much higher than the numbers scheduled to relocate. Someone in power in the US is planning to help Iran by transporting individuals from the secure facilities to the ports as well. This would make the number of casualties so much higher."

I sit quietly for a moment. I let Kristi register this information. I think about the severity of what is about to happen to our world. To my people.

"It's almost too much to believe," Kristi finally says.

"I know it is. The terrorists planning this are counting on the fact that the puzzle will not be put together because it seems too preposterous. Much like people could not fathom Hitler's concentration camps. It was a horror too difficult to even comprehend."

Kristi's head nods up and down. Her brow furrowed in concentration. "What about the people being moved from the facilities? Wouldn't they alert someone of what was happening?"

"I have not figured that out. I assume electronics will have been taken away, but there would still be television crews. I don't understand it all, but once people are in the vicinity of the ports, it is too late for any rescue. Much of the military will be occupied with the relocation effort and unable to quickly respond. Of course, there is no chance of completely decimating the Jews. This is a statement of hate with the purpose of inflicting a wound. The Jews will not be destroyed; we know that from the past and from what we know of the future."

"Kristi, listen very carefully. There is a man in the White House who has the ear of the president," I begin.

"Phillip Stone?" She breaks in.

"Yes, Phillip Stone. He advised the president to withhold help from Israel after their conflict with Iran in the first place. I don't have evidence, but I think the violence first perpetrated by the Jews against other Americans was a set-up. When the violence got worse, it was Phillip Stone who suggested the idea of separating Jewish Americans for their own protection. He was the one who introduced the relocation option. I believe he must be working with Iran."

I can feel my blood starting to boil just talking about Stone. He is manipulating the whole country in order to massacre thousands. "Kristi, listen to me. Esther has to do something. The media is not listening. The public won't believe. The president is blinded, but he is the only one who has the power to stop the unthinkable."

Understanding and concern is written all over her face as she nods her head in agreement.

"I have a folder will all the information. Can you get it to Esther safely? It has to be in her hands only so she can see for herself."

"Yes, I should be able to get it to her."

"Kristi, are you a praying woman?"

"Yes, I truly am."

"Then please pray. Pray for Esther to receive your message. Pray she will have strength. Pray she will act despite her fears."

"I will, Mr. Allenby—Cai. I will be praying."

"Kristi, you must help Esther see the importance of talking to her husband. She must help him see the truth and break free of the blinders he is wearing. President Susa must see what is about to happen and then we have to pray he will do something to stop it."

"I will do my best. I will give her the information and try to explain it with the same passion you have shared with me." She pauses for a moment before she speaks in a quiet tone. "But Cai, what if Esther won't believe enough to do something?"

I think for a moment about this possibility. *I always assumed if she could hear the truth, she would do whatever she could. What if she doesn't? What if her fear overpowers her?* "If Esther does not respond it is probably because she is afraid. Remind her that her silence will not save herself or anyone else. Phillip has already come between her and Xander and as far as we know, he doesn't even know that she is a Jew. God has protected that information of her background from Phillip. When he finds out, she will not be safe."

I think of all Esther has sacrificed these last few years. Her efforts to be strong and brave in the midst of a difficult situation.

"Tell her this is why God brought her to the White House to be Xander's wife. She has the opportunity to save her people. God's plan for Esther's life is for such a time as this."

~~

Chapter 21

THE UGLY TRUTH
ESTHER

Where is she? Kristi should have been here more than an hour ago. She was supposed to come around nine o'clock. I start walking down to the visitor's entrance. *I'll check and see if she is having trouble getting in.*

"Morning, Mrs. President." I turn to see one of the secret service agents at the visitor's final security entrance. An older, southern gentlemen who always makes me smile.

When I am allowed out of my residence, which seems only when Xander is gone, this is my wall to the outside world at the moment. Mr. Stone doesn't want me taking any appointments and have made it clear I have no reason to leave the White House. Thankfully, he does allow me to have a friend in.

"Good Morning, Jasper. How are you today?" I've been getting to know all the staff on a first name basis these last few weeks of my sequestering. Since I'm stuck in the White House, I've explored every inch of it when I can.

"I'm doing just dandy. Especially since our First Lady has graced us with her presence again."

I can't help but smile, even with the stress of waiting for what Kristi has to tell me on my mind.

How can I not smile when I hear the word "dandy" in normal conversation?

"Thank you so much, Jasper. I always appreciate your hard work, done in such a friendly fashion." We both pause. I don't want to seem pushy, but do want to ask about Kristi.

"Mrs. President, is there anything I can help you with this morning?"

"You know—there is. I have a friend coming to visit. I want to make sure there wasn't any problem with her getting in today."

Jasper walks over to his computer screen and types something in. "Mrs. President, I see you have a Kristi Wright slated to visit this morning."

"Yes, that is who I am looking for. Has she checked in through the first gate yet?"

"Yes, ma'am, she did. Just a few minutes ago, so she should be here at any time."

"Oh, good, Jasper. Thank you so much."

I look out the window onto the sidewalk I know Kristi will come down. She is just turning the corner into my line of vision. Her walk is brisk. *I'm guessing she is almost as anxious to see me as I am to see her.*

"Oh, there she is now." I have to hold back as she comes in. Jasper quickly runs her through the final security checks.

"You made it," I try to say calmly.

"Yes, I'm so sorry I am late." Her eyes are telling me there is much more to say.

"No problem. I just wanted to make sure you got through okay, so I came on down."

Metal scan done. Purse back over her shoulder, which she holds onto tightly. Shoes back on her feet. Watch back on her wrist. We can finally give each other a hug.

"Thanks so much, Jasper. I'll bring some more of my blueberry scones next time I come visit."

"Mrs. President, you know I do love them. But you are always welcome for a visit—blueberry scones or not."

Hardly a word is spoken between Kristi and me until we get upstairs. As we walk through the living room, I pause to turn on some music. I turn it up extra loud just in case there are listening ears. When we are safely locked away in my personal office, I turn to Kristi.

"Tell me everything. Did you see him? What did he say?" I can hardly wait for the answers. I have so many more questions.

"Where should I start?"

"Did he say he would stop talking? That is really the most important thing." My patience is ragged. I can hardly wait to know my uncle will be careful and quiet.

"Esther, how about we sit down?

I nod in agreement and we settle into two chairs. Kristi takes a deep breath.

"I want you to know I did deliver your message to your Uncle Cai. I told him exactly what you asked me to. For the next hour or so, your uncle explained everything to me. You'll be happy to know he is done talking to the press."

"Oh, thank goodness. He has only been making things worse."

"There is so much more that your uncle needs you to understand about this situation."

I sit in stunned silence minutes later, or maybe it has been an hour, I'm really not sure. The folder of information open on my lap and my belief that everything will be okay is shattered into a nightmare.

"There have always been questions in my mind. Never in my far-reaching imagination could I have come up with an explanation as horrible as this." I sit with the silence between us. My mind wavers between trying to wrap my head around the truth and holding onto my false beliefs of reality.

"I thought if we could just ride this out. If Uncle Cai would be patient and wait. I actually thought it might go away."

Grief over this new reality hits me. "My people have already gone through this scenario before. Targeted for death by a madman. Why? Why do we have to be so hated?"

Kristi gently puts her hand on my arm. Her simple act reminds me I am not alone. It takes me a few moments to compose myself.

"Esther, your uncle said he has done and said what he can. He told me to tell you that now it is your turn."

"He wants me to talk to the press? That doesn't make any sense. It will only tell the world I'm Jewish and let Mr. Stone immediately know I am against him. If I repeated everything you just told me to the press, they would dismiss me as being crazy too."

I realize my statement's implication to my uncle. "Basically, what they have done to Uncle Cai," I say with sadness.

"Your uncle agrees with you completely. He believes you need to speak the truth, but only to one person. Cai wants you to talk to your husband and tell him what is going to happen. The president can put a stop to all this."

I am shaking my head from side to side before she even finishes. "Kristi, I have not seen Xander for weeks. I have no access to him. Even if I do get a chance to talk to him, he isn't going to listen to me."

"Your Uncle Cai believes you're the only one with the position to help the president see the truth and stop this from happening."

My slightly shaking head tells Kristi I do not agree. She stands up and walks to the window. Kristi gently pulls the curtain to the side and looks out over the garden.

"Esther, are you scared?"

I don't answer—thoughts rush in and consume me. *I just don't think it's practical, that's all. What if Xander won't listen? What if Mr. Stone finds out? This information could be untrue. Or what if I say it all wrong? Then the deaths of so many will partly be my fault. So yes, I am scared.*

"Your uncle thought you might be scared to take a stand. He wants me to make it clear this calamity is going to touch all Jews—those in secure facilities as well as you living here in the White House."

Kristi continues to look outside. *Maybe she can't look me in the face and say what Uncle Cai told her to tell me.*

"Esther, isn't that the garden where Xander asked you to marry him? I recognize it from the video clip."

Her question seems out of context. "Yes, that's it. He asked me exactly where the pink rose bush is now."

Turning away from the window and looking right at me, Kristi asks, "Esther, why do you think God moved all the details in place for you to become Xander's wife?"

"I don't know, I have wondered that a lot."

In the pause following my answer, the still small voice of the Lord speaks. "You don't have to wonder anymore." In that

211

moment, I realize why God has brought me here. Tears begin to form.

I have been such a coward. Convincing myself that I cannot do anything just so I would not have to try. My fear has been controlling me all along.

As I speak, tears are sliding down my cheeks. "Uncle Cai is right. I am the First Lady of the United States. I am married to the president. I am a Jew. My people need me. It does not matter if I'm scared. It does not matter what it might cost me. He's right." My confident words come out even as my voice wavers.

"Would you please keep praying for me Kristi? I don't think I can do it without prayer."

"Of course I will," she quickly assures me. Bowing our heads, she begins praying for me—for strength. I slowly raise my head, feeling more resolve.

"I don't feel strong enough to do this, not with the way my relationship is with Xander right now."

An idea comes to me. "Kristi, I am going to pray and fast for three days. During that time I will beg the Lord for his help before I go talk to my husband. *Am I stalling because I am scared? I don't think so.*

"Kristi, will you fast and pray with me for three days? Pray that I will have the opportunity, that Xander will listen, and that he will do something."

"Yes, I will—of course I will."

Kristi has done so much for me. I still have to ask one more thing of her.

"Could you get a message to my Uncle Cai? Please ask him to pray and fast with us too. Ask him to get as many people as he can to join us in praying for a miracle."

~~

Chapter 22

PRESS CONFERENCE
ESTHER

"Three days. Seventy-two hours of fasting."

Gabriella is helping me get ready for the day. This is part of her job when I have an engagement. Today is a very important one.

"So, how did it feel?" she asks me.

"The first six hours were fine. Then my stomach started growling followed by a slight headache. The second day I just felt weak. I was a little dizzy when I tried to move too quickly. By last night, I had come around the other side of my dizziness. I think by then my stomach had given up on complaining too." *I can't seem to stop my chatter today. It must be the nerves.* "Seventy-two hours will be up in about thirty minutes. I am doing okay, but not much energy."

Gabriella looks at me as though she doesn't understand.

"They say dieting does not work as well when you starve yourself. Your body will just hold on to everything it has."

Not eating for three days was tough on me. The fate of my people will be so much worse if Stone carries out this plan.

"No, this has nothing to do with dieting. It is all about praying and asking God for his help in my life."

The shock is apparent on Gabriella's face. She does not see God as a being to have a personal relationship with. *I talk to her often about the Lord's love. The Lord's character, but this is the first time I have fasted and prayed.*

"Well, did it work? Did you get help?"

How can I honestly answer this question for my friend? "When I find out, I'll let you know. I am choosing to believe in faith that I will get the help I need."

Gabriella gives me a little shrug and a quick smile. She walks into my closet to help me decide what I will wear.

I am not trying to force God to move because I fasted, that isn't how it works. I just know it will be impossible for me to make any difference without Him. When I fast it takes me to the place of needing God's help desperately. The same feeling as when I run.

"Gabriella, today is a big day. I need an outfit that will draw attention. Not too flashy that I look like it is a night out. Not at all boring that I might be overlooked."

"Hmm, sounds like a challenge. You have hair and make-up coming in about an hour, as you requested. You really need to eat something though. Your color is pale."

"I've already requested some soup and toast to come in about thirty minutes. I think I need to start small."

"So, what is the big occasion? Are you headed out of the White House today?" Gabriella has been here in the White House with me for these weeks. It is obvious she is excited by the prospect of getting out too.

"No sorry, not going anywhere. I'm staying right here at the White House. Today is the day I'm going to get some time with my husband."

"Really?!" Her outburst shows genuine excitement for me. She comes from the closet, hangs up the clothes over her arm and gives me a hug.

Wow, I haven't been hugged for weeks. It almost feels foreign.

"I am so happy for you Esther that finally Stone scheduled some time for you with the president. Dinner? Lunch? Coffee?"

I'm not sure how Gabriella will react to my plan. I hope she will be supportive as I need her help.

"Actually, Mr. Stone has not agreed to give me any time with Xander as I requested. Stone always tells me Xander's schedule is packed. Or he gives me the excuse that he is getting ready to travel. Or he is traveling. Or he is recuperating from travel. Too many meetings. Always some reason. I have tried jumping through his hoops. It is no use. He is blocking me completely from seeing my husband."

"I'm so sorry, Esther. How can he do that to you?"

"He told me this is a critical time in Xander's presidency. That I have to understand the priority is not our relationship." I take a big gulp.

Gabriella looks at me with pity. *It does sound pretty pathetic.*

"At first I took it at face value that Xander was too busy with meetings and appointments to even sleep in his own bed. I know Mr. Stone has even had a makeshift bedroom made up near his office for him to sleep. Then he has been gone for a few days here and there."

I pause for a moment to think about how I want to phrase this next part.

"Gabriella, I have wondered if maybe this block is not only from Mr. Stone, but from Xander too." I gulp down my emotions and try to hold strong. "What if it is because there is someone else?"

Gabriella looks uncomfortable with where this conversation is going.

"Maybe this is how it was for Xander's first wife at the end of their marriage. Kept away from Xander. Not even the chance to try and work it out."

"No Esther. Please don't think that way. I'm sure he's just busy right now."

Or maybe Phillip did find out about my Jewish heritage and that is why he is keeping us apart.

I try to shake off my fearful emotions once again.

"You know, it doesn't really matter why I haven't had time with Xander, but I need to have it today. And Gabriella, I need your help to do it."

My assistant has proven herself a loyal and compassionate woman. Not just as an aide anymore, but also as a friend.

"I need you to do some information gathering if you will. Nothing that will get you in trouble with Mr. Stone I hope."

"Of course I will. What do you need?"

"I would like to see Xander in his office this morning. I need you to find out exactly what the secret service has been told about letting me in. Maybe there is some way around the blockade."

She smiles. "No problem. I've become friends with some of the men with all of our extra time around the house lately."

"If you can't find a way for me to reach Xander in his office, I do have one last plan. Xander is giving a press conference later today. Would you please find out some details about it? The exact time? How many guards will be at the private entrance? I would appreciate any information that could help me gain access to the press conference. If I can't get to Xander in his office, then I'm going to him during the press conference."

"Are you serious? Going into a press conference to talk to your husband?"

I nod my head solemnly.

"That is bold. I will try to find out what I can for you Esther, but have you really thought this through? You know Stone will have a fit, right?"

"I know, but I need to do this. I have to talk to my husband today."

"If you really want to see him that badly," Gabriella's tone tells me she does not agree.

Hopefully I can count on her to help me and keep this quiet. I don't have much choice anyway. I need her.

Gabriella leaves to find out the information I am looking for. I look through the clothes she has brought out and choose my outfit. Food is coming in ten minutes. Hair and make-up in forty.

I don't know if I'll be able to eat much anyway. My stomach is tied in knots.

I leave the closet and go to the window to look out—back across the room and sit in a chair — get up and go to the closet and consider a pair of shoes—decide against them and go back to the chair. *This is ridiculous. Lord, I need to relax. It is in your hands.* Peace begins to wash over me.

A quick knock followed by the entrance of a food cart. "Good morning, Charles."

"Good morning, Mrs. President. Please enjoy," as he takes the cover off of my meal. "Are you sure you would not like anything else?"

I look at the clear soup and lightly buttered toast. "No, this is just perfect. Thank you."

Time creeps on. Food eaten, hair done, make-up perfect, and I am all dressed. *Where in the world could Gabriella be? I will have a much harder time getting to Xander today without her help. Would she have gone to Mr. Stone?*

I am starting to feel like a wreck again. A quick knock jolts me even though I have been waiting for it. It is Gabriella's face that comes around the corner of the door. I rush over to greet her.

"Thank goodness, I was getting worried."

"I'm here. I think I have all the information you need."

"Excellent, I cannot tell you how much I appreciate this."

"Probably shouldn't thank me yet as it isn't all good news."

I nod intently, fearing the worst.

"Okay, there are direct instructions to the guards at the president's office not to let you through when your husband is in. Stone told them that he needs to focus without any distractions. There are also clear instructions to not let Xander see you. If at all possible, they were to divert any interaction between the two of you. It does not seem like it will be possible for you to get through when your husband is in his office."

That explains why I only get in when his office is empty.

"Why would Mr. Stone be doing this?"

Gabriella looks uncomfortable at my question and begins speaking more formally in her assistant's voice.

"If you really want to talk about that, let's sit down."

This cannot be good.

"I am so sorry to report this to you, but one of the guards told me he thinks the reason you are not allowed near the president is because there might be another woman. Possibly more than one other woman."

I can't help the sigh that escapes me. I look down into my lap through the tears pooling in my eyes. "So, there it is. I hardly wanted to admit it, even to myself. Deep inside I had a hunch." My voice is calm and quiet. "Is there more?"

"Are you sure?" Gabriella asks carefully.

"Yes, just tell me it all. I want to know."

"I guess there have been two other women who have been coming in and out of the White House lately. Stone takes them directly into the Oval Office himself. No one knows who they are."

Even though I wish it didn't, this news still cuts me to the core. Discarded. Humiliated. Xander doesn't want to see me, it's not just Stone keeping us apart.

I shake off my realization and the feelings that go with it for the moment. I have to.

In the grand picture, the fact that my marriage is about over does not really matter very much.

"Tomorrow I can process Xander's unfaithfulness. Today I have to talk to him about something else. Did you find anything out about the press conference?"

Gabriella looked surprised. "If you still want to go to the press conference, there I do have some good news for you."

"Thank goodness. I need it Gabriella."

"The press conference you mentioned will be starting…" she consults her watch, "in just over forty minutes."

"So soon!"

A notepad comes out of Gabriella's pocket and she refers to it as she speaks. "Don't worry, I have it figured out." She seems excited, I can sense it in her voice.

"Okay, there are guards at all the press doors and general entrance. However, your husband goes in through the president's entrance which is down a private hall from his office; guarded of course. There are usually guards on the outside of this door. During a press conference these guards walk with him and stand at either side of the podium." Gabriella is talking so quickly that I work to digest it all. "Your husband and his entourage, including Stone, are scheduled to enter at exactly five minutes after one. The conference is anticipated to last for about twenty minutes, although it could depend on how many questions the president answers."

"So, are you saying no one will be at the president's entrance? I can just walk right in?"

This sounds too good to be true.

"You can, as long as you can get past his assistant and the guards at his door."

My face falls. *I can't just barge my way through Cyrus and a set of security guards.*

"Esther, think about it; Cyrus and the guards have been letting you through when the president is not inside, right? Well, the president won't technically be inside his office."

Gabriella's smile and voice show her optimism.

"Do you really think this plan can work to get me into the press conference?"

"Well, I can't promise you anything." Gabriella pauses before continuing, "Esther, are you positive this is what you want to do? You do have your image to think of and you can always see Xander later. We could work on a plan."

"No question! I need to do this today!"

I can't believe I am going to break into a press conference. To speak to my own husband no less.

"Esther, what is your plan when you get in there?"

"I need to talk to him about something important. I just hope Xander still has enough love left for me that I can have a few minutes of his time."

"What is it you need to talk to him so urgently about? About the other women?"

"It's not about the women. It is way more important than that. I won't go into detail now as our time is short and I don't want to get emotional. You'll know soon enough." My hands are slightly shaking. The butterflies in my stomach have multiplied and are doing laps. "Before I go Gabriella, let me just say thank you from the bottom of my heart. You do not even know how important your help has been."

"You sound like you are going down there without me. I am going to make sure you get through that door."

"Are you sure? It could mean your job."

"Since I don't know what you are talking to the president about, I'm not truly an accomplice. I'll get you into your husband's office and then you are on your own."

"Thank you Gabriella." I start picturing the scenario about to come. *The secret service might pull me out of the press conference as soon as I enter the room. If I can't talk to Xander alone, I'll yell out as much as I can. The press will hear along with Xander.* I check the clock. 12:32 pm.

What will Stone do to me afterwards? I'm scared that with his Iranian connections, he could even have me killed for telling what is about to come. He will not let me outmaneuver him without repercussions.

Gabriella breaks into my thoughts. "Do you want to go down early or wait here until it is time to go in?"

"I think it's better to wait here. I don't want to cause any suspicion by milling around."

Gabriella nods her agreement.

"How about we leave here right as Xander is scheduled to take the stage? That would put you at his office by ten minutes after one. Hopefully into the press conference by one fifteen. Does that sound okay?"

I nod. We both sit in silence. I will the seconds to tick faster. Then I beg them to slow down so one o'clock never comes. *"God, I don't know if I can do this. I am not that strong of a person—I used to feel stronger, but right now I am so worn down."*

In the silence, I can feel his love. I feel I am enough because I am His. Gabriella looks energized by the excitement. I am a wreck.

The quiet is broken by Gabriella. "You look very beautiful by the way. I meant to tell you when I first came in, but I had so many details on my mind."

"Thank you. I figured it would not hurt to try and look my best. It feels cheap in a way to do it, but I am hoping it might help me get some time with Xander."

I check the clock. Sixteen intolerable minutes later, we set out. Gabriella and I walk side by side, not saying a word.

Outside Xander's office, Cyrus is sitting at his desk. A security guard is sitting next to the door. *Cyrus does not like me. Maybe I should just make a run for it and try to get in before they can stop me.*

As we get closer and before I can make a decision, Gabriella steps in front of me and starts talking. "Hi again Cyrus, how you doing?" Her voice almost sounds like she's flirting.

"So, I got those Knicks tickets we were talking about. Did you want to go? Cause if not, I am pretty sure Jasper would like to go."

Cyrus laughs. *I guess he doesn't think Jasper is much competition.* "I would love to."

I can't believe the way he is looking at her. Gabriella didn't mention that Cyrus has a crush on her. He straightens up just a bit. *Still, I have never seen him look so relaxed. He actually has a nice looking face when it isn't all scrunched up.*

"What can I do for you, Mrs. Susa?"

Gabriella jumps in again before I can speak. "Mrs. Susa just wants to leave a note on her husband's desk. Kind of a romantic gesture. It's the three year anniversary since she knew he was the one for her."

His face scrunches up in the look I am used to seeing.

"Mrs. Susa, leave the note with me and I'll be sure your husband gets it."

Gabriella steps closer to Cyrus and leans in. "Come on, Cyrus, let her go in and leave the note for her honey." She lowers her voice to a whisper, which I can barely make out. "Give her a break. You know she's had a tough go."

His serious look cracks and he nods his head with a little smile on his face and whispers back, "Okay, Gabriella, only for you."

"Thank you," we both say at the same time. My assistant straightens up and hooks her arm in mine as she says. "Let's go."

"You too?" Cyrus asks. Gabriella just winks at him.

We head into the office and casually swing the door shut behind us. Immediately, I head towards the hallway leading to the press conference room with Gabriella following.

"Gabriella, I can hardly breathe. You shouldn't have come inside with me though. And how do you have Knicks tickets?"

"I hope you don't think less of me Esther. I don't have Knicks tickets yet, but I'll get them. That is if Cyrus and I are not both fired." Her statement is serious, but she says it with a small smile. *I think she is enjoying this, meanwhile I feel like I am having a heart attack.*

"I have a few lies of my own weighing on me, Gabriella. I hope you won't think less of me when you learn about mine."

She looks over at me in confusion as we quickly walk down the hall. I turn to look behind us, half expecting Cyrus and the guard to come chasing after.

"I don't know if I can do this. I feel as though my heart is going to explode." My lungs are pumping. I'm starting to feel dizzy.

"It's okay Esther. You don't have to do this if you don't want to. Let's just go back and it will be like it never happened."

Her words jolt me back to reality. "No, I need to talk to Xander."

I force myself to slow down my breathing and relax. *The last thing I need is to pass out.* As we approach the presidential entrance to the press conference, it is just as Gabriella said. There is no one in sight. When we get to the door I turn to Gabriella.

"You need to put all the blame on me for this–even now with Cyrus. Tell him that I went through the door into the press conference."

She turns to head back down the hallway. "Okay, but I will walk slowly back out. You'll be great in there, Esther."

I may start hyperventilating. I might throw up. I am not even confident my legs will work to walk me inside.

With my hand on the door handle I quickly bow my head in prayer. *"Lord, please help me. Give me the words to speak."*

After inhaling a long breath and slowly blowing it out between pursed lips, I open the door more confidently than I feel. I walk inside briskly. The room is packed with press and the White House staff. Most of the press is furiously scribbling notes. Xander is at the podium, his face showing concern as he speaks.

Keep focusing on Xander. Just look at him while I walk. Don't think about anyone else except Xander. As I walk towards Xander I hear someone whisper, "Look at the First Lady. What is she doing?" People are starting to notice me, but I don't turn to look.

Keep looking at Xander. Just keep walking towards him. I have to will my legs to keep moving forward. *I have missed him. Enough of that thinking. All that matters right now is telling Xander what is about to happen to my people.*

Xander catches sight of me and his eyes show confusion. He continues speaking, but is obviously distracted as he looks over at me again. I force myself to give him a smile.

This reminds me of when I walked down the aisle in our wedding. Different room, different observers, and different clothes. But I am the same woman walking to meet the same man. The emotions are much the same. Fear about my future intertwining with his. Hoping everything will turn out well in the end.

As I get closer to Xander, a peace fills me. I am moving in the right direction. *This is the exact same overwhelming peace I had during my walk down the aisle at our wedding.*

Out of the corner of my eye, I see the guards step forward on alert as I get closer to the podium. *I don't see Mr. Stone.*

Xander stops speaking at the same moment I stop in front of the podium. The room is silent. *I'm sure they are ready to scribble down whatever comes out of Xander's mouth. Focus. Focus on what you need to say.*

"Hi," is all I can manage to squeak out.

His face breaks out into a huge smile. *That's the last look I expected to see.*

"Excuse me for just a moment," he says to the crowded room. He moves from behind the podium and down the steps to meet me.

"My love, are you okay?" Xander takes my hands in his as he leans in close to talk.

"Well, yes and no. Yes, because it is so good to see you. No, because there is something extremely important I need to talk to you about." *Part of me didn't think I would get this far. I imagined yelling about the fate of the Jews as I was dragged from the room. I am so flustered I can't even focus on what I need to say.*

"I'm sorry to interrupt you, Xander. I just need to talk to you about something urgent."

"It's okay honey. I'm just so glad to see you are feeling better."

Feeling better? What is he talking about?

"Xander, can we go talk for a few minutes?"

"Well, you can see I'm kind of in the middle of something here," he says with a smile.

I love the way his eyes twinkle when he smiles. "I know you are busy. If it were not so important, I would not have interrupted you."

Waiting for Xander's response, I notice Mr. Stone approaching us. *Where did he come from?* "What in the world is going on, Mrs. Susa? You are interrupting a vital press conference." He is whispering, but his tone is harsh.

Mr. Stone turns to wedge his body part way between us and leans in towards Xander. "Mr. President, this disruption cannot happen right now. Think of the message you are sending to the American people."

Xander nods agreement, but with a smile on his face and a chuckle in his voice. "I will be right back to it in just a minute, Phillip. But look at my beautiful wife, back to health and here. I just can't help but spend a moment with her."

There is the topic of my health again. Why does Xander think I've been sick?

I begin again, "Xander, I just need to talk to you about something extremely important," both my words and face plead with him.

Mr. Stone cuts in again. "Mr. President, you are putting your personal life above your country at this moment. Right now, you need to speak to your country. You and your wife can have a chat later."

Oh no, he's going to hustle me out of here. I might not get another chance. I can feel panic beginning to rise in me. *Should I just blurt it all out?* A thought pops into my head.

"I would like to have dinner with you tonight. All your favorites. Will you come?" I look directly in Xander's eyes.

"The president is extremely busy tonight," Stone replies.

With every ounce of self-control and womanly poise I possess, I turn directly to Phillip Stone. "Mr. Stone, I was hoping you would join us too. The three of us could have a little time together."

The surprise on Mr. Stone's face is obvious.

"Yes Phillip, join Esther and I for dinner. We can get right to work afterwards." Xander sounds like a school boy trying to talk his mom into having a cookie before dinner.

My husband gives me a quick wink and a squeeze of my hand. "We'll be there at seven, won't we Phillip?"

Mr. Stone's angry face is gone; replaced by something resembling pleasure. He nods in agreement.

"Now, I have to get back to work, my love."

As quickly as he came away from it, Xander is back up to the podium. I briskly walk down the aisle and out the media entrance. A guard follows behind me. I can hear Xander say something to lighten the mood. The press all laugh supportively.

I just blew it – I didn't even say anything. I am sure they won't even show for dinner. The moment I am out the door, all the strength I have mustered is now gone. My knees buckle under me and I start to go down. I feel a hand around my back. The invisible support stays and guides me to a nearby chair. The guard stays next to me, silently supporting for a moment. Once my dizziness mildly subsides, I look up at the man who caught me.

"Mrs. Susa, what you just did took a lot of courage." All I can manage is a small smile.

"I hope you have a wonderful dinner tonight with your husband."

And Stone. If they come. "I appreciate your kindness."

"It's my pleasure, Mrs. Susa. Whenever you are ready, I'll be happy to accompany you back to your residence."

His words jolt me to reality that I have to have dinner ready for Xander and Phillip in just a few hours. *I don't feel like myself with the lack of food coupled with the stress of the day.*

My brain tells my body to hop up and get moving back home. My body slowly responds.

Why in the world did I invite Stone to come? Even if they do come, how can I possibly talk to Xander with him sitting right there? I have blown my chance already.

~~

233

Chapter 23

ALL THE FAVORITES
XANDER

"Hi honey, I'm home!" I burst through the door with Phillip in tow. *It feels good to be here after weeks away. I've missed home. I've especially missed Esther. I can't help the smile that comes across my face.*

"Xander, you are really here!" Esther comes from the dining room towards me.

Why does she look so surprised to see me? "Come here beautiful." I walk towards her and hold her at arm's length once I reach her. I look her up and down and take in the sight of my wife. "You look absolutely stunning." I can see color coming into her cheeks.

"You know I love this dress on you. I remember the first time you wore it. I couldn't keep my eyes off of you all night, just like now."

"I remember that night." She steals a glance behind me at Stone, obviously embarrassed.

I pull Esther into my arms and kiss her right on the mouth. *Phillip understands. He unsuccessfully tried to keep me occupied*

234

during Esther's illness, but I know I am a changed man because I had no interest in the other women and waited for my wife.

Once we finally pull apart I say, "Today at the press conference, that is exactly what I wanted to do the whole time we were talking."

"Xander, I have missed you so much. Thank you for coming." Esther looks like she might cry.

"Where else would I be?" I look behind me and motion Stone to come closer. "With my wife and my right hand man."

"I'm so glad you could join us for dinner as well, Mr. Stone." Esther, the ultimate hostess, greets Phillip formally.

"Thank you for inviting me, Mrs. Susa." Phillip's voice shows he is comfortable here. "It is a pleasure to join you."

"Thank you for taking time out of your busy schedule."

I can see the pleased look in Phillip's eyes. *With time, I knew that they would come to appreciate each other.*

"It is time for a drink." I walk towards the living room.

"Phillip your usual? Esther, red wine for you tonight?" I don't wait for a response.

"Honey, I'm glad you are finally over that nasty virus. I feel like it has been forever since I have seen you. You know I just couldn't risk getting sick at a time like this." I look up at

Esther. A moment of confusion crosses her face before understanding.

"Well, it is good to have you back," she responds.

"Phillip, you didn't let on that Esther was all better."

"I guess I wanted it to be a surprise," he says as I hand him his scotch.

"Well, I am pleasantly surprised. That is for sure." A look I don't understand passes between the two of them for just a moment. Esther gives Phillip a small smile and their tension is broken. *Maybe they were in on today's surprise together. Maybe they are getting along better than I realized.*

I pass Esther her wine. Holding up my glass, they both follow suit.

"To a day full of surprises."

A small wink for my wife. She goes red again.

"Mrs. Susa, are you sure you are feeling alright? You look lovely, but you don't quite seem like yourself tonight." Phillip looks at Esther concerned.

"Yes, I'm just fine, thank you. Let me check if the food is ready. Then we can eat. You two just sit and relax." Esther gives me a big smile and touches my arm as she walks past. Her touch sends chills through me. *How is it this woman so enthralls me?* I watch her walk out of the room. Stone interrupts my thoughts.

"Xander, you can see how sick your wife still is. Her coloring is so pale. She didn't even take a sip of her wine."

"I'm sure she's fine Phillip."

"Mr. President, she may be rushing herself to get better for your benefit when she is not ready. I have to advise you not to make yourself susceptible to this virus by any more physical contact tonight with your wife. Definitely not staying here yet."

"Come on Phillip. You have to be joking."

"I'm not at all, Xander. The strain of virus your wife had, or still has, can be deadly. You cannot put yourself at any risk right now."

"She looks great to me."

"I'm telling you she is not well, Xander. Really look at her and you can see it."

I shake my head, not believing him at all. "How about this, if she eats a normal dinner then we'll know she's fine and I'm staying."

"Mr. President, you can't stay. Your entire cabinet is coming for a meeting immediately after dinner."

"They can wait for a while. I'm planning on staying longer than just for dinner." I give Stone a knowing smile. He does not smile back.

"Please, Xander, listen—"

Esther's entrance interrupts him mid-sentence. He stops talking and gives her a smile.

"Is dinner ready, love? I'm starving."

Esther stands at the end of the couch awkwardly as though she has something she would like to say.

She almost seems tongue-tied tonight. Maybe Stone is right. Maybe she isn't feeling so well.

"Yes?" I ask. She takes a deep breath and blows it out.

"No nothing, it's just that dinner is ready."

"Great, let's go eat. I'm sure you are hungry too."

I shoot Stone a knowing glance.

Once Esther eats and shows she is feeling fine, I'm sending Phillip straight downstairs and he can figure out how to stall the cabinet.

The table is filled with food. "Honey, you weren't kidding when you said you would make all my favorites. Smoked salmon, roasted duck, sweet potatoes and artichokes with your delicious butter sauce." I can hardly wait to dig in. "Let me guess, caramel cheesecake for dessert?"

"Yes, you know it." Esther smiles at me and I start to lean towards her.

Phillip clears his throat. *I forgot, no contact until after dinner.*

"I can't take the credit though. The staff cooked it all. I just planned it."

"That is plenty to take the credit for," I say with a smile. "I guess you aren't going to be talking to me tonight about healthy eating?" Esther is usually the one encouraging my health.

"Tonight is a special night," she says.

Stone and I enjoy the meal thoroughly; talking and laughing. To my dismay however, Esther sits quietly and hardly eats anything. She picks at a few things on her plate. Sitting quietly listening to our conversation for most of the meal. *Phillip must be right. She must not be completely well yet. I can't believe this.*

"My love, this was an amazing meal. Thank you."

"My pleasure, Xander," Esther clears her throat as though she has something to say.

Stone abruptly scoots back his chair and stands up. "Mr. President, don't forget your cabinet is waiting to begin. We really should have been down there ten minutes ago."

I shoot him a silencing look. *I'm sure I won't get sick if she is almost over whatever it was she had.*

"You know, Phillip, I think I'll just let you head on down there. I'll be a few minutes behind you."

"Yes, Xander, please stay for a little bit longer," my bride quietly adds. "I would love some more time with you." Her look tells me I can have more than just cheesecake for dessert.

Stone's relaxed face of the evening falls off and his serious face goes back on. "I'm sorry, Mr. President, but I'm going to have to insist we get down to the cabinet meeting as we agreed upon."

He is so much like a mother sometimes. So worried about the slight chance of me getting sick.

"Mrs. Susa, thank you so much for the lovely meal. I'm sorry I have to take your husband away. Duty calls."

"Xander, I really want some more time with you though. Could I just have a few more minutes?"

One look in those eyes. *Yes, I will stay.*

One look over at Stone. *Oh fine, Mother Hen.*

"I'm sorry Esther. I would love to, but I really have to go."

She looks like she can hardly take the thought of me leaving. *Poor thing. She has obviously been missing me.*

I stand up to join Stone. Esther looks stricken. "How about we all do dinner again tomorrow night?" She blurts out. "You both need a little more pampering after all your hard work."

"Phillip, isn't she the best?" He returns my smile. "Of course, baby. Let's do it again tomorrow." I look pointedly at Stone who nods in agreement.

He bows to her gallantly. "Mrs. President, I will be honored."

"And tomorrow night there will be no late meetings, understand Phillip?"

"We will have to see," he smiles. We both start walking towards the door, Phillip stays behind me. *He's obviously afraid I'm going to turn and bolt back in.*

As I get ready to say goodbye from the door, a memory comes to me from the press conference.

"Esther, I completely forgot. Today, you said you wanted to talk about something."

"Yes, Xander, I do." Before she can get another word out, Stone cuts her off.

"Mrs. Susa, can we put a pin in that conversation until tomorrow night? "

"Tomorrow night?" I ask her gently.

Esther just nods. Her smile looks forced. *I hate leaving her this way, but tomorrow we will catch up more.* I blow Esther a kiss over Stone who is corralling me from behind.

Once we are out in the corridor, Stone sounds apologetic, "Sorry Xander, but there is too much going on for you to get sick. It is such a critical time for the country."

"I know, Phillip. You are just looking out for my best. My voice of reason. I'm just missing my wife."

We walk in silence for a moment. *I really do miss and love that woman. The time apart has made that crystal clear.*

"What do you think she wants to talk to me about anyway?" I wonder aloud. *Phillip has been married for a long time. He probably understands women a whole lot better than I do.*

"Esther probably just wants a house at the beach or some piece of new jewelry. Who knows with women? I'm sure it's nothing to worry about."

"Yeah, I'm sure you are right. Probably not a big deal."

~~

Chapter 24

KING OF THE CASTLE
PHILLIP

I love driving this car down the highway. Tonight I had a driver bring me my own car instead of driving me home. *I just want to feel the power of my Z4 beneath me.* The wind all around me, my music up loud, going way faster than I should be. *I am the king of my BMW and the road. The king of so much more.*

"I am controlling this country and soon my mission will be complete!" I yell to the wind that is accompanying me to my home. Virginia is just a quick thirty minute commute this time of night with a quick stop to pick up my oldest son.

Why have I been worrying so much about Esther? I thought she might sway Xander, but she's harmless. She is more skittish than I thought. Best part is she is smart enough to know who is boss. When she found out I lied to Xander about her being sick, she kept her mouth shut. She's like the puppy that rolls over on her back because she knows to be submissive to the big dog.

"Of course, I've already had the President of the United States in that position for a long, long time." I laugh out loud to the night sky who is witness to my celebration.

I push the voice command button. "Call home."

There is a loud commotion in the background behind my wife's voice. "Hello Phillip."

"Tricia, is everything ready? I'm on my way to pick up Jack and then I'll be there."

"Yes, of course. Since you called earlier, I've set up everything. Our friends, and enemies, have been invited to celebrate as you said. The caterers are almost all set up and ready to go. We doubled the drinks from usual and have the caviar brioche that you like. I was able to get that DJ you wanted."

"Good, I even want Douglas there. I want to rub his face in my success." *My old tennis partner always thought he was something special. Never did appreciate who I was. Now look at him, still running some sales company, while I'm running this country.* "And be sure to spare no expense."

"I haven't Phillip. It has already been a small fortune in bonuses to put on this short notice party, but it will be worth every penny."

"Well done Tricia, you are a powerful woman in your own right. And do you even realize the power of the man you are married to? Do you know I control this country?"

"Of course I do, Phillip," she says with a chuckle.

"Do you have the usual security arrangement; bodyguards, metal detectors, no electronics allowed inside?"

"Phillip, I have everything planned. Don't worry."

Tricia learned a long time ago that I get what I want. We would not be married today if I had not gone after what I wanted and got it. I was just a poor, struggling politician and her daddy was one of the richest oil tycoons in Texas. He did not want me anywhere near his little beauty queen. But here we are, married with three boys; living off of all his money now that he is dead and gone.

I gun the motor and the beautiful machine beneath me races even faster.

When my oldest son and I pull through the wrought iron gates of my house, more of a modern day mansion, it is alive with energy. There is music pumping, lights flashing, and people swarming inside.

Tricia comes outside with our younger two boys to greet us. A scotch is in her hand for me.

"We are ready and waiting for you, Phillip."

I put my arm around my wife's waist and kiss her on the lips. *It will be a shame to not have these lips to kiss anymore.*

"Get the drinks flowing. I want everyone in a good mood."

"People are already drinking. It is pretty lively in there."

I enter my house to cheers. My fist pumps the air like a champion and the cheers grow even louder.

"Drink, my friends. Eat. Enjoy yourselves," I yell above the noise.

I down my first scotch and call for another.

"Bring out rounds for everyone in the house," I yell to the servers.

Over an hour later, there must be triple the amount of people in the house. Some I don't even recognize.

I instruct the servers to bring champagne around to everyone. I tell the DJ to turn the music down and I step onto the top of a coffee table. A glass of champagne is handed up to me.

"Thank you all for coming. I hope you are having a good time."

Cheers, yells, and whistles answer my question.

"Friends, my reason in asking you to come tonight is to celebrate. To celebrate this great country of America, where a man of humble beginnings can rise up to become—I pause for a breath before I begin shouting, my arm held up high—"To become the most powerful man in the entire country."

The cheers, yells, and whistles come back at me even stronger. The crowd's energy is feeding mine as mine is to them. After a few moments, I pat the air with my hand, asking for my fans to be quiet.

"You all know that I am a self-made man. I have been wise with how I have spent my life. I saw the most beautiful woman in the world and I married her."

The cat calls go out as I gesture towards Tricia.

"We have three boys who are making their way in this world."

I see my boys acknowledge the clapping and cheers, each in their own way. I raise my glass to them and all three return the gesture.

Again I ask for quiet.

"I have climbed my way up the political ranks to the top. And tonight I want you to know you are in the home of the man who is guiding the White House and our country."

I pause for emphasis with a smirk on my face. Everyone pays attention just a little closer.

I yell. "Amazing things are about to happen. When they do, remember it was me, Phillip Stone, who made them happen."

My crowd begins to cheer wildly as they raise their glasses towards me and we all take a drink.

I call out to my adoring fans, "Who is the most powerful man?" I cup my hand to my ear, waiting for a response.

"You are," Jack yells out in a strong voice. A few chuckles around the room.

"That's right," I respond, beaming at my son. *I need to take that boy along.*

Again I repeat louder, "Who is the most powerful man?"

This time most of the room answers with smiles on their faces.

"You are."

This time I yell my question at the top of my lungs. "Who is the most powerful man?"

My people match my volume and scream back at me. "You are, you are, you are!"

I throw up my arms and slowly circle around on the table top. There is a voice screaming wildly above the rest. It takes me a moment to realize it is my own.

Laughter begins flowing out of me. Eerie laughter to join the clapping, whistling, and yells coming from the crowd. Slowly, the noise subsides and I stand still on top of the table. *I have no idea where the drink I was holding went.*

"Give me another drink." Someone hands one up to me immediately.

"I want to raise my glass one last time tonight." I raise my glass towards my wife and sons. "To you, my family."

"To all of you, my friends." I slowly tip the edge of my glass all the way around the room.

"And even to those of you who are competitors," I find Douglas in the room and salute him with my glass.

"I feel nostalgic tonight about this life I have created. It is allowing me to do something I feel is worthwhile. Someday, when I am gone you will think of me as a man who lived with passion. A man who lived with principal. A man who gave it all."

This is also my farewell speech. In just a short time, I will be whisked away to my Iran forever.

The room is completely silent for the first time all night. I look down into my glass, trying to hold back my emotions about the culmination of my life's work. I take in all the people around me. *I love the feeling of admiration I see. They envy me too.*

A thought comes into my head that blemishes the perfection —Mordecai Allenby. *With all this power, how can that man still disrespect me so?*

My countenance changes from nostalgic pride to anger. I begin to pace on the top of my coffee table like a caged lion. My hand clenches into fists and my breathing becomes ragged. My fans watch me with rapt attention.

"What is it Phillip?" Tricia calls out to me, obviously worried.

"There is one reason I cannot be completely happy at this time of celebration. One person ruins my peace."

My friends and family start looking around at each other accusingly.

"There is a man who is beneath scum who does not respect my position. He is an enemy of the state."

The crowd boos and hisses as though they are watching a British pantomime where hate for the villain is verbalized.

"I know the man," Tricia joins into my one man show. "It is Mordecai Allenby, but he is nothing compared to you."

I guess she has heard me talk about him enough times.

"Allenby does not respect the good I am doing for this country. He spews garbage and is garbage."

"You should make him respect you once and for all," calls out Tricia. I can see the heads of my sons nodding in agreement. Ideas start flying from all around the room.

"Get his taxes audited."

"Trump up legal charges against him."

"Maybe there are rumors about him and a young intern you could exploit."

"Show him you are the boss, Phillip."

"Who is he compared to you? He is nothing."

I look at Tricia across the room. She beckons me with her finger and I step down from my coffee table pedestal. My friends begin milling, looking for more drinks. The DJ turns on the music, seeing that my speech is over.

Tricia pulls me close to her and whispers in my ear.

"Phillip, what do you really want to do about Mordecai Allenby?" She pulls back and gives me a look that shows me she has an idea of what I am really capable of.

"I want him gone. Dead."

"Then make it happen." Her smile is not one I have ever seen on her before. "I know that you can if you want to."

Maybe I underestimate Tricia. I love the way her mind is working. For all her Texas charm, she sure has a dark side. It is almost a shame that I have to leave her behind. A blonde Texan beauty hiding in Iran is just not practical.

I give her a kiss on the mouth and literally run towards my office. The party behind me is all but forgotten.

"It has to happen in the next forty eight hours," I tell my comrade on the phone after explaining what I want. He is one of the sleeper agents here in the states who was crucial in starting all the violence among the Jews.

It will be nothing for him to take out Mordecai. Like a walk in the park.

"Yes, of course everything is on schedule." I respond to his question. "This is just side business. Ahmed said you are at my disposal." I listen to his agreement.

"Good. Let me know when it is done." I lean back in my chair. The secure satellite phone sits on my desk.

Ahmed said he would confirm the relocation date by tomorrow. Maybe he knows tonight. I dial his number and wait expectantly.

"Brother," he answers in high spirits. "You cannot wait either, can you? It is almost time. Are you ready?"

"Of course, just tell me when."

"Relocation day will be next Saturday, the Jewish holy day. That gives you five days."

"Perfect timing," I respond in joy. "I was hoping it would be within the week."

"Do not let anything get in the way, Phillip."

"Of course not, Ahmed. There will be no complications," I assure him.

"What are these protests against the secure facilities I have seen on the news? I've been told there were thousands there."

"The numbers are inflated, Ahmed. It is nothing. You know how Americans love to make a sign and protest almost anything. Save the trees. Save the Jews." I laugh out loud. "Protests mean nothing."

"Good, that is what I want to hear," he says relaxing.

"Everything is moving forward exactly as planned. The president is putty. The numbers of Jews are increasing just as we hoped."

"Excellent." Ahmed pauses and then speaks in a softer tone. "I look forward to seeing you here this time next week, brother."

"My plane will leave simultaneous to the attacks."

"There will be celebrating when you arrive."

"Thank you, brother." The emotion of earlier rises in my throat again. "Thank you for giving me the opportunity to complete my life's work."

"It is mutual, Phillip. We have both given our lives in service. Now is the time to reap our rewards."

We end the call. *I can't believe the moment is almost here. So many details still to be finalized, but almost here. At least I will get to see Mordecai die before I go. The only shame is he won't get to watch his people go through the pain and suffering I have planned for them.* I smile at the thought.

The irony of it all is that Mordecai Allenby is the only one who is right. He sees the truth. It is a conspiracy. Jewish Americans are walking themselves into their deaths. Mordecai Allenby will be proven right, but by then it will be much too late.

I laugh out loud to my filing cabinet and desk—the two observers of my evil ways.

I head back upstairs. Tricia is across the room and I walk to her briskly.

"Well?" she asks with anticipation.

"It is taken care of," I tell her with a smirk on my face.

The excitement in her eyes is priceless. *I think she likes feeling the power I have. Just wait until Sunday. She will be in awe of me once she realizes what I have done. Maybe she will speak of me with honor after I am gone. Doesn't really matter though. The more shame on this side, the more honor on the other.* "I have to get back to the White House."

"What? No, stay here. The party is going strong," she begs me.

"I have to get back and babysit the president. He was fast asleep on his office couch when I left, but I don't want him to get into any mischief without me." I give my wife another kiss.

"Thank you for tonight. It was perfect."

"You are welcome, Phillip."

I walk out of my castle. The king in every way.

~~

Chapter 25

CAUGHT IN THE MIDDLE
XANDER

"Cyrus, are you out there?" I call to my assistant from my reclined position on my office couch. "Cyrus? Cyrus!"

Maybe it is too early for him to be in yet. I guess it is still dark outside.

"I need to ask you something, Cyrus. Are you there?"

A brisk knock on the door.

"Come in Cyrus." The head that comes inside is not Cyrus's, but Secret Service.

"Mr. President, can I help you with anything? I heard you calling."

My mind is fuzzy from a drink-induced sleep that I never quite settled into.

"I just need to ask Cyrus a question. Is he here?"

"No, sir, I have not seen him yet."

"What time is it?" I ask, trying to rub my eyes clear.

"It is just before four, Sir."

A groan escapes me. "Short night—I've been waking up on and off all through."

"I'm sorry, Mr. President. Is there anything you need?"

I remember turning on the projector at some point during the night. Last year's news clips were interesting to watch, until I dozed off again.

"A question is nagging me from something I saw last night. I need to ask Cyrus about it."

"I'll call him in for you if you would like, Mr. President."

I nod. My eyes already heavy again.

They don't open again until I hear a knock on the office door and Cyrus walks in.

"There you are. How long have I been out?" I ask him groggily, not feeling like myself as I struggle to sit up.

"I'm not sure, Mr. President. It is just after 5:00 am."

Cyrus looks a little tired himself, but he does not say anything.

"Sorry to wake you. According to Phillip, you owe me anyway for letting my wife through to the press conference."

Cyrus's face drops.

"Don't worry buddy. I thought it was awesome. You might actually have to get a raise."

"Really? You aren't upset?"

"Upset? Are you kidding me? I can't buy that kind of press. My wife is so in love with me she can't stay away and crashes a press conference just to be with me. The people love it. I owe you."

His face visibly relaxes.

"That has nothing to do with why I want to talk to you this morning."

Back to business. Cyrus stands up straighter.

"You know how I sometimes like to watch past news?"

Cyrus nods in agreement.

"Last night, a few hours ago actually, I was watching some. I had forgotten Mordecai Allenby was the one who discovered my assassination plot."

Cyrus nods again, but does not say anything.

"You know Allenby, the attorney general, who is being so vocal about our peace plan?"

"Yes, Mr. President, of course."

"Sorry, I'm not still thinking too clearly this morning." I try to laugh off my question.

"He's a good guy though. Just a little confused right now about things. Love his passion. He'll come around to our side once he sees the peace plan clearly."

Where was I going here...oh yes, "Well, I completely forgot he was involved with protecting me in that guard debacle. It's funny—parts of that day are crystal clear in my mind while other parts are foggy."

"Yes, Mr. President. As I remember, his involvement was crucial to your safety."

"So what did I do to thank him?"

"I was not in my current position at that time, Mr. President, so I don't know off the top of my head what was done. Let me do a little checking through the records. I'll find out."

"Appreciate it, Cyrus. Just hate the idea the man saved my life and I never did anything for him regardless of what is happening now."

I lay my head back down on the couch as Cyrus stands up.

"Was there anything else, Mr. President?"

"That's it, just let me know as soon as you find out anything. I feel like it is hanging over me and I want to take care of it immediately."

I close my eyes as Cyrus closes my office door.

"Mr. President, Mr. President."

In my dream, Mordecai Allenby is standing on the deck of a large ship floating farther and farther away from me. He is surrounded by children and they are all yelling to me. I reach for him.

"Mr. President."

This time I jolt awake. I quickly sit up. "I couldn't reach him," he looks at me strangely.

"Never mind. What did you find out?"

"There was nothing done for Mordecai Allenby."

"Nothing, really? Are you sure?"

"Yes, sir, I checked all the records." He watches my reaction of disbelief. "Mr. Stone is here if you would like to confirm it with him."

"Stone's here? Excellent, please ask him to come in. And bring me a coffee too."

"Oh, and by the way," Cyrus adds, "Allenby is in DC right now. Yesterday he was answering questions from the steps of the Lincoln Memorial."

"Thanks for checking on that Cyrus."

A few minutes later Stone arrives, right after my coffee. I have freshened up and am at my desk getting to work.

"Good morning, Phillip." I notice my chief of staff looks a little disheveled this morning.

"Did you get any sleep last night, President Susa?" Phillip asks.

"Yes a little. I just woke up a while ago. I was wondering the same about you." I reply with curiosity. *I think that's the same shirt Phillip was wearing at our meeting last night.*

Phillip's face breaks into a wide grin. "Too many thoughts flowing last night for any sleep. There will always be time to sleep later."

"Perfect," I boom, "Because I need some ideas this morning. Then I want you to take those ideas and make them happen for me immediately."

"Of course, Mr. President. That is what I am here for."

"Phillip, there is someone that has gone the extra mile for me. I want to show my gratitude. I want the American people to know how much I value him. You get where I'm going with this?"

"Of course, Mr. President. You want to make your appreciation clear. You want to honor this man for what he has done."

"Exactly, but I don't want to just send a gift with a thank you card. I want a grand gesture to show the impact this man has had on my life. I want it to happen today as it should have happened a long time ago."

A huge smile spreads onto Phillip's face. He stands up and starts walking back and forth as he likes to do when he is thinking. "Xander, your act of gratitude needs to be something that has never been done before. Something that will let the American people see the importance of this man."

"Sounds good. What should we do?"

Phillip paces back and forth a few more times, his hands rubbing together as he thinks. He stops and turns to look at me. *I can see he is in idea mode. He has presented ideas to me many times before with these same actions. Although never with such a huge smile on his face as today.*

"The most important thing is the honor must be bestowed publically," Phillip begins. "It must be a show. It must be unique so it will make the news again and again."

I take a drink of my coffee ready to be wowed.

"Mr. President, I suggest beginning with a press conference where you will present him with 'The American Hero' award."

"Sounds okay. A little boring though. I was hoping for something more."

"That's only the beginning, Mr. President," he says with a smile. "I've got a lot more in mind."

I just smile at his enthusiasm.

"From the press conference, our hero will get out with the people. Of course, the press will be invited to come along and cover the whole event. Our hero riding on the back of your convertible through downtown D.C. would be a nice touch."

"My convertible? Why not yours? They are the same except for the color."

"It will mean so much more if it is yours," he responds back seriously.

"We can get the crowds out on short notice through social media. Thousands will come to our impromptu parade."

Now we are talking. I nod my appreciation.

"Love it, Phillip. Let's make it happen today."

"I have more, Mr. President."

"Oh really? What else are you thinking?" I smile at my over-achieving right-hand man.

"Our parade should conclude at the National Mall. We can have the national anthem sung directly to our hero, of course by a big name female singer. You can call in some favors and do the introduction yourself. We'll continue the block party into a full-blown concert."

"Love it, Phillip." I stand up and move to my desk. "Now, can you make it happen today? You know how I hate to let a good idea sit."

"Of course, Mr. President. Impromptu events are in fashion. I'll get the PR and marketing teams to drop everything else just for the day and put their efforts into this. I think it's that important."

I can tell he is calculating details in his head. Although he's speaking out loud, it is more to himself, as he is looking down.

"Two o'clock press conference, Three o'clock parade, Five thirty the concert starts. No, maybe better to push everything back by an hour. That gives us almost twelve hours before the concert start."

Phillip looks up at me again with a confident smile on his face. "No problem; plenty of time."

"This celebration is an excellent step in line with the peace plan. I am glad you see it that way as well. I'm sure you will make it an event to remember."

I think I'm going to need one more cup of coffee. With this impromptu celebration, I will have to make some changes to my schedule. I buzz Cyrus and ask him to come in.

Phillip is still standing in front of my desk, oddly, he looks uncomfortable. *Not a look I have seen on Phillip very often during the time I have known him.* "Is there something else, Phillip?"

"Before I go, I just want to hear it come out of your mouth— the hero you would like to honor today." Phillip stands up a little straighter in front of my desk. *What is he talking about?*

"Phillip, I told you at the beginning of this conversation that I want to honor Mordecai Allenby. Who did you think we were talking about?"

Confusion stands still on Phillip's face.

"To thank him for saving my life, of course."

"The Mordecai Allenby?" Phillip asks as he continues to stand rigid before me.

"How many Mordecai Allenby's do you know?"

"Mr. President, he is speaking out against you. He is trying to turn the country against your peace plan with his vicious attacks."

"That's why it's the perfect time for an over the top gesture of thanks for him. It will send a message to the world that the peace plan is to help all American Jews. It will show that Allenby's views really are irrational."

Phillip stands still and silent.

"Isn't that the strategy you were thinking too?"

Awakening from his trance, Phillip finally speaks. "Mr. President, things like this don't happen to me."

"What do you mean? You are the one who came up with all the ideas. Now, let's do it, Phillip. We have talked enough."

Cyrus has been standing by the door waiting. I wave him forward.

What is wrong with Phillip today? I'm going to give him the benefit of the doubt that he is just tired. Maybe he's sick.

Phillip is still standing in front of my desk unmoving. I ignore him and Cyrus begins to look over the day's schedule with me.

"Mr. President," Phillip interrupts us. "Allenby might not even be in D.C."

With a big sigh, I look up from my schedule to Phillip. *He must see how annoyed I am getting with him.*

"Don't worry, Phillip. Allenby is here."

"Mr. President, this is a mistake."

I have never seen Stone so weak and confused. I'll build him as he has built me so many times before. "You can do this, Phillip Stone. Your country needs to see your strength and leadership and this is the perfect way to forward the plans for peace. It will be done today. No more discussion."

His countenance changes. Phillip's look of confusion is replaced by sudden resolve. "Mr. President, it will be done as we discussed," he concludes formally.

"Glad to hear it, Phillip." And with a nod, I excuse Stone from my office.

~~

Chapter 26

A MOST UNCERTAIN DAY
MORDECAI

"Good morning, Mr. Allenby. This is Jana calling from Mr. Phillip Stone's office."

The call to my cell phone surprises me. I've been waiting for the moment Phillip Stone takes me to a facility, but not a call. I am standing at the open office door of a DC judge, about to enter for a meeting. Instead of walking through, I hold up my index finger to let him know I'm going to be a minute more. I step away from the office door and out into the hallway.

"Good morning, Jana." I try to stay polite. *It isn't this lady's fault her boss hates me.*

"Mr. Stone would like to extend an invitation for you to come to the White House this afternoon. Please be ready at one o'clock. Please have your schedule cleared for the rest of the day. There is something special being planned for you, Mr. Allenby."

Here it is. I'm going to a secure facility. The term "something special" is an interesting choice of words in this circumstance.

"Can you please tell me more details?" I ask, trying to keep my voice polite and calm.

"I can tell you that you are requested to dress nicely. A blue suit and red tie would be best." *He wants to dress me up before he takes me away. Sounds like he is using this for some angle.*

"A car will pick you up and bring you to the White House." Jana continues. "Where will you be at that time sir?"

"Well, probably at the hotel. I'll need to get changed and pick up my luggage to bring. I'll have my assistant call you back with the details."

A moment's hesitation on Jana's part.

"Of course, Mr. Allenby. You are more than welcome to stay at the White House tonight if you would like. I will have a room prepared for you."

"Stay at the White House? What exactly is happening today, Jana?"

"I'm so sorry, Mr. Allenby, but I am under strict orders. Mr. Stone will tell you about it himself." Her voice is full of excitement.

I bet he will tell me about it himself. He's been waiting to tell me this for a long time.

"Okay, Jana, I'll be ready at one." My voice is resigned to the inevitable.

There is no point to even think about running. I can't talk to the press now with Esther so close to speaking to Xander either.

The rest of the morning is a blur. I cancel all my afternoon meetings. A fellow lawyer takes a briefing for me so I can go get ready. I head back to my hotel before noon. That gives me time to pray.

When I am inside the car sent by Phillip Stone, my fear begins to mount.

I wonder if I'm really going to the White House at all. Maybe just directly to a secure facility. Then it will be to my death along with thousands of others.

When we actually pull up to the White House, I am truly surprised. I am shown into a waiting room where a buffet of drinks and snacks are prepared. Then I am left alone.

Suddenly, Esther's assistant, Gabriella, pops her head into the room. "Good afternoon Mr. Allenby. I'm the First Lady's personal assis—"

"Yes, yes, I know exactly who you are. Hello, Gabriella."

She smiles at my recognition. "Mr. Allenby, the First Lady asked me to come see you."

"And why would she do that?" I ask cautiously, not sure how much she knows.

"Don't worry Mr. Allenby, Esther has explained your connection and I am helping her in any way I can."

I nod. *I don't want to give away anything in case this is a trap from Stone.*

Gabriella goes on, "Esther wants me to let you know how excited she is for you. She will try to sneak into the back of the ceremony to watch. That is all she will be able to attend."

My face is a window to the confusion I feel inside.

"Help me understand all this, Gabriella. I don't know why I am here, except I assume it is to go to a secure facility. What kind of ceremony is this and why would the First Lady be excited for it?"

"What do you mean? No one has told you why you were brought here?"

I shake my head no. Like a student who has to admit they don't know how to do long division yet.

"You have been brought here to be honored as a hero for the time you saved President Susa's life."

"What? Honored? I don't believe it. There must be something else going on."

"Esther thought so too at first. Then we found out it was actually the president's idea to give you this honor. Mr. Stone got roped into it without even realizing and he is not too happy about it either."

Could this be true? I am being honored against Stone's wishes?

Gabriella sounds almost giddy, "Honestly, the staff all think it's hilarious. He has been so difficult to everyone. And now to see him so upset about this—it's poetic justice."

"But why would the president want to honor me now?" My confusion is not gone. "I've been speaking out against his peace plan and this happened so long ago."

"We are not sure of his reasons, although there is speculation. His assistant told me that the president just realized he never did anything for you and he put Mr. Stone in charge. I guess the president doesn't realize how Mr. Stone feels."

"It's hard to believe the president doesn't know his right hand man well enough to realize how humiliating this would be for him. I think most of the world knows that. Although it's true that Xander does not take time to really notice the people in his life."

"I don't actually know the real reason, Mr. Allenby. I peeked in the press room right before I came here and it is almost ready. And your parade should be well attended with all the tweets and posts."

"My parade?" *I must have panic written on my face again because Gabriella jumps in.*

"Don't worry. You'll have the press corps cameras and body guards around you the whole time. Esther thinks the cameras will be extra safety for you."

"That might be true, but you never know." I am getting over my shock at the news.

"Gabriella, how is Esther? Did she say anything else?" *If Esther is not going to talk to Xander, I may need to use this opportunity to speak out.*

"She is okay, although she seems a little anxious. There are the dinner preparations for Xander and Mr. Stone again and she seems to want everything just right."

Her anxiety is because of what she needs to tell her husband. Lord, please give her the strength to speak and let him really hear her.

"Thank you, Gabriella." I feel renewed by this news. "Please tell Esther that I love her."

"Of course, Mr. Allenby. Oh, and she did ask you to pray for her. She said you would know what to pray about."

"Tell her that I will pray for her to be brave."

A quizzical look crosses Gabriella's face. *Obviously she doesn't know everything, which is good. That information needs to be given only to the president.*

Over an hour later, I am on the stage in front of a slew of cameras. *I've been in front of the cameras many times, but this unexpected conference is different.* Phillip Stone is speaking. It is a speech about heroism and the American spirit. His expression is stoic and formal.

"Mordecai Allenby is an example of each one doing our part to make our country a better place. His heroic actions saved the president's life. That is why we are here to honor him today." Phillip's voice chokes up at the end of his sentence.

To the outside observer it might look like he is getting emotional. I know it is Phillip is literally trying to swallow his pride.

I can hardly keep from smiling. Not at him or because I am happy, but at the irony of the situation. *The press, of all people, who daily report on Phillip Stone pushing forward the peace plan as I daily speak against it.*

Looking out over the reports, I can see Esther standing against the back wall.

I wish I could go to her now and encourage her in the words she still needs to say tonight. Regardless of what is happening today, the president's response tonight is all that matters for our future.

The president takes the stage. With a smile, he motions me to step forward. "Today, I personally want to thank Mordecai Allenby. Cai, it is because of you that I am standing here today. Without your bravery and quick thinking, my life could have ended in a tragic story of hatred. Instead, you are an example to us all of the strong American spirit."

The president puts one hand on my shoulder while he shakes my other hand. "Cai, I cannot thank you enough." The camera clicks engulf us as we smile at one another.

"It was my pleasure, Mr. President. I believe that we should stand up for any American that is in danger."

Should I speak now – to be specific and say something more? I can try to explain to the whole world the hidden agenda for the Jewish Americans. Something holds me back. I need to trust that Esther will speak. That her words will make the difference to the one person who matters, when mine have not been able to.

Phillip Stone takes center stage again. "We would request all of you to join us on our day's activities. The parade will begin in approximately twenty minutes. There are maps of our route at the back."

If Stone has a plan to kill me, this is probably the most dangerous part of my day.

"There will be an open air concert at the conclusion of our event. It will be a day to remember," Stone concludes flatly.

I am guessing by his tone, Stone would much rather remember this as the day that I die.

~~

Chapter 27

LIFE COMES CRASHING DOWN
PHILLIP

The last note of the national anthem is still hanging in the air. I turn to the staff member next to me with disgust.

"That is all I can take. You are responsible for him during the concert. Take Allenby wherever he wants when it's over." *It doesn't matter where he is, my comrade will find him—hopefully tonight.*

I walk towards the entourage of cars that came with us. The drivers perk up as I walk towards them. I choose a car and order the driver to take me home.

"Mr. Stone, we have orders to wait until the end of the—"

"Those orders were from me—new orders—take me home." He shows reluctance to comply. I lean into his face and yell. "Now, you idiot!" Spit from my last word sprays onto his face. He quickly moves to open the door for me to get inside.

I sit in the back of the car, stunned as we drive. *What happened today? I need back the confident feel from last night. I need to focus for what is really important; relocation day.*

I can feel tension in my house as soon as I enter. The television is on. I hear the national anthem.

They are already watching my day on the news. All because I came up with the idea to have the press cover the entire event so thoroughly. As I walk towards the living room, I hear crying.

"Tricia, is that you?" I turn the corner into the living room to see my wife huddled on the couch, her eyes red. A box of tissues sits next to her. The floor is littered with the used and discarded.

My three boys sit mesmerized in front of the flat screen television. The news is reporting Mordecai Allenby's honor; my humiliation. No one even acknowledges my entrance.

"I'm here."

Tricia looks up at me. She shakes her head and then buries it into her arms. *Is that a look of disgust in her eyes? Or is it pity?*

"Boys, I'm home," I say to them.

"I can see why you would want to come home after a day like today." My oldest, Jack, says sarcastically.

"Who do you think you are?" I raise my voice at him. All three boys turn to look at me. I walk directly in front of the television and turn it off.

"You have no idea!" I yell at my boys.

I walk back towards Tricia. Her head is still in her arms.

"Tricia, look at me." I demand of her.

"I can't. I'm just so humiliated. After all that you said last night in front of all our friends. Then for you to go and honor the very man you said you hated."

"It just happened." I reach towards Tricia, looking for comfort. Instead, she puts her hand out in front, pushing me away.

Her action snaps something inside of me. I begin to scream at her. "Don't you think I am humiliated enough? Who are you? You mean nothing. You are nothing."

I grab her arms roughly and pull her to stand in front of me. I can see the fear in her eyes. *Good, she needs a little more respect for me.*

"Who are you to look down on me? You dare to snub your nose at me because I made one mistake?"

Out of the corner of my eye, I can see my boys edging closer. *I have never seen these looks on their faces before; a look of fear coupled with contempt.* I drop my wife's arms and turn towards my sons.

"You boys have something to say?" I stare at them. "Jack?"

He stands up taller and looks me right in the eye. "Last night we were chanting how you are the most powerful man in the country. Today I watched you grovel before your worst enemy. Why?"

Before I can answer, my wife's phone rings. No one moves.

"You answer it, Phillip. People have been calling. I don't know what to say."

I pick up her phone. Instead of answering it, I throw it against the wall as hard as I can. The noise is shocking for an instant. I see my family jump.

Now I have their attention. If I can explain, they will understand. I take a deep breath and try to regain control. "Everything is just fine. Today was just an off day, that's all."

My family stares at me in silence.

"This morning the president was talking to me about honoring someone. I had no idea that it was for Mordecai Allenby." I change my tone from explanation to my usual mode of confidence and control. "This does not matter at all. It doesn't change anything."

I paste a smirk onto my face. "I am still the most powerful man in the White House."

My three boys stand tall, just staring at me. Tricia won't make eye contact with me. She dabs her eyes with a tissue as she looks out of the window.

"That's all the support I get from you four? For all I have given you"

"Phillip, you know that I have stood beside you." Tricia finally looks at me. "I have always known that you would rise to the top." My wife of twenty-three years stands up and faces me. "But today, you are not the Phillip Stone that I married. You are not the Phillip Stone from last night. For the first time in our marriage, I am embarrassed."

My anger rises. I feel my jaw clench as I try to hold on. *I'm losing control—with Mordecai—in my own house—with my anger.*

"Phillip, I have a bad, bad feeling about this. About you prancing Mordecai Allenby around D.C. today as the hero. After all you have said in this house about how detrimental he is to our society."

This woman better be careful. She is about to cross a line.

Tricia looks straight at me, but speaks tentatively. "Phillip, you know that I want you to succeed. I just have this horrible feeling that Mordecai Allenby and the Jews are going to bring you crashing down."

"How can you say that?" I step aggressively towards her as I speak. Tricia shudders in front of me.

"You really should learn to control that mouth of yours." My jaw is tight as I speak. *I'm losing it.*

I grab my wife's throat. *I want to choke out the words she has just spoken. She is saying my worst nightmare.*

"You don't even know what you are talking about. Mordecai will be dead soon. They'll all be dead soon. Just wait and see."

Her eyes look at me in panic as she grabs at my hand on her throat. My other fist comes crashing towards my wife's temple.

"Stop!" The yell of my oldest son attacks my ear just before I feel the weight of him crash into me. I lose my balance and fall to the ground with Jack on top of me.

For a moment, time stands still in disbelief. *I just hit Tricia. But she deserved it for what she said.*

In the next instant everyone is moving. Jack jumps up. Chest out towards me—back to his mother—ready to fight. My second son moves in next to Jack—fists clenched at his sides, steely cold eyes. My youngest, now fifteen, moves towards his crumpled mother.

"Are you okay?" He quietly asks her.

"I need him to get away from me."

Tricia glares up at me and for a moment I feel regret. *This is not the way I want to leave them. Humiliated by the scum, Mordecai. Hurting Tricia. Losing the boys respect. I had a plan to leave as their hero.* I stand back up with my hands raised in surrender. The fight in me is gone.

This doesn't really matter. My time with them is almost over.

"I'm okay, boys. I just lost my head for a minute there."

They relax just a bit, although still creating a blockade between me and their mother. Our youngest leads Tricia out of the room and upstairs.

I don't say a word, just head directly downstairs to my office. The first thing I do is pour myself a drink. *How could the last seventeen hours have gone so wrong? I was on top of the world.* Over and over I replay the day in my mind. *With just one question to Xander, this day could have been so different.*

I down one drink after another. I am counting on them to cover my regret. Suddenly, I sit up straight in my chair.

What did Ahmed and our comrades think when they saw the news? I should call him and explain.

"How can I make him believe this was a part of my plan?" I ask myself.

I'll wait until tomorrow. Maybe they will figure it is all under control if they don't hear. Another drink.

Hurting Tricia was not part of my plan. And the boys too. This isn't how I wanted it to end with them.

Speaking out loud to only myself and my listening office, "But she should know by now to hold her tongue."

Doesn't even matter. Maybe it will make it easier for her and the boys to move forward without me. Since I will be seen as a traitor to the country – and now the family as well.

"Keep your eye on the goal, Phillip. Mordecai will be dead soon. Thousands of Jews to follow. I will have the last laugh." I exhort myself as I look to my office walls, almost expecting agreement.

280

I look out the window as I drink. The sky turns from shades of pink, to a deep orange and finally to a dusky blue. My office is dark, but I don't make a move to turn on a light.

My cell phone rings. It is the president's private number. I clear my throat and try to shake the drunken fuzz from my mind. "Hello Mr. President."

"Phillip, why aren't you here? *The president's tone seems to be somewhere between annoyed and jovial.* "We should already be heading to dinner."

I can't think of what to say. My brain is in slow motion. The president fills in my gap.

"Get here as fast as you can."

Finally, I remember. "Right, Mr. President, of course— dinner with you and the First Lady. I would not miss it for the world. I had pressing matters, but I am coming. Please wait for me."

How could I have been so stupid to forget? What am I doing here drinking when I should be there? I can't afford to let things get off track.

"I knew you wouldn't want to miss it, so I already sent a driver to your house."

"Thank you," is all I can muster.

"The team is meeting in my office so come on in when you get here. You should have been here for this meeting also instead of at home, playing hooky with your beautiful wife,"

Xander chuckles. "Don't worry, I'll debrief you before we head up for dinner. A few transportation numbers I need to ask you about."

"Yes, sir. I will see you soon." I get off the phone and let out a yell of frustration.

The team has been meeting. What was I thinking coming home? It is too easy for something to go wrong without me guiding everything. Looking out the window, I see the car already sitting outside. I walk upstairs the best I can, holding onto the rail. *I wish I hadn't drank so much. It will be fine though. I can keep it together.*

Tricia and Jack are in the kitchen as I walk by. She looks at me with cold, fearful eyes.

"You told me that this would all come crashing down. Guess you were wrong. I am off to dinner with the president and First Lady. You should never have doubted me." I don't even bother to say goodbye. I just slam the door at them as my parting farewell. My confidence is starting to come back to me as I carefully walk towards the waiting car.

~~

Chapter 28

PLOT EXPOSED
ESTHER

"I just couldn't say anything," I confide in Kristi. She has come over to give me moral support after my failure last night. "It was like something was blocking my words. Suddenly, they were leaving. I could not get anything out except another dinner invitation." *I can't start crying again. My make-up is already done.*

"You have another chance to tell him tonight."

"I'm just so scared." The tears are brimming. "I am scared to fail. I am scared to become a target."

"He will give you the strength that you need in the moment to speak." Kristi's tone is encouraging, but firm.

"I know. I am right where I'm supposed to be. Trying to help my people. It's what I should have done a long time ago. It's just..." I can't find the words to say.

"What is it?"

"I just think maybe God made a mistake with me. I can't seem to muster my courage anymore. What if I can't get the words out tonight? What then?" I hang my head, feeling shame at my inadequacies.

"Esther, you are more than equipped. You love the Lord. You are a good speaker. Your husband obviously still adores you."

I just shake my head with doubt.

"I keep feeling like I am supposed to be the superhero of some movie. Problem is, I don't feel strong."

"You don't have to be a superhero. God promises to use the weak as long as they are willing. Look at Moses. He said he couldn't speak well, but he was used to deliver his people."

"Yes, but he had Aaron by his side," I complain.

"And you have your Uncle Cai. You have me."

I look up at my friend and smile. "You have been here for me and I am thankful."

"You also have thousands right now that are in prayer for you. So you are not alone tonight as you talk to your husband."

I somehow feel stronger now. *Kristi is right, there are so many with me. So many in prayer.*

"Thank you, Kristi. Will you pray with me right now?" We clasp one another's hands and bow our heads in unison.

Two hours later, I am pacing back and forth in my dining room. *They aren't coming. Already over an hour late. I might have blown my one chance last night to talk to Xander.*

Finally, I hear the door open. My heart begins racing as I hear Xander's upbeat voice coming towards me.

"Hi Esther, sorry we are late."

I put a big smile on to greet Xander and linger with him in our embrace for just a moment.

I address Phillip Stone, my dinner guest for the second night in a row. "Hello, Mr. Stone. How are you tonight?"

He looks like a disaster. So glossy eyed and disheveled.

"Never better Mrs. Susa. You look lovely tonight."

"Thank you. Would you like something to drink?"

"Just some water please." *That is not like Stone at all, but he looks like he has already had a few.*

"Water, no he won't be having water," Xander slaps Mr. Stone on the back and laughs. "Phillip will have a scotch just like me."

The conversation during dinner is not nearly as animated as the night before. *Mr. Stone seems extremely subdued. I'm not surprised with the day he had. Tonight he seems like an angry, bitter man.*

"Esther, this meal is delicious," Xander takes my hand across the table as he says it. "I love your lasagna. Did you make it for us yourself?"

"Yes, I did. I know how much you like it."

I take a deep breath as I prepare for what I need to say.

I hope the dessert will open the door to talk.

"I made the dessert that is coming too. It's a honey cake, which is a traditional dish from my family." *We would have it the first night of Rosh Hashanah with hope that the coming year would be sweet.*

Stone looks up at me with questions in his eyes.

Xander doesn't seem to even notice my comment. Please...ask about my family.

Xander leans across the table and gives me a kiss. "How did I get such an amazing woman as my wife? My staff must have given you something on the side to seal the deal and get you to marry me."

My husband looks adoringly at me. I smile and nod my head no. *I need to start talking now.*

"Nothing? Well, if you did not get anything special to marry me, what would you like now? There must be something I can give you, or something I can do for you?" Xander's tone is light, but he also sounds serious. There is a moment of silence at the table.

This is it! This is the moment!

The butterflies in my stomach begin flapping wildly. I take a deep breath and say a quick prayer inside before I begin.

"Xander, there is something that I want to ask for."

"Of course, my love. I'll give you anything."

Xander looks genuinely pleased. He looks directly into my eyes, as he did that first time we were together at the river.

"I want you to save my life. I beg of you to save the lives of my people."

Stone's head jerks to attention across the table from me. I ignore him and hold my husband's gaze. Xander's face is full of confusion as his eyebrows wrinkle down in concentration.

I lean closer to my husband. "There is a plan in motion to kill thousands of Jewish Americans on Relocation Day. Without your knowledge, this day has been planned as a day for murder, not a day to protect."

I glance over at Stone. His face is draining of color—quickly going white.

Xander's eyebrows furl even deeper into his forehead. He is slightly shaking his head back and forth in disagreement.

I have to explain quickly. "Iran is going to use this day to attack ships loaded with Jews going back to Israel. Thousands from the secure facilities will be brought to the attack site. There will also be simultaneous attacks on Israel."

Xander still holds my hand. His face relaxes and he speaks to me in a gentle tone. "Esther, you can't believe every rumor you hear. There has been a lot of crazy talk going on, but it's all fabricated to hurt the peace process."

He pauses for a moment and scrunches his brows together again. "And what do you mean about saving your life?"

"Xander, my mother was a Jew. I am Jewish. Iran hates us and wants to kill my people–to kill me. I am begging you as the president, as my husband, and as the only one who can possibly stop this atrocity."

Stone has not jumped in yet like I thought he would, belittling and refuting what I am saying. He is just sitting there—looking shocked.

Xander continues to shake his head questioning. "Esther, you never told me you were a Jew before, did you? Not that it matters to me. I just didn't know that you were."

Has he heard anything I just said about the attack?

He continues, "My love, you are so sweet to want to be involved, but I think you have somehow misunderstood the purpose of the relocation option. This is something to be happy about for your people, as you call them. The purpose of the facilities and the relocation is to protect the Jews. It gives them the option to stay safe here in the states or they can be supported to move back to Israel if they would like. So you can see, I am trying to help Jews, not hurt them."

288

I'm completely blowing this. No wonder Stone is not jumping in, he doesn't have to. Xander is never going to see the truth.

"Xander, I know that is your purpose. You believe the peace plan is in the best interest for Jewish Americans, but someone is planning to use your kind-hearted gestures for violence. You have unknowingly been involved in preparing your own citizens for a massacre."

I briefly get up from the table and grab the file folder Uncle Cai prepared with information to show Xander.

"I need you to look at these documents. They show the true intent for Relocation Day."

Phillip has snapped out of his stupor and is ready for action. He reaches out to grab the folder. "You are involving yourself in matters you know nothing about, Mrs. Susa."

Xander puts his hand on top of the folder so Mr. Stone cannot take it. The two men look at one another.

"Xander, you know how poorly it worked out when your last wife tried to get involved with matters that were above her. This is a waste of your time. Just ridiculous accusations by someone who does not even understand politics."

"Phillip, I can take a few minutes to listen to my wife. She is obviously very passionate and has something to show me." Xander looks back to me, takes hold of the file folder and opens it.

I probably only have a couple more minutes. I have to make them count.

"Thank you, Xander. There is information in here that shows the violence with Jewish Americans was started by an outside group, most probably Iran."

My husband looks confused. "Are you telling me Jewish Americans were set up?"

"Exactly. That is how the cycle of violence began; Iran setting up our citizens to fight against one another. And there is evidence of still so much more violence to come."

I glance at Phillip who keeps eyeing the folder as though about to pounce on it. *Keep going. Just ignore him.*

"You will find copies of emails showing communication between Iran and someone in our government planning a coming attack. There is a transcript of part of a recorded phone call where details are discussed. There are the numbers of naval ships and commercial ships being deployed to the relocation stations in much larger numbers than required."

Xander interrupts me, "That sounds like what we were discussing on our way up here, Phillip. Some of the ships numbers are much higher than we need."

"Xander, this is ridiculous to discuss this here with your wife. Let's head downstairs and we will look at the numbers in your office where business should be done."

My window of time to talk could close quickly. "Xander, there is also documentation of movement by the Iranian military putting them into position for an attack on the United States.

See, look at these maps." I quickly put the attack map on top.

Xander's brow furrows deeper as he flips through the papers.

"And Xander," I pause until he looks up at. "There is a possibility that the attacks will be nuclear."

"Mrs. Susa, really, where did you get this ludicrous information?" Stone breaks in. "Mr. President, this is the exact reason why political wives are to be seen and not heard. They stir up drama that you do not need."

Xander does not seem to hear him as he pours over the documents in the folder.

"Mr. President, why don't you let me take a look at those?" Stone tries again in a much calmer tone with his hand expectantly open.

Lord, please open Xander's eyes. Let him see the truth.

A paper passes from Xander to Phillip.

"Esther, what is the significance of these commercial cargo ships being at the relocation docks on the same day? I don't understand."

"The cargo that will be put on those ships are all the Jewish Americans currently in secure facilities." *I am feeling more confident.*

"Do you see all the transportation scheduled for the day before? Those buses and trains will bring the people to the ports so they are in range for the imminent attack."

Stone shakes his head and starts to laugh as he looks over the paper in front of him.

"Mrs. Susa, it is sad to see that a woman of your caliber is taken in by these lies. Someone has falsified these documents for attention or entertainment. This is impossible and there is not any truth to them."

Xander puts his hand up towards Mr. Stone to stop his talking. Stone's face reddens. He glares over at me while my husband is visibly trying to put the pieces of this puzzle together.

"But, how could Iran know all the details to attack? Who would have ordered all the extra transportation?" Xander is speaking to himself as though we are not there.

"If this information is true that Iran is using my peace plan for an attack – there must be someone inside our government helping." He looks up at both of us. "Here is my question for you both—who would be working with Iran?"

"No one, Mr. President," Stone pipes in quickly. "This is nonsense—complete and utter nonsense."

Xander turns to look at me. I don't say a word. I just shift my eyes towards Stone and raise my finger to point directly at him.

Xander follows my finger and looks at his trusted right-hand man—a glimmer of understanding beginning in his eyes.

I work to find my voice. "Phillip Stone is the one who is turning your dreams of peace into a mass murder of American Jews."

Phillip starts to chuckle as though I have just made a joke. He works to accelerate it to a full out laugh.

"What an absurd statement."

He leans towards Xander and speaks to him in a quieter tone, as though I am not sitting right here next to them.

"It is shocking what a seemingly stable woman will do when she is jealous. Your wife is obviously an insecure young bride. She does not realize the time commitments of your position as President of the United States. Instead she accuses me of something ridiculous—to push me away."

I don't know what to say. Please Xander, do not be duped by Mr. Stone again.

Suddenly, I see a look come over Xander's face. A change as he looks at Phillip intently. The emotion of distrust, of disbelief, is dawning. His eyes narrow at Phillip. At someone he knows is lying to him.

Xander looks as though a veil is being lifted. I think he is seeing the truth.

He sits quietly for a moment, both Mr. Stone and I do the same, watching him. Finally Xander speaks, softly and calmly.

"There were questions in my mind Phillip. Worries I would push away because I trusted you. All this time and I did not see what was really happening. Everything is suddenly clear." He stands up and starts pacing in front of us.

"How could I have been so stupid?" His volume increases as does his confidence level.

"No Xander, you are wrong," Mr. Stone responds.

Now he turns to speak directly to Mr. Stone. "I put you on a pedestal since the first moment I met you. I have let you have control of my presidency. I believed that you were making good choices for America and our people."

My husband points his finger at Mr. Stone. "You were just using me."

"No, Mr. President, what are you talking about?"

"You slowly implanted the idea of separating the Jews for safety. You created this whole scenario. You were using my presidency for your own vendetta."

Xander turns to me quickly. "Esther, have you been sick the last few weeks?"

"No, I have not been sick at all."

"You have even been creating a wall between me and my wife, and between me and the rest of my staff, since the day you came to work for me."

Mr. Stone stands up and steps towards Xander gingerly. "Xander, you are seeing this all wrong. I have always been on your side. Helping you, supporting you and your ideas." He emphasizes the word your—placing the responsibility on Xander.

"Stop! I don't want to hear your lies any more. I think I've been manipulated by you too many times already!"

"Xander, really…"

Xander holds his hand up. "I don't want to hear it. Not another word."

I am so proud of my husband right now. The strength it is taking for him to stand up to someone he has admired. The wisdom to see the truth, even though it is difficult. Now, I hope he has the integrity to do something about it.

"All the pieces of a puzzle are coming together. Reports of Jewish protests that you would dispute the numbers and downplay as nothing. Iran—I never understood your tight connection. Late night phone calls. Large amounts of ground transport that you did not explain, but assured me were necessary."

"Xander, you are putting the pieces together all wrong. Let me explain." Mr. Stone is starting to sound desperate.

"No, Phillip. You listen for once. I remember you talking once about how life would be better if the Jews were gone. I took it lightly because I thought you were joking. I see that you were completely serious. You are truly a terrorist—working to kill Americans."

"Xander, you have it all wrong. Don't make a horrible mistake."

"You sit down, Phillip." Xander roars at him.

Phillip sits on the edge of a chair looking like he is about to explode. Xander paces back and forth in front of us both.

Xander stops in front of me. "Esther, I am sorry I let Phillip come between us. I'm ashamed of what I have let happen in our home and in our country."

"Xander, the worst hasn't happened yet. You can still stop it." *The hardest part for him is yet to come.*

My husband pulls me into his arms and holds me tight. He whispers into my ear, "Esther, what am I going to do?"

"You know what has to be done," I whisper back into his ear. *This moment of intimacy with my husband is one I have longed for. I wish it was not under these circumstances.*

Mr. Stone stands up defiantly and approaches Xander. His stance is aggressive. He talks as though commanding.

"Xander, we both have the best intentions in mind for our citizens. I won't let you throw it all away because your wife is putting crazy thoughts into your head."

I can feel Xander tense where his arm is still around me.

"You are a liar, Phillip Stone. You do not have good intentions towards all our citizens. I am done with you."

Xander strides to the table where the file is and picks it up. He shakes it in Mr. Stone's face as he speaks. "You have used my presidency for your prejudice. You are going to be the death of my political career." Xander spits the words into Stone's face. "But I will not let you be the death of Americans."

Xander is pacing again. Running his fingers through his hair. He is mumbling words I cannot comprehend. Xander's jaw clenches tightly between his mumblings.

"I need some fresh air."

Without another word, my husband stomps down the hallway of our home. I can hear the balcony door open. Then from outside, a slamming sound, again and again. It must be Xander's fist slamming against the railing.

I believe he will do what is right to speak up and stop these plans. It could mean the end of his political career—probably will be.

I look up from my thoughts. Stone is eyeing me. A sly smile comes onto his face as he slowly gets up and walks towards me.

~~

Chapter 29

LOSING CONTROL
PHILLIP

I hold Esther's gaze while I walk towards her. I want to make her nervous. To let her know that I am still in control.

I hate her–trying to ruin my work–now to know she is a Jew. I knew not to trust her. Should never have let Xander near her. Now, she will help me.

Sitting down on the couch next to the First Lady, I soften my face to let her know she can trust me.

"Mrs. Susa…Esther, I am as disturbed as you to hear about these possible plans. You can rest assured that I have no intention of harming anyone. Whatever sources your information came from are blatantly deceiving you about me."

I reach out my hands towards hers and gently grasp them as I continue. She tries to slide her hands away from mine. *I want her to feel connected to me as I sway her.*

"If there is any truth to a coming attack, I know enough about Iranian agents to know that they will kill you and Xander immediately if you speak out. We must all keep quiet for now as we gather more intelligence. For your protection, for the president's protection, we must be patient until we find out the truth. Then if an attack is truly coming, we can stop it and go public."

If I can get them to stall. Everything will go as planned. I can see fear building in Esther's eyes. She begins to look around for help and sees that no one is there.

"Please Esther, see the truth. I am not the horrible man you are making me out to be."

Just a moment more and she will believe me. Her apprehension is only because she wants to believe me.

"Mr. Stone, I want you to let go of my hands." Esther's fear is still there, but her voice is firm.

"Just listen to me for a moment more."

Her face is hard towards me. "Mr. Stone, there is no question that you are the one working with Iran. My husband cannot keep quiet because that will only give you more time to carry out these plans."

"No, my dear, no, you are mistaken."

"Now let go of my hands!" She raises her voice to me.

I will not let her go until she understands me. If she and Xander speak up, that is the end for me. Esther tries to pull out of my grasp again. I hold her hands tighter. She tries to stand up. I pull her in closer to me. *Doesn't she understand how important this is? This girl is going to ruin my life.* I can see her fear rising and feel my own panic as well.

"Esther, you don't need to be scared of me. I will never hurt you, just like I would never hurt anyone in our country. Listen to me." I lean in even closer to her. "You have to help me, please."

I'm losing control. She is not listening.

Her strength surprises me as she tries to pull away again and almost slips out of my grasp. Her mouth opens as though she is trying to yell, but nothing comes out. I quickly grab her mouth to silence her. Her eyes widen and now her voice is screaming behind my hand. With my other hand, I grab around the back of her head to hold her. I lean onto her to secure her against the couch. I harshly whisper into her ear.

"Esther, you have to talk to him and tell him to keep quiet. You have to help me. I will die. We will all die."

I can feel her tears streaming over my hand. *This is not how this was supposed to go. Why does she not trust me? Why won't she listen?*

My body is being pulled upward by the back of my hair and an arm around my chest, away from Esther. Her screaming now pierces the air. *I did not even realize that someone else was in the room.*

I turn around to find the president there. "You low life!" He hisses as he grabs the front of my shirt with one hand. He punches me right in the face with the other fist.

"What are you doing to my wife - in my own house?" Another blow, square on the nose. "Or were you trying to seduce her?"

I think to put my hands up to shield my face this time. The blow comes to the stomach. I begin to cough and double over in pain. Xander pushes me and I fall sideways onto the couch in pain.

Laying on the couch, I take in the scene from my sideways view. A bodyguard is standing over me. The president shaking out his hand. His wife next to him, keeping a wary eye on me.

Xander turns to her. "Esther, I am so sorry. I left you alone with him." Xander begins to choke up. "When I saw him on you like that—" He can't finish his sentence.

Esther clings to her husband's arm, "I am okay. Really. But thousands of my people are not. Xander, you are their only hope. You have to do something to save them."

This is the end for me. I am the outsider now. Turned against.

Xander does not answer. He is trying to regain his composure. His gaze settles on me. All his emotions seem to settle in on anger. His face turns hard.

"Sit him up, I want to talk to him." Xander stares at me as he instructs the guards. "Esther, do you want to go out?"

I don't make a move. I want the guards to have to sit me up. *I'm not going to give an inch. If they want to play hardball, I can do that.*

301

"No, Xander, I want to stay," Esther says. "I am afraid his lies are going to continue."

"Esther, don't worry. My eyes are open now."

Two guards pull me to a sitting position. My head is spinning. I can taste blood from my nose. I turn sideways and spit the blood directly onto the president and First Lady's couch. I stare at him in defiance.

"Mr. President, it is too late to try and be the hero now. You are the one who approved all of these decisions since the beginning. If you did not see the truth of what you were doing, you should have. Do you really believe that anyone will think you didn't know what was going to happen?"

I smirk at him and continue, "If you really didn't figure out anything, that just proves what an idiot you are. Whether you knew or you didn't, you will take the blame for all of it. You will lose your presidency. You will lose your dignity. You will be a traitor to your country." My smirk grows bigger as I see the worried look on his face.

"Most likely, an Iranian agent will kill you immediately if you choose to speak up."

I am glad that he is worried; that is exactly where I want him.

He is quiet, contemplating. *Probably thinking how to apologize to me and smooth this over.*

"Xander, I know you well. You are not the kind of man who does anything for anyone but himself. I see that as a good thing. You know what you want. You do what you need to do. That is how you have gotten to be the President of the United States and stayed there."

I pause for effect. I'm speaking calmly again as Xander's wise advisor. "Now is no time to start acting heroic. Keep your head down, Xander. Be smart. Let this play out and I will leave the country as the traitor. You can place all the blame on me and be the heroic president who brings his country out of crisis. It's a win-win for everyone."

If he is smart, he will see that my proposal is his only option. And I love how nervous the First Lady looks—twisting her hands and biting her lip. I have them right where I want them.

"Xander, listen to me as someone who knows politics and has been doing this for a long time. This is your only chance at survival. Not only politically but for your life. And the same goes for your wife too."

I nod in Esther's direction to remind her of the threat of death as well.

The president stands up taller. His face is different than I've seen it before. *More strength. More calm. I hope this means he has decided to listen to reason.*

"Stone, I have listened to you for long enough. You are right about one thing though. I have been selfish in the past. I have thought of myself first." The president looks over at his wife. He looks down. She moves closer to him and takes his arm.

"If it means losing my office, I probably deserve it. If it means I am seen as a traitor, I'll take that punishment as well. If I lose my life—" He pauses for a moment. "I don't want to die, but I can't live if I have sent thousands to their deaths."

Xander has an unnerving calm. I feel myself coming unglued. My life's work is ruined. My life. Everything. Over. Done. Finished.

I begin to scream, "What are you saying? This isn't you talking. Now you are weak. You are worthless."

"Guards," Xander says calmly, "Take the chief of staff into custody for treason against the United States of America."

The guards quickly move to either side of me. My hands are behind my back before I even realize they are doing it. They call for backup as they walk me towards the front door.

"You are going to regret this, Alexander Susa." I yell at him over my shoulder. "You are going to regret this decision every minute for the rest of your life, which will not be very long. The Iranians are going to kill you. All the Jews will still die and you will go down in history as the president who helped kill them."

My anger turns to humor at the situation. I begin to laugh uncontrollably. *They think they have beaten me. But look at me, I am still in control. I am the one saying what will happen.*

I continue laughing all the way down the halls of the White House. I feel the same power I felt less than twenty-four hours ago in my own living room. Unbridled ecstasy. I laugh on and on and on.

These guards don't even know they are walking with the most powerful man in the world.

~~

Chapter 30

HONEST REVELATIONS

XANDER

Phillip's laughter still lingers in my home. Chills run down my back. I turn towards my wife. She is shuddering.

"Come here, it is okay," I tell Esther as I pull her towards me and put my arms around her. After a minute, I feel her shoulders relax. I try to breathe deeply and slowly.

"Everything is going to be fine," I try to sound confident.

Esther clings tightly to me. "I can't believe it. It's almost too horrible to be real."

"Esther, you were so courageous. I was blind. I'm ashamed of what I have been a part of." *I want to be brave for her, but honestly I am scared.* "It might be too late."

"No, Xander, you can still make it right. I believe in you. That you can stop my people from being killed."

She has more faith in me than I have in myself. It feels hypocritical to try and be the hero when I helped to create this mess. But I will try. I switch from emotional mode to planning mode.

"We have to get the Jewish Americans out of the secure facilities as quickly as possible. They are in danger there. I'll have to tell everyone the truth to make it happen quickly."

Once I say it out loud, I'll probably be impeached and imprisoned.

"I will probably lose my presidency, Esther. I might be tried right along with Stone. And if he is right, my life could be in danger."

Esther arms tighten around me as I continue. "I haven't always been the most upstanding man in the past, but lives are at stake."

"Xander, I am so proud to be your wife."

Love for this woman overwhelms me. I realize how blessed I am. *How can she be so loyal?*

"There is no doubt that I don't deserve you, Esther. Will you stand with me when I tell the world the truth? No matter what comes, will you be by my side?"

Her reply is immediate with no time for thought. "Of course, Xander. I will be by your side in the days, months, and years ahead. No matter what comes, I will support and love you."

Tears spring to my eyes. I bury my head into Esther's hair.

This woman loves me unconditionally. Not because I am the president. Not because I am powerful.

I pull back and look at Esther. "You told me about unconditional love once. You are the best example of it that I have ever seen."

"That is the way God loves me. I'm learning from him, even though I have a long way to go."

I compare what she has just said to my past beliefs. "My parents taught me that we didn't need God. I believed I

307

didn't really need anyone or anything else, including my parents too. I worked my way to the top—grabbing as many pleasures as I could along the way. There has always been something missing though."

"God wants you to know Him."

I don't see lightning strike. There is no voice from heaven, but I do feel peace.

Considering I am in the middle of the worst crisis I can imagine, it amazes me to feel peace. Maybe it is Esther's God.

With peace, comes clarity of mind.

"Precious minutes are passing. It's time to move." I gather up Esther's file folder of evidence as I speak. "I'll get my team together immediately. I want you there. We'll make a statement to the press as quickly as possible."

"Xander, there is someone else you need there as well. My uncle is the person who gave me this information."

We spend the night working with my crisis management team and Esther with more pots of coffee than I can count. Esther's informant joins us as well. *I'm not surprised Cai Allenby is the one supplying her the information. I am surprised that he is her uncle. Can this night get any weirder?*

The press is hastily assembled in the early morning again. *They are probably getting used to these impromptu gatherings, although the news cannot be what they are expecting.*

"Ready?" I ask my beautiful bride. *No sleep, but look at her—as gorgeous as ever.* "Do you have anything else to tell me before I go out there? You have been full of surprises tonight."

"That is everything Xander. You now know I am a Jew and that Cai is my uncle. I think God knew we needed to keep it quiet for the right moment. But there are no more surprises."

"I'm okay with it as I am grateful to both of you."

"Do you have your notes?" She asks me as she straightens my tie. "You don't want to miss any points."

"I've got them and will cover everything."

"You'll do amazing. I have no doubt."

"The calls are already going out, right? I don't want to say that people are leaving the facilities and the transportation is being cancelled if the calls have not started yet." I am worrying about every detail now. Maybe just stalling for minutes.

"Yes, Xander, they are already calling. Have been for over thirty minutes now."

"It's only 5:00 in the morning. Who can they be calling this early?"

"Many of the ships are international. Their companies are up. They are waking everyone else." Esther looks at me funny.

"What?" I ask.

"I want you to know how proud I am of you. Before you go out there Xander, can I pray for you?"

I smile at her words. "I don't know that God is listening, but please go ahead and try."

Esther prays for me as though I am a man worthy to be prayed over. When she finishes, I feel the urge to say something as well.

"Hello God, I haven't talked to you much. Thank you for giving me Esther. This the worst time of my life—please help us to get through this alive. I don't really know you, but somehow today, you feel more real to me, so ... thank you."

I look up and grab Esther into a hug.

I put on my confident political look. "Here we go."

We step onto the podium together, holding hands. I see the double security forces, working hard today to keep us safe. The press is extra jovial today. *Probably wondering what the second impromptu press conference in two days will bring.*

"Good morning, although it hardly feels like one." I let them know by my serious tone that today's topic is not a light-hearted one.

Everyone goes completely quiet except for intent writing and the click of buttons being pressed.

"Today I come before you with an urgent message for the American people. A message that is imperative for the safety of our citizens. Today I come with a heavy heart because I am partly to blame for the message that I must bring to you. My job as President of the United States is to serve and protect my people. Without even being aware of it, I have failed at protecting all of my citizens. This morning I stand before you, humbled, ready to make things right, and to do just that—protect everyone."

The next thirty minutes I spend explaining what was just revealed to me. I share Iran's intent to attack Americans on American soil. There are intermittent gasps from the press.

I can tell they are in shock, but not sure if they are placing the blame on Iran or at my door?

I tell them everything we know about the plans of attack from Iran. I let the American people know that there was an "insider" in our own government working with Iran. *It will come out later who it is.*

I wonder if what Phillip said is really true about Iranian sleeper agents killing Esther and me. There could be someone in this room right now with that intent. Don't think about it, Xander. Just keep going.

I outline the steps our strategy team has drawn up to keep our citizens safe, to clear the secure facilities, and to get people back to their homes as quickly as possible. I announce the cancellation of the relocation option until further notice, as well as the military's move to high alert in preparation for an attack from Iran.

This next part is the vital step to moving the country in a positive direction. To work together towards a real peace plan.

"My fellow Americans," I slow down my words for a moment to make the importance apparent.

"We will not let those who hate America win this battle. We cannot allow fear and hatred towards one another to continue. I have new information that shows Iran was behind the deaths that started this cycle of hatred and violence in our country. Our enemies succeeded in turning us against each other for a time."

I pause to glance at Esther. Her look encourages me

"Continuing this cycle of violence and hatred will divide us. At this crucial time in our country, we need to unite as Americans regardless of race, religion, or cultural background. There have been mistakes made by many—myself included. Now is the time to join together as Americans in moving forward. Today I ask each of you to lay down your anger, lay down your fear and seek forgiveness."

I take a moment to look around at the press.

I have to trust these men and women to present my message to the country as intended. That they will not spin it in a way that will continue the divisions in our country.

"To Jewish Americans who will be coming out of secure facilities and heading home, I ask you to please soften your hearts to forgive. An evil few planned a horrible atrocity against you. We are all grateful it has been stopped. I ask your forgiveness that it went as far as it did."

"To Iranian Americans as well as Iran's citizens who wish Americans well. We will move forward together with all who want unity and peace."

"You will have neighbors coming back to their homes, employees returning to their jobs, and friends re-joining you. Please welcome them and reach out to them with open arms. This is a time of reconciliation and renewal for our country. Let us join together instead of continuing our divisions."

I look to the side of the room where my surprise guest is waiting. This will be his second time in front of this press corps in as many days.

"I would like to ask Attorney General Mordecai Allenby to join me. You all know him well."

A few chuckles are heard around the room. Cai steps forward to greet me.

"Mr. Allenby saw the truth long before anyone else. He tried to tell me. He tried to tell you and we did not listen."

I turn to Cai. Genuine regret grips me. "Attorney General Allenby, with our country as my witness, I humbly need to apologize to you. I am sorry I did not listen to your wisdom sooner. As a step towards reconciliation and unity, I would like to ask you to join me in leadership in the White House?"

"President Susa, I am honored. We will work towards a unified future together."

Cai and I shake hands to a chorus of cameras clicking. I step away from the microphones and motion Esther forward. Cai steps up to stand by her side.

Esther begins, her voice shaking, "Thank you in advance for sharing this message of peace and reconciliation to our country and the world. I would like to tell you the reason that these events are so close to my heart."

My sweet wife continues and I can see her confidence grow.

"When I was very young, my mother, father, and brother were killed in a car accident. I went to live with my mother's brother. I kept my father's last name and went by Esther

Thompson. What I don't think most of you know is my mother's family name is Allenby."

The room is silent for split second as the connection is made. A collective gasp passes through the room

"This is my uncle, who raised me as his own daughter." Esther looks to Cai, who puts his arm around her back.

"I am a Jewish American. The threat to my people has been excruciating to go through. There will still be challenging times ahead as we rebuild trust and unity in our country, but I believe this is a time for celebration as this disaster has been averted."

I look through wet eyes as my wife turns to me. *My emotions are so real. So raw. Appreciation, humility and love.*

Cai steps back from Esther and I step up, reaching for my wife's hand as I speak.

"Are there any questions?"

"What more can you tell us about the government insider?" A member of the press calls out. "Where is he now and what is your plan to bring him to justice?"

"More information will be given as we are able. The individual is in custody and is in the process of being transferred to a maximum security facility."

"Mr. President, you mentioned a possible attack still coming from Iran."

"We have thwarted Iran's attack plan towards our Jewish American citizens. However, the possibility is still there. Our military and Homeland Security is vigilantly working. I have full confidence that no Iranian attack will penetrate U.S. soil."

The press conference continues much longer with questions I can answer and questions I cannot. By the end, I am exhausted. I share everything I know, except for the name of Phillip Stone. Esther and Cai share openly as well. The tone focuses on peace and reconciliation. Our front is unified and hopeful for the future.

Hopefully the country will grab onto these feelings of hope and peace and move forward. Who knows, maybe their feelings of forgiveness and reconciliation will extend to me as well.

~~

Chapter 31

Three Months Later
Esther

"Mrs. Susa, what were the first few days like for you after the president revealed Iran's plan of attack?"

I am in the middle of another interview, this one for a morning show with Libby Wright. Xander is encouraging me to do as many interviews as I can, which tells me that he trusts what I will say.

"The first few days after the press conference were extremely stressful. There were so many worries. We were worried about an Iranian attack—both on the country and against Xander and myself personally. Then there was the worry about the public reaction to the Jewish Americans suddenly coming home. We did not know if the country would rally together for peace or continue the violence."

"Was there a worry for your husband in his role as president?"

"Of course, we did not know if the country would rally together or be looking to place blame. If so, it could have been the end of his presidency."

"Now three months later, how are things different from those first few days?"

"The American people and their spirit have amazed us. Early on, I helped families move from the secure facilities back to their homes. I was able to see their neighbors welcoming them back with open arms. To see the Jewish Americans reunited to the rest of society in peace was more than we could have hoped for."

Libby's face takes on a serious look. *I know what she is about to ask.*

"Tell us how you felt when you heard about the death of Phillip Stone at the hands of Iranian agents."

"I was and am still grieved for Mr. Stone and his family. I'm sad for the way that he chose to live his life as well as the way that it ended."

"Was there any satisfaction that his death brought justice? After all, he not only planned for thousands of Americans to be killed, but he also personally attacked you."

"He did do those things, but my only satisfaction came when so many lives were saved. There was no satisfaction in Mr. Stone dying, especially the gruesome murder he experienced."

"Mrs. Susa, your husband's ratings are as high as ever. Instead of taking the blame for this incident, President Susa is seen as a hero. What do you think made the public view him in this way?"

"Xander acted immediately when he learned of the coming attacks. I think his willingness to put himself on the line spoke to the country. Xander spoke with humility and asked forgiveness for his part, which is something we do not hear

317

every day. I believe he was genuine and the country saw this."

Libby leans in as though talking with a girlfriend rather than conducting an interview. Her tone is much lighter. "It is rumored that you are changing the president's party boy ways."

I laugh out loud. "Xander Susa is his own man. Any changes he makes are completely his own. I am so proud of who he is—proud of how his presidency is making a difference."

"And I hear talk of little feet in the White House, will that be happening soon?" Libby lowers her voice.

"I sure do hope so." I reveal to an extremely pleased look on Libby's face. "There are many children in need of families, so we are beginning the adoption process. If God gives us a baby biologically as well, we will be happy with more."

"Esther, are you saying it is possible there could be two sets of little feet running around the White House?"

I laugh out loud at the thought. *God has given me a peace about having children. When the time is right, I believe one way or another He will give us a child or even two.*

"I am as excited as you are to see what God has for the future."

"What about this surprise uncle you kept a secret from all of us?" She scolds me. "How is the president enjoying having your father figure as his chief of staff?"

"It is a gift to both Xander and I to have Uncle Cai in our lives. The two men are meshing well—both professionally and personally."

"You have also been busy. Tell us more about the commemorative celebration that you and your uncle are planning."

"Yes, I am so excited. We are planning a nationwide celebration based on the Jewish holiday of Purim. It is a holiday to celebrate all that God has done for us in the past and well as recently. When I was a child, we would observe this holiday. I remember dressing up in costume and blowing noise makers. We would spend time fasting and praying—thanking God."

"With everything that has recently happened, this is the perfect time to celebrate Purim again. We want to include the entire country in this celebration as everyone has been affected. It will be a nationwide day of thanksgiving called 'Celebrate Peace'."

"We will look forward to hearing more about it."

"Mrs. President, many people don't know the important role that you played in bringing out the truth of Iran's coming attack on our citizens. That you were the one who stood up against Phillip Stone and told your husband what was happening. Can you tell us more about that?"

"Libby, I am grateful I was able to help, even though I did not do it perfectly by any means. I could have been braver, or more articulate. It certainly was not because of me that this disaster for the Jewish people was averted. God chose to put me where he did, as the president's wife. He allowed my uncle to gain the information about the coming attacks. He gave me the words to speak against the lies that Mr. Stone was telling. God asked me to obey him in faith and that is all I did."

I look over to the reporter who for the first time in our interview does not seem to know what to say, but I do.

"All that I did was be willing to do what He asked me to do. Although I am no one special—my God is. That is my story."

~~

ACKNOWLEDGMENTS

I love the acknowledgment page of a book because it shows the relationships that helped a book come to life. Over this nine year process, I am grateful for many friends and family and the part they played in the completion of this work.

My amazing husband, Brian Remsburg – You supported my desire to write this book and gave me the confidence that it was time well spent. Thank you for the practical ways you helped me find time to write with our busy home. You encourage me to be brave and step out in faith, doing it right alongside me. I love you forever!

Mom and Dad, Warren & Shirley Fleischmann – Thank you for raising me to love and trust the Lord. For encouraging me in all that I pursue, including writing. I am so blessed to have you as my parents.

David and Libby Beaty – My first draft had a long way to go, but you read it enthusiastically during our road trip to Oman. That was priceless to me, as is your friendship.

Mark Fleischmann – I appreciate the confidence you helped instill in me since childhood to put myself out there and try new things. Thanks for being a support and encouragement to me in this project and in life.

Elaine Wright Colvin – Our meeting was orchestrated by God. How he knit together two Western Baptist grads so quickly in an airport boarding line is a miracle. Thank you for the vision, expertise, and time you gave to this book.

Cyndi Boes –As my first editor, you were kind and gentle with this new writer. Ginger Chirgwin – It was fun brainstorming the title with you from across the world. With Jodi Martin, you three are rocks of support!

For the dear friends and small groups in Udhailiyah, Saudi Arabia who read, commented, encouraged or prayed with me during this journey. Especially to Tom Wrightman, Doranne de Montigny, Jana Edgington, Kara Green, Catherine McLandress, Lesley Wood and Kate McClellen. From other spots of the world, friends and family who did the same; Tony & Kathryn Diedi, Toni Fleischmann, Kristi Barnes, Greg Remsburg, Andrea Pickett, Sue Remsburg, Kara Kropf, Jim Kosmack, Jason VanGalder, Gretchen Swinger and Malia Heil.

Over the years, so many others have shared words of interest and encouragement that reminded me to move forward with my story to glorify God through the process.

About The Author

Maryann Remsburg has been surprised by the adventures of life. With her husband, a short adventure overseas turned into eighteen years counseling and teaching at international schools in Kenya, Saudi Arabia, and South Korea. Raising four Third Culture Kids, both biological and adopted, born in three different countries is an amazing adventure that also keeps her on her knees. Maryann loves getting out in nature to cycle, hike, run, and compete in triathlons or other races as often as possible. Her latest adventure has been moving back to the US and becoming a stateside sports mom along with other endeavors! God's faithfulness has grown Maryann's trust and excitement for the next adventure He might have around the corner.

Maryann would love to hear from you as well as have the opportunity to share more to individuals or groups about stepping out in faith: maryannremsburg@gmail.com

Made in the USA
San Bernardino, CA
29 September 2018